Broken People

Scott Hildreth

Published by
Eralde Publishing

Cover Design Copyright © Creative Book Concepts
Text Copyright © Scott Hildreth
Formatting by Creative Book Concepts

ISBN 13: 978-0692322277
All Rights Reserved

DEDICATION

This book is dedicated to Michelle Basilious, who opened my eyes to the art of sitting still.

A special thanks to my children, Erin, Alec, and Derek for believing. If even for only a fleeting moment, they believed.

My life's experiences created this book, but my good friend Dave Bowlin at A&H Electric made it possible.

1

JUST THE TIP

FAT KID

Managing my time wisely had never been one of my strengths. In fact, my inability to effectively organize my day's activities was one reason I typically sat in the coffee shop all damned day. As I looked down at my watch, I realized I had been sitting in the same place for nearly five hours. The majority of the time had been spent on my blog responding to posts or returning personal emails. I generally came for at least a few hours a day and often for the entire work day. I dressed comfortably and always wore the same basic attire - a white V-neck tee, khakis, and black canvas Converse sneakers. My work consisted of running a website which offered help to those who were incapable of dealing with the day-to-day difficulties associated with life. This primarily involved people in their teens to early twenties and their associated problems - pregnancy, having been abused, parent problems, boyfriend or girlfriend issues, eating disorders, suicidal thoughts, or depression.

Just to name a few.

My current primary focus was a suicidal girl named Shellie. Earlier, however, I had received a message from a girl who was fifteen, scared and pregnant. She had not yet advised her family of the pregnancy and it appeared from the content of her email she hadn't told her boyfriend either.

I looked into the parking lot and considered what I may want to tell her. Being fifteen and pregnant wasn't her life goal when she was fourteen, but it was a slice of reality now.

Fifteen and pregnant.

It seemed strange saying it. Try as I might, I was drawing a blank on any meaningful advice. Incapable of recalling the last time I had eaten, I decided maybe I needed nourishment. Eagerly, I reached into my left pocket to retrieve a snack. To satisfy my never ending hunger and to maintain my non-diet, I generally carried some form of chocolate in my left pocket. As I fumbled through the contents of my pocket I felt many things, none of which resembled a Hershey bar.

Nail clippers.

Lip balm.

Money clip.

Loose change.

Fuck. I really needed chocolate.

I made some room between my fat stomach and the edge of the table, allowing me to reach a little deeper into my pocket.

Nothing.

I looked at my right hand. It resembled the fat kid's hand in the movie Willy Wonka & the Chocolate Factory. Reluctantly, I shoved my sausage-like fingers into my right pocket.

Empty.

I rarely carried anything in my right pocket. Actually, I had developed some deep seated issues about using or utilizing things on my right side.

I always started walking with my left foot first. I used the left door when entering a movie, and always sat on the left side of the theatre. I sometimes wondered if the movie theatre caught fire in the left rear - would I simply burn or would I attempt to exit through the other side? The thought of even walking on the right of the theatre to *get* to the left side caused me terrible anxiety. I imagined a 320 pound carcass of burnt flesh on the left-hand side of the theatre. In my left pocket a money clip covered in melted chocolate would identify my remains.

Typically I weighed myself several times a day and tried to maintain my weight at 320 pounds. If it fell two or three pounds below 320, the obsessive/compulsive part of me took over and I would eat frantically in an effort to restore my weight to 320 - the exact opposite of being on a diet. Throughout the course of the day I would count calories and make certain I was taking in enough to keep my weight on track. I felt if I maintained my obese appearance people would be less attracted to me. As a form of assurance I would never become anything less than fat, I purchased a small digital scale and carried it with me in my laptop bag. Historically, I checked my weight multiple times a day. Anything below 317, and I would eat whatever I had to just to maintain my target weight.

In most of my adult years I weighed 185 and was often approached by strangers who were intrigued by my unique ways or my odd nature. Frustrated after years of approach by outsiders, I made a decision to gain weight, become less inviting to the eye, and try my luck at physical fatness instead of physical fitness. Immediately following the weight gain program, I shed my contact lenses and purchased some black horn-rimmed *birth control* glasses. So far my experiment worked well and far less people found me interesting. My shaved head caused me to be fractionally more repulsive and the 320 pounds, glasses and shitty

3

attitude did the rest. Far less people approached me and I was much more satisfied.

I reached into my bag, removed my scale, and tossed it onto the tile floor. I stood in front of it, tapped it with my toe and I stood on it. I stared down at the numbers displayed on the screen and blinked. I blinked again.

316.

Jesus.

Are you fucking kidding?

I stepped off.

I waited a moment and climbed back on.

316.

Fuck me running.

I needed chocolate, and I needed it *now*. I put the scale back in the bag. I turned to face the cash register and was immediately relieved, as there was not a line of patrons waiting to order. *Thank God.* I needed chocolate bad. I felt nauseous. I attempted to walk to the cashier. My head spun. It was no more than a hundred feet away. Thirty three steps at most. No reason for concern. Within minutes I would be eating *something*.

As I began to slowly waddle toward the cashier I caught a glimpse of him out of the corner of my eye. *The Nigerian nightmare.* A man I truly detested. Daily dress for this annoying fraction of a man was a pair of dark brown slacks and an argyle sweater vest that was two sizes too small. The vest was always worn over a wrinkled dark earth-tone dress shirt. He wore a version of the same clothes every day.

We made eye contact as he was about to open the front door and enter the coffee shop. As he reached for the door handle I began to run toward the cashier – the thought of him making it to the counter before me caused me to feel ill. As I hustled toward the display of snacks several people looked up in awe - my running sounded like a rhinoceros loose on a gymnasium floor.

The Nightmare appeared to be hot-footing it toward the counter as well. *Perfect, a race between a 316 pound fat kid and a 121 pound six foot tall African professor.* In an all-out run, I was headed for the cashier. I stepped in front of him with six feet to spare. As my rubber soled sneakers screeched to a stop on the tile floor, my 320 pound body continued to move forward. Dizzy and hungry, I almost tipped over. As I looked up I noticed the entire store staring at the two of us - most in disbelief. As I opened my mouth and attempted to speak, I realized I was out of breath.

"I…"

Exhausted, my heart pounding and seconds from collapse, I couldn't continue speaking.

My voice broke as I tried.

"…need…chocolate."

As I finished my sentence I let out a long sigh, hesitated, and inhaled a slow breath. My hands now resting on my knees, I stood and stared.

The newly hired twenty one year old barista looked at me and smiled, "Would you like a white chocolate mocha, they're good?"

Her face looked like a porcelain doll and her ears resembled Dumbo the elephant.

Fucking great, one hundred and five pounds of pale skinned incompetence.

As I heaved for my next breath I pressed my hands into my thighs and struggled to speak.

"No," I finally responded.

I straightened my stance and tried unsuccessfully to continue.

She smiled and repeated the menu of chocolate offerings she had memorized, "A mocha, chocolate chip vanilla smoothie, or a….."

I was becoming rather disgusted with her. Her eyes barely cleared the top of the cash register.

They really should provide this girl a crate to stand on.

I needed chocolate. I couldn't take it anymore. My legs felt weak. My 316 pound frame was mere seconds from collapse. I envisioned falling on the floor and being unable to get up. My arms and legs flailing aimlessly. My death imminent.

Who would help me back to my feet?

I heard the Nigerian Nightmare clear his throat. I turned and attempted to glare. My field of vision slowly narrowed as if I were peering through a pin hole in a sheet of paper. As I turned my head toward the cashier the room spun. Sweat formed on my brow. I reached under my tee shirt. I felt wet. Clammy. As my vision blurred I looked at the barista and word vomited.

"Chocolate," I bellowed.

"I need fucking chocolate. Not a drink," I breathed.

I waved my hands back and forth like an umpire calling someone safe at home plate.

I extended my arms with my palms up, as if begging, "Fucking chocolate. Chocolate covered *something*. A chocolate bar. Candy. Chocolate of some solid form. Choc-O-Late. What do you have?"

As I daydreamed about falling to the floor and the Nigerian Nightmare reaching to help me to my feet, I decided I would rather expire than have him assist me. I would simply lay there and die. Certainly someone else

6

would come to assist me - especially if I screamed for him to go away. He would eventually be forced take a few steps back and one of the regulars would come bring me to my feet.

I glanced down at my sneakers.

I looked up toward the porcelain faced Dumbo.

Her lip began to quiver, "Uhhhhm. Sir, we have chocolate covered almonds, trail mix with chocolate, and…."

I interrupted her. I was incapable of putting up with any more of her meaningless bullshit, "Almonds, give me the fucking almonds. All you have."

I stood and waited as she reached around to the display counter, emptying it of the remaining cylindrical plastic packets of chocolate covered almonds.

"Sir, that will be $24.94," she said as she offered a portion of a smile.

"What, twenty fucking what?" I bellowed.

I felt as if I was going to be sick.

But what?

What would spill form my lips?

Nothing.

"Sir, its seven packages of almonds at $3.29 each, plus tax. The total is…" she sounded frustrated.

With my hearing impaired from malnutrition, I didn't even comprehend the remaining statement. *Thirty dollars. She needed thirty fucking dollars.* I tossed her a ten and a twenty. The money fell in front of her on the counter. As she handed me the almonds and my change I visually measured the distance to my seat and wondered if I could make it. Weak and wobbly, my half-hearted attempt to open the package was unsuccessful. The lid was taped to the cylinder.

Are you serious?

I frantically bit at the top as I tried to pry it free. Finally, I successfully removed the lid to one of the tubes of almonds and immediately dumped half the packet in my mouth. As I began to walk to my seat I could feel the effect of the chocolate. I was regaining composure. Half way to my seat I stopped and began an attempt to calculate the cross sectional area of the almonds, the thickness of the chocolate shell, and the actual relief I would receive from an entire packet. I emptied the remaining cylinder into my mouth, allowing the disgusting nuts to mix with the sweet chocolate as I chewed.

Each step became easier than the last.

As I began to sit in my chair my phone rang. I looked at the screen. The caller ID and the photo from the caller's profile confirmed it was Michelle. Reaching for the phone, I noticed the Nightmare scanning the coffee shop looking for a nonexistent seat. *Thank God.* Someone must have taken the last chair while he was ordering his coffee – possibly while I was purchasing my chocolate almonds. I smiled as I picked up the phone and answered.

"Kid, what are you doing?" she asked.

"Hey Michelle. I'm watching the Nightmare look for a seat. It looks like he isn't going to have a place to sit. I hope no one gets up," I responded excitedly.

"Why are you obsessed with that guy? Can you just leave him be? He didn't do anything to you. He's as entitled to sit there as anyone else. This *is* America, Kid," she complained.

Michelle was right.

She was always right.

I both loved and hated her for it. I rarely agreed with her but I often followed her advice. We had met on the Internet and although we lived at opposite ends of the United States we had become extremely close. Our friendship consisted of texting and an occasional phone call. We had never met in person but I could probably pick her out of a group of ten thousand people. She would certainly stand out in any crowd; she was five foot seven with the most inviting brown eyes I had ever seen. Her long black hair was to the middle of her back and she had perfect olive colored skin. It would, however, be the Texas sized attitude that would allow me to immediately recognize her. She was intelligent and tactful, but she made it crystal clear she was an independent woman.

She stood alone, and there was certainly not another like her.

I drew a shallow breath and dumped a half packet of almonds in my mouth, "He doesn't speak English and he's just fucking gross, Michelle. He disgusts me. I can't work around him, he creeps me out. He comes in here like he owns this place, and camps out. Hell, he never leaves."

"Kid, *you* go in there, camp out and never leave. He speaks English, but with an accent. Now leave him alone. You say you're not prejudiced, yet you get so aggravated with that guy."

I watched as the Nightmare lowered his head and gathered his coffee, laptop and book bag. Slowly and sheepishly, he began walking to the door. I raised my clenched fist and pumped it in the air as if I were the victor.

"Okay, Michelle, Okay. I will leave him alone for a bit."

"Before I forget, did you have a chance to look at that picture of my friend Lucas I gave you? You know, and *read* him?" she asked.

"Oh. Yeah, I looked at it last night. You ready?" I asked.

"Yes Kid, I'm ready," she responded.

"Well, he is very intelligent. For some reason, he struggles with math. The rest of his education comes easy. He's almost bored with the degree of education he receives. He needs to be about two years further advanced. He loves politics, it's what drives him. He will eventually be a politician, or work in a political field. He abides by the rules and regulations his parents expect him to, but internally he is opposed. As he gets older he'll oppose them. He is extremely independent. Extremely. He enjoys his alone time – to think. That's about all I remember. How did I do?"

"That's insane. I can't believe from looking at a photograph you can get all of that information. It's like you can look into a person's soul. But you're a hundred percent accurate, Kid. That's crazy, just crazy. Now, why did you text me?" she asked.

"Well, I have a girl that's fifteen and pregnant. And, I wanted your advice on a few things." I dropped a few more of the almonds in my mouth and turned my head to prevent from making chomping noises into the phone.

The phone was silent for what seemed like an eternity.

"Michelle, are you there?" I asked.

My phone beeped, indicating I had received a text message. As I often did, I extended my arm and listened to the phone for Michelle's voice as I checked my text messages.

Opening the screen for receiving text messages, it appeared.

MICHELLE: *eye roll*

I placed the phone to my cheek and smiled.

"Michelle, I *need* your opinion," I insisted.

The phone beeped again. I didn't dare look. She was rolling her eyes at me again. Michelle had started the entire *eye roll* thing with me when we first met. On almost every occasion we spoke, she rolled her eyes at me. She indicated this rolling of the eyes by sending me the "*eye roll*" text message. She claimed she frequently rolled her eyes so far back into her head they actually hurt. I envisioned her tossing her head backward at the same time as the eye rolling.

"Michelle, are you too busy to talk?"

"No, I am just. Well no, I am not busy at all," she said in a preoccupied tone.

"Well, I want to talk to this girl when I get home. As soon as I catch my breath and regain some energy from this chocolate I will go. And for what it's worth, I am not prejudiced. I *did* pick up on the comment. It has nothing to do with prejudices; he's a God damned idiot – and an irritating one at that. I've spent the majority of this morning at the coffee shop and I need to go home, I'm hungry."

"Already eat all of your chocolate?" she asked.

"That's a long story. I have some, but it is covering a disgusting almond. Let's get back to the girl. She is fifteen, pregnant, and just wants to feel better about things. She's embarrassed and hasn't told her boyfriend or her parents. According to her they are going to kill her."

Raising the tone of her voice, Michele responded, "Well, I doubt that they'll *kill* her. So what's the deal with the boyfriend? Is he in the picture or is he out?"

"Well, Michelle," I sighed, "I'm not sure. We have only shared a few emails. In the first one she stated he was still with her. In the second, although she didn't say, she indicated she was alone. I suppose it's hard to say at this point. I just really wanted to know what the thought process is for a fifteen year old going through a pregnancy. What she may be thinking. I suspect I know the answer – fear, embarrassment, raising the child alone, not attending college, living with her parents for the next ten years.”

“How did this happen?” Michelle asked.

“Are you serious? *How* did it happen? Michelle, hold on a minute….”

“Not *how* did it happen, but how did it *happen*?” she interrupted.

“Well, you are going to love this,” I began to explain.

“As we have discussed before, in different locales things are different. I have given my opinion to you regarding the differences of people based on education, upbringing, parental involvement and even the family income. Get this,” I paused as my mouth formed a grin.

“Just the tip. The boyfriend lured her in with *Just. The. Tip.* She said she didn’t think she could get pregnant from the tip. In fact, she asked me if I had ever heard of such a thing.”

“Oh. My. God, I am soooooo rolling my eyes. So, where is this little pregnant jewel from?”

“Kansas,” I chuckled, “of all places.”

“Anyway, I told her the tip was enough. In fact, I explained to her it was the *business* end of the penis and it would be all that should be required to make her pregnant. That is if it were inserted or in close proximity. Or…”

Before I could finish my thought, Michelle interrupted.

“And you say you hate stupidity,” she huffed.

“Well, I hate it when people *choose* to act in a stupid manner. I do not hate people in general and I certainly do not hate people who are uninformed. Or if they’re slow to catch on,” I smiled.

I began to laugh out loud, thinking of the girl agreeing to accept *just the tip.*

“What happened?” Michelle asked.

“Oh nothing, I was just thinking of the event that brought this on,

12

and how special it must have been. I bet it was a real nice time for them both. *Just the tip.* That's so nice," I laughed.

"Sometimes," Michelle sighed and paused for a moment, "I wonder why you *really* run that blog. Why you spend your life helping those who, in your own words, are *incapable of helping themselves.*"

"I'm just a nice guy, Michelle."

"There's more to it than that, and we both know it."

Knowing she was right but not wanting to get into a heated discussion about my inner self or about *the incident,* I opted to change the subject. I hoped to get home before it was time for lunch, so I began my departure comments.

"Well, I have emailed her from here. I will check my emails when I get home, and I will text you as soon as she responds. So, if we don't talk sooner, I will text you in a bit, okay?"

"Ok, Kid. I'm headed to a movie with Brianna and staying at her house tonight. I guess we will talk in the morning. Sweet dreams, Kid."

I hadn't had a dream which I had recalled in almost eighteen years and Michelle was fascinated by the fact my mind didn't *remember* the dreams. She was convinced I *had* them, but my mind was incapable of the recollection. Often sarcastically, she said *sweet dreams* as an inside joke. Eighteen years, nine months and four days. Not one dream.

Not a single one.

"I'm sure I won't and I am fine with that, Michelle. Enjoy the movie. Think about this girl, please," I hung up and shoved the phone into my left pocket.

After placing my bag over my shoulder I dumped another tube of almonds in my mouth. I tried to determine what the caloric value would be of this almond littered chocolate. I rotated the sleeve and stared.

Nothing. As I walked to the door I tipped it on end and looked for a sticker. *Nothing.* Frustrated, I opened the door, leaned back, and tossed the useless empty sleeve into the trash.

As I waddled across the parking lot, I tried to recall the calories of an almond. *Seven? Ten? Twelve?* I opened the car door and scanned the parking lot for the Nigerian Nightmare's Toyota. *Not a sign.* Perfect. I couldn't help but feel nothing less than satisfied. He made my skin crawl. Content, I tossed my laptop bag into the rear seat and forced my 320 pounds of flesh into the front seat. As I backed out of the parking spot I thought of my phone call with Michelle. Immediately, I erupted into laughter.

Just. The. Tip.

2

GOD HATES FAGS

DAVID

"Inside the auditorium, people stood and cheered. They were all wearing pastel colors and dressed rather nicely. As they clapped their hands and smiled at me I stood on the stage, microphone in hand, and said it again. *I am proud, and I am gay. I am gay and I am proud.* The auditorium erupted. I could *feel* the noise. A few people started clapping a rhythm, and one began to cheer. I couldn't make it out at first. His hands held high over his head, he clapped as if he were at a concert cheering for the performer. Slowly, others joined in the rhythm of the clapping. Their mouths moved in unison. After a short time it became clear. They were cheering my name."

"Da-vid.....Da-vid....Da-vid...DA-VID."

"I was wearing the sweater Bethany told me to buy that one day in the mall. After I got home I had decided I didn't like it, but I looked fabulous standing there on stage. Oh, and khaki's. I was wearing khaki's. Looking around the auditorium, I clutched the microphone and I felt myself fill with pride. I saw him approaching on my right. Paul. He was there. My life was complete. And he was wearing the sweater I had told him was *my* favorite. The one he wore during the weekend of the trip to

15

Washington, D.C. when we all went to the mall. It was the sweater from Saks. God I love that sweater. I just wanted to hold him - he looked so cute."

"He stretched his arm out toward me. Placing the microphone in my other hand, I extended my arm and we held hands. I held the microphone in the air. The crowd continued to cheer, but the chant changed. *Kiss, Kiss, Kiss*. They chanted as they clapped. So, I leaned toward Paul and our lips just about touched. And the fire alarm erupted. Sirens sounded in the auditorium. The fire sprinkler started spraying putrid water. It smelled so bad. And our sweaters were ruined."

"Oh, there was an owl flying around at the end. But it was massive. Like uhm, the size of a huge turkey. How big are owls, anyway?"

"Is that the end of the dream, David?" she asked as she twirled her pen between her fingers.

"Oh, yes. I suppose so. Yeah, the owl was the end, or at least as much as I can remember. Is that crazy, or what?"

Dr. Baritz had been my Doctor since I was about twelve. She was in her mid-forties and was gorgeous. She had red hair, bold black glasses, and was very petite. Her skin was pale, smooth and without a blemish. She was small - but very curvaceous. Sometimes the buttons on her top would come undone. For her size, her breasts were rather large. If I wasn't gay I could simply love her. She was adorable, had excellent posture and she liked yogurt.

I liked yogurt.

We had several things in common besides yogurt, and we never argued.

She smelled of summer.

My parents had sent me to her because according to them, I was a disciplinary problem. I had *issues*. Truthfully, I was *not* a disciplinary problem and the only *issue* I had was the fact I felt I could not tell my parents I was gay. I had told Dr. Baritz I was gay when I was fourteen or fifteen. Now, at eighteen, my parents seemed to lack a good level of understanding of *who* I actually was. My entire life was a lie. It sometimes seemed as if my parents were adopted – not my real parents – and maybe they were merely switched at birth. I felt as if I was the real child but they were the wrong parents.

Why couldn't they just *understand*?

"Well, David," she spoke softly, "It is not crazy, no. Tell me what you felt after you woke up - when the dream was over and you had a few moments to clear your head. How at that point in time did you *feel?* Talk to me about your *feelings*," she said as continued to twirl her pen.

I always enjoyed our open conversations. She made me feel as if I could tell her anything. Actually, I *could* tell her anything. She never got angry with me and she rarely acted as if there was anything I could do or say which was wrong. She supported me fully in all of my thoughts, feelings, needs, wants or desires. Additionally, she was so conscious of fashion as well. It made me feel so good when she complimented me regarding my clothes, and she did so quite frequently. My parents never complimented me on my attire, ever - and their constant complaints about my spending habits got so old.

It seemed as if all they were concerned about was how much money I was spending. *David, stop buying that yogurt. David, stop buying so many clothes. David, stop this. David, stop that. Oh my, David, how many pairs of shoes do you have?*

I sat up in the loveseat and sighed, "My parents are assholes, Dr. Baritz. They complain about my spending. And they hate the way I dress."

I glanced down and noticed my khakis were wrinkled. As I spoke I tried to stretch my legs out on the loveseat cushion to eliminate the wrinkles.

"David, do you want to talk about the dream? About how you *felt* after you woke up," she said as she tapped her pen on her lip.

"Well, I felt. Well I suppose if you get right down to it, I felt - well, proud - like it actually *happened*. As if I were announcing to the auditorium. Well, actually as if I were announcing to the world. I was gay and I was proud. I remember feeling for the entire day following the dream that I *was* proud. I walked through the school as if everyone knew. And as the day progressed I remember sometimes actually feeling as if they *did* know. It was," I paused.

"I guess it was somewhat surreal. But to answer your question, I felt prideful - like I had accomplished something. And all of those people in the auditorium had recognized me for doing so. Yes, Doctor Baritz, prideful," I nodded my head and smiled.

I partially stood up and pulled my pants at the thighs attempting to eliminate the wrinkles. As I sat down I carefully repositioned myself in the seat, feeling somewhat self-conscious about my pants.

"That's a great bit of sharing David. Now we haven't got a tremendous amount of time left, only twenty minutes. I'd like for you to tell me if you have told anyone about your homosexuality since we last spoke. Additionally, I want you to think about when you think you may be able to tell your parents or at least begin discussing things with them," she said as she shifted in her seat.

As she stood, she continued. "I am going to go get a bottle of water, would you like something?"

Happy for the offering of a cold bottle of water, I responded quickly, "Yes, ma'am, I will drink a Perrier. If you're out, I would rather not have the others, please. Oh, and I thought of something else. The entire dream, even the parts I didn't tell you about, I just realized I never tugged on my pants in the dream. And they never wrinkled. They never *needed* tugging. What do you think about that?"

She turned and looked over her shoulder as she reached the door, "Think about what, David? Your pants?"

"Yes ma'am. Not the pants, but the lack of wrinkles. There's no way all that could have *really* happened without wrinkles," I shrugged.

"We will discuss it when I get back, David. Okay?" she said as she turned to the door.

As she left the room I tugged at my pants again and thought of my parents.

Was she kidding me?

Tell my parents?

I would rather die than speak to my parents. Especially my father, who had no capacity to comprehend the thought of having a gay child. I always felt if my little sister announced she was gay, they would embrace and everything would be grand. If I even indicated anything that wasn't masculine or sports related, I was questioned of my manhood. It was as if I couldn't be gay *and* be masculine. Or, I couldn't be gay and be a man. Since I can remember, I detested both my parents for making me feel as if there was something wrong with me. There was nothing wrong with me. Not any more than there was something wrong with them. They were born heterosexual and I was born homosexual.

It was how God made me.

No differently than he made the sky, the sea and the flowers.

I turned and looked out the window, disappointed there were no flowers in the planters. The office building was in an old brownstone which sat immediately beside the adjacent buildings. There wasn't room for foot traffic between the buildings, and the windows housed planters which held fresh flowers during the appropriate months. During this particular visit it was winter time and there were no flowers. As I sat and stared out the window, a feeling of sadness washed over me. I had always found the flowers to be so soothing.

How did she expect me to tell my parents?

I felt as if I could tell my parents nothing.

What did she ask me?

When, or how?

I felt as if it didn't matter, I couldn't accurately answer either. My father would have a heart attack if I attempted to speak to him. It really didn't matter if he was forty-two years old or seventy-seven. Homosexuality was not acceptable *behavior* to him. Not with his son, and not in his world. A former Marine officer, he was a man's man and he despised homosexuals. He was as much of a homophobe as could ever exist.

As I lowered myself into the loveseat I began to consider her request. My father, being the insistent former Marine, had always stressed physical conditioning. I never opposed him regarding maintaining a good physique - I was in good health, six foot two, and a lean 180 pounds. I was muscular and appeared to be a Marine myself. I was proud of my chiseled torso. But nothing could be further from the truth regarding the Marine in me. The thought repulsed me. As I began to think of my father and his hatred for homosexuals, I felt ill.

Fags, as he loved to say.

20

One day as we watched television there was a special news segment about a church in the Midwest. Protestors had gathered at a funeral and several motorcycles were parked in a fashion which formed a blockade between them and the family of the deceased. Motorcycles lined the streets of the cemetery. A line of bikers standing with their arms crossed separated the protesters from the people attending the funeral. Several bikers held flags. The angry protestors waved signs reading *God hates fags* and *God killed your soldier son*. Outraged, my father stood from his chair and placed his hands on his temples as he began complaining. Although angry, he still appeared very much a military man and a Marine. His six foot four height and two hundred and twenty pound frame was intimidating to most people. He wore his hair short, probably as short as it could be cut with scissors.

"Are you fucking *kidding* me?" he screamed as he waved his arms at the television.

"These asshats are protesting the funeral of a Marine that was killed in Afghanistan defending this country. God fucking damn them. Someone should put a bullet in each of their God forsaken heads. This world would be a better place without these communist bastards in it. Chesty would turn over in his grave if he saw this. Out-fucking-standing. Out-fucking-standing. Mary, come look at this horseshit!" he yelled.

When he was disgusted with television, it was fairly common for my father to call my mother into the media room and witness what he was watching. It was as if he required some form of confirmation of what his feelings were regarding whatever issue he was ranting about. She seemed to make him feel as if his thoughts and feelings were justified.

As she entered the room, my mother turned and looked at my father. Now pacing back and forth in sheer disgust, he noticed her and raised his arms in obvious wonder. Standing in her wrinkled dress and house slippers, she glanced at the television and turned to my father again. As if she didn't know what to say for sure, she simply said *something*.

"Oh my," she gasped as she raised her hand to her mouth.

Standing in the doorway, she barely filled half of the opening. At five foot two and a hundred and ten pounds, there wasn't much to my mother from a physical standpoint.

"Joseph, I am so sorry," she offered.

"Sorry? Don't be *sorry*," he said as he motioned toward the television.

"That Marine is a hero. Needs a proper God damned burial. God fucking damn, Mary, I can't take this. How on God's earth can this be happening. These fuck-tards need shot, Mary. Do you see them? *Where* is this happening?" he shouted.

Hating to say anything, yet feeling as if I must confirm my father's feelings regarding his fallen Marine brethren, I spoke, "That is just awful. But the Constitution gives them the *right* to be there, doesn't it?"

My mother covered her mouth and gasped again. She looked at me as if I had stabbed my father in the back. He turned and glared at me as if I had done the same. He placed his hands on his hips and bent at the waist. As his face reddened, he started to scream.

"I can't God damn *believe* you just said that. What in the absolute fuck are you thinking? Clearly you're fucking God damned retarded, right? Listen, these Communist sissies don't have a fucking *right*. I commanded troops in the Gulf War. I do not have to look at this shit. Where's the God fucking damned remote?"

As he looked for the remote the television went into a commercial. The entire thing didn't last two minutes. It wasn't so much watching the protestors at the funeral, but what followed that truly bothered me.

Standing with the remote in his hand and still red-faced, he began, "Son, I *wonder* about you. You're going to have to man up."

He paced back and forth as he continued to speak.

"Become a man. You're going to graduate soon, and then life gets *real.* And it gets real *quick.* And having a soft spot in your heart for everyone isn't going to work. Not in life. I hoped when you were young you'd grow out of this God damned sissy attitude when you were older - but Jesus fucking Christ, son. Be a real man. And those fucking weirdoes do *not* have rights. Remember that. That was a fucking US Marine being buried. One of God's own. Good God son, we defend the Gates of Heaven. Don't you remember?" he asked.

He stared at me with his Marine eyes. It was as if there were two people inside my father; the day-to-day inconsiderate father and the insane Marine.

This was the insane Marine for sure.

With her shoulder-length brown hair pulled back with a hair clip, my mother continued to stand in the doorway in disbelief. I wasn't sure if she couldn't believe I had said something, or if she was incapable of comprehending my father *hadn't* reacted differently. At this point it was difficult to say.

She stood with her hand on her mouth, frozen.

My father took a deep breath and glared toward the television. He must have realized the news was on, and the segment about the protestors was long over. With his hands resting on his knees, he slowly stood arrow straight and took another slow breath. As he exhaled he spoke firmly, but not in a screaming voice.

It was then that he dropped the f-bomb.

"Let me tell you what. I don't like those Goddamned weirdo

protestors but I will tell you something. If there is one thing they have right it's their position on fags. Fucking queers. *God hates fags.* That's what they say. Well, *no shit* is my response. Who doesn't know that? God hates fags. Fags go to hell. That's simple. We don't need *them* telling the world, but I do agree whole heartedly. God hates fags. And I tell you what; I won't be defending the Gates into Heaven for the passage of any fags. They fall straight to hell. Isn't that right, Mary?"

"That's right Joseph, straight to hell," my mother agreed as she took her hand from her mouth.

It was as if she was relieved we were now killing fags, and leaving the sacred Marines alone. I looked toward her, paused, and glanced back at my father. As my mother walked out of the room my father looked at me and raised his hands into the air as if asking the question, *What?.* Before I had a chance to even think of what I may want to offer to the conversation, he sighed again.

"I have to pee." I said as if seeking permission to leave the room.

He stared at me and shook his head, "Piss, son. You have to *piss.* Men don't pee. See, that's what I am talking about. You're eighteen years old now. You are a man. Do you understand, son? The *instant* you turn eighteen, you become a man. Start acting like one."

Dr. Baritz' office was typically warm in the winter. As I tried to get comfortable in the seat I felt a cool breeze in my armpits. In surveying the room, I noticed a fan was blowing. I realized as I felt the chill I was sweating profusely.

Dr. Baritz entered the room and handed me the bottle of Perrier. I thanked her and began to take a drink. I was sweaty and cold. I felt miserable. As I tipped the bottle to my mouth, I could see I was shaking. *Maybe I'm having a seizure.* I always felt embarrassed when I shook, and it happened quite frequently. Nervous, I looked down at my pants and I noticed my khakis were still wrinkled.

A brain hemorrhage.

A brain hemorrhage could cause shaking. Or possibly a swollen brain.

I felt my head. It did not feel enlarged.

"Well, have you had time to think about the questions we discussed, David?" she asked as she began to sit.

The third button on her shirt was unbuttoned. As I tried not to stare, I wondered what she had been doing in the bathroom.

"Yes ma'am, regarding the homosexuality and telling anyone? Well, I have not told anyone *yet*. I have, as we said last session, never been with anyone of my own sex. That remains unchanged. I have, however, felt as if I may be able to tell a few of my girlfriends, but I am not totally comfortable doing so. Not yet," I said as I took another drink.

As I lifted the bottle to my mouth I felt the fan on my wet armpits. Embarrassed, I lowered my arm.

"It's just well," I hesitated.

"As we have talked in the past ma'am, in this community there isn't a tremendous support system for homosexuals. I know of no one in school who is homosexual. And, other than speaking to people on the internet, I have no knowledge of any homosexuals actually existing, if you know what I mean."

As I finished speaking my hands felt numb. I rubbed them together as I wondered if my heart was working properly.

The sound of trickling water played over the sound system in the office. It was on some form of rotation, and during the course of our meetings the sound generally changed three times. It was calming, but the more I thought of living a homosexual life, the more I felt sick. I tried to focus on the sound of the water, hoping to become lost in the sound. I loved listening to certain things, and found tremendous comfort in some things other people did not. Sometimes, I would take my iPod into the media room and listen to Jazz. John Coltrane. The sound of his music gave me reason to believe there was a God.

I knew God existed, and I was quite certain *his* blood flowed through Coltrane's veins as he played his music. God's blood. Coltrane had the ability to make me forget being homosexual, and just *exist*. Just be myself. I could simply listen and get lost in being me. And as the music played, nothing mattered. There were no strange stares, no feelings of guilt for secretly admiring other classmate's clothes, and no thoughts of driving my car into oncoming traffic - just soothing music. Coltrane was magical.

"David, did I lose you?" Dr. Baritz asked as she tapped her lip with the pen.

"No ma'am. I was thinking about music, what music does, and where it can take the mind. Music frees me, Doctor. Does that make sense?" I smiled as I asked her the question, thinking of Coltrane's music.

"Yes, David, it does. Have you had time to consider what we talked about? It's about time to end the session," she said as she looked down buttoned her shirt.

"No ma'am," I lied.

Not necessarily feeling like thinking about the day of my father and his reaction to the protestors on television, I stood from the couch. Hopeful of her ending the session, I stretched and walked to the trash. As I bent down and placed the bottle in the trash, I wondered how John Coltrane discarded trash. I disliked tossing things into the trash, and

26

preferred placing them there instead. It was quieter and more peaceful. I bet John Coltrane placed his trash in a receptacle. I bet he did.

"Well, do you want to think about the questions I asked, and we can discuss them in the next session?" she stood and slowly walked toward me as she twirled the pen in her hand.

"Yes. I would prefer that. I feel cold. I am ready to leave," I said as I crossed my arms and tried to hide my armpits.

I continued to feel the breeze from the fan. I walked toward her, meeting her half way across the office. As always, we shook hands. She watched me as I turned to walk to the door. As I reached the door I turned back to her, smiled and waved.

She smiled in return.

I walked to the parking lot to get in my car, wishing the entire way we would hug at the end of the sessions. I would really like a hug. Hugs were like Coltrane's music. Hugs healed the soul. At least for a little while, but heal they did. I bet John Coltrane hugged people. I bet he did. I straightened my pants and looked for my car. Not immediately seeing it, I feared it had been stolen. I feared calling the police more, so I continued to look. Eventually I found it, certain it was parked elsewhere from where I had left it.

A brain hemorrhage, without a doubt.

I drove the entire way home in some form of a trance having forgotten the entire trip when I arrived. My brain often failed. I vaguely remembered thinking of Paul, and how much I liked him in the dream. He sure was a fantastic friend. I often felt guilty for feeling as if he *may* be gay. I always told myself I didn't feel he was gay, I hoped. I cherished him as a friend. He was splendid. I had very few male friends, and always felt somewhat intimidated by them. Paul was different, he would

27

allow me to just be me and never question my thoughts or opinions. He was a true friend.

Once he told me *if we can't be ourselves, why even be?*

I always wondered if there was an underlying reason for the statement, or if there was possibly some hidden meaning. Eventually I dismissed my thoughts, feeling as if it was merely hope. Hope there was someone who could reassure me I was normal, this was okay, and one day I could possibly find love - true love from someone who appreciated me for simply being me.

Me being me.

The thought was laughable.

As I pulled into the driveway of the house, I came out of my mental state of vacancy. In realizing my parents weren't home, I regretted not stopping at *Cups*. I loved that place. A frozen yogurt hangout for high school aged kids; it was one of my favorite stops. The yogurt was fabulous and almonds or peanut butter cups were my favorite toppings to add. Sometimes on special occasions I would get red gummie bears.

My mouth watered as I pulled into the garage and parked.

As I stepped from the car I considered getting back in and going to *Cups* for a yogurt. It was possible Michelle and her friends would be there. She was so nice, considerate and so off limits. She was Egyptian. I often wondered if she knew I was gay. She seemed so intelligent and street wise, but such a bitch to most people who approached her. I respected her for having the guts to be an individual. She wore combat boots to school every day, and took shit from no one. Seeing her with her friends always made me comfortable. It was the way she looked at me. Her eyes were inviting, and the eyes never lie.

As I stepped up the step from the garage into the house, I stumbled.

I realized I was tired and a nap was probably my best option. As I turned the handle from the mud room door to enter the house, I thought of my father.

God hates fags.

3

I'M WORRIED ABOUT THE BEAVER

FAT KID

As I drove home from the coffee shop I began to think about Shellie. She had continued emailing me regarding having thoughts of suicide. She reached a point where the pain of living life, to her, was unbearable. Her resources for coping with her misery had been exceeded by the pain itself. I had not heard from her in a few days, and was considering emailing her to see how she was doing.

Feeling.

Thinking.

Threats of suicide were something I did not take lightly. In fact, earlier in life I lost a girlfriend to suicide. I had gone to her house to see her one day after being away for some time. Her father answered the door, handed me a poem, and shut the door. I stood on the porch with the poem in hand and wondered just what happened. After reading it, I understood. I never recovered from losing her. I probably never will. Survivors of suicide are often consumed with guilt for not being able to prevent the suicide. I was no exception.

"She left this for you," her father said as he handed me a folded sheet of paper.

"Where is she," I asked.

"She's gone. Suicide. While you were away," he said flatly.

And he shut the door.

Suicide is almost impossible to digest and all of those exposed are affected. I didn't want anyone else to ever feel the pain and loss I had felt in losing her. Dealing with natural death is difficult but eventually we all seem to recover. Suicide passes the pain from the victim to the survivors. For the survivors, the pain lasts a lifetime.

A lifetime of trying to make sense of something that never will.

Now, a recent series of problems with Shellie's family and her boyfriend had prompted her initial email to me. She felt alone and as if she did not know where her life was headed. Not that any sixteen year old *knows* where her life is headed, but she was truly worried. Typically when I assisted people over the internet, I requested a personal photo shortly after the initial correspondence. I was surprised at what the photo she provided depicted. I deduced the photo was taken in the winter, as the trees were without leaves, and the people posing with her were wearing sweaters. She appeared to be a hundred pounds at best. She wouldn't give me her weight, but that was my educated guess. She said she was five foot seven; and for sixteen years old she was certainly tall. Her complexion was dark and she had very smooth skin. She was, or could certainly *be*, gorgeous. The people posing with her in the photo were school mates and they truly looked worried. My initial surprise came from their appearance. The look on the faces of the two people standing next to the otherwise beautiful waif was the same. It was genuine and not some form of theatrical pose.

It was as if they were sending a message.

Help. This. Girl.

Few people ever understood the extent of my ability, but since I was a child I had the capacity to look at someone and see inside of them. See who they were. Not *what* they were, but *who*. The sum of their character defects, personality traits, strengths and weaknesses all rolled up into what appeared to be a normal human being.

Define normal.

I wasn't always capable of performing the *trick* as many called it with just anyone. Some people I could *read* and yet others I could not. It was not uncommon for me to mentally critique people as they walked into or through a restaurant or as they happened into the coffee shop. This gift allowed me to categorize people as I met them, and often prevented me from meeting someone that wasn't necessarily appealing to me.

I allowed very few people into my world and tried to maintain the same posture through my day-today living. I had no part-time friends, only full-time friends as I called them. If someone stopped talking to me, communicating with me, or caring about me I deleted them from my telephone's address book entirely. It wasn't uncommon for me to receive a rambling text message from an unidentified number which included two or three well phrased paragraphs.

Typically, my response was *"Who the fuck are you?"*

I always made a big issue right then and there about their having been excluded from my life. They knew the rules coming in. If they couldn't live up to their end of the bargain, they were out. Kaput. Gone. Sayonara. Bye.

"Yes, this is Fat Kid, and you are excluded from my life. You aren't allowed to speak to me any longer. You made this decision, I didn't. Good bye. Do not text me or call again..."

For fear of exposure, Shellie had not told me where she lived. It was obvious the location in the photo had definite seasons. Spring. Summer. Fall. Winter. Her physical location was not important, but I always *wondered*. I needed details in order for things to make sense in my head. The more details, the better I felt. I understood little about her, but what I had learned was pretty textbook stuff. Typical. Same story, different girl. She suffered from bulimia and often binged, eating way too much food. Guilt would follow the eating and purging herself of the food would happen almost immediately afterwards. She had self-esteem issues and viewed herself as fat, regardless of her weight. As with many people who suffer from bulimia she had other things she obsessed about. Shopping and exercise to name a few. Additionally, she craved attention and didn't feel she received any at home. Her parents were an anesthesiologist mother and an architect father, neither of which had time to include her in their lives.

Their feeling of necessity to obtain the largest possible savings account all the while claiming they were *broke* prevented them from including themselves in her simple life of attending high school.

Work trumps children.

Welcome to 2014.

I often found myself wishing we were in the 1950's again.

Leave it to Beaver.

June and Ward would pay attention to their children's needs and necessities. The Beav' wouldn't need to ask his father to attend a school function; Ward would be there for certain. And upon completion, rest assured June would have a pie for the boys, including Eddie Haskell. *Eddie fucking Haskell*. I wondered how many of today's parents would allow an Eddie Haskell to even enter the premises of their home? Parents

34

today seemed to be far more concerned with *who* their kids befriended and were far less concerned with being friendly to their own children.

"Ward, I am worried about the Beaver…"

I suspected, and I am certain rightfully so, no one ever said, "Dear, I am worried about Shellie."

At sixteen years old she was in a relationship with an eighteen year old. On the surface this didn't seem overly strange. She had initially indicated there was some concern of him possibly taking advantage of her and that he may have distributed nude photos of her to classmates. Additionally, there was concern with her parents regarding the relationship in general. Egyptian Americans girls were not to mingle with the white boys.

After considering all of the issues, she felt she couldn't separate herself from the boy.

And so the pattern began to develop.

Codependence.

I had learned through experience that codependent woman sought relationships earlier than normal. Shellie, considering all things, clearly fell well within the limits of what would be the makings of a codependent woman. Frequently, they dated older and often abusive male partners - men who may resemble their father. Seeking recognition, praise and love from a partner and often not receiving these things at home caused the initial desire to develop. Codependent women were willing to sacrifice themselves as well as their health for the relationship they were in. Poor treatment and abuse, at some level, were a guarantee with the textbook codependent relationship.

Starting *this* early, Shellie was typical of every girl in America these days - at least the ones who were neglected by their parents. As their parents were earning their next million, their daughter was out performing orally for an eighteen year old *bad boy* in the parking lot of the local 7-Eleven. For one sentence of praise, a fifteen year old codependent girl would generally do *whatever* her abusive partner required of her. The lack of self-esteem and codependency were almost always hand-in-hand. So as mother and father earned another day's wages, working late and nonstop, their daughters formed lines in the parking lots. Filling the passenger seats of their abusive boyfriends' car, they would agree to almost any sexually request in hope for a moment of praise.

Maybe tonight he will tell me that I did a great job, that he's proud of me. He might say I'm a good girl or I make him happy. Or he loves me. I hope he doesn't say it feels good again. I know it feels good. I want him to be pleased. I want him to stay. I want him to hold me tonight when we are finished, and tell me how important I am to him. Please don't let him tell me "that felt good" again. Maybe if I swallow he will be pleased. I'm going to swallow. He will surely say he is proud of me if I swallow...I think next week I will tell him that I want to call him Daddy when we are doing this. I wish he would bring it up. I wonder if we could just call it role play? Surely he will agree to that. I just hate to bring it up. What if he gets mad and leaves me? Okay, I will not bring it up. That was a bad idea. Bad. Bad idea. I love him so much.

And, as the mother completes one more scheduled late night careful administration of anesthesia, their daughter swallows in the parking lot of a 7-Eleven. The preteen cries for help went unanswered. Teenagers eventually turn into adults. Adults get married, have children, and expose their children to the abusive behaviors of a codependent relationship. And the cycle continues. Shellie would be no exception.

But it was the suicide threat that concerned me.

As I drove, I wondered what was *behind* the suicide. There was always a reason. Something. Typically there's an event which takes them over the edge - making the pain unbearable. Sometimes it may be a combination of items the person just can't comprehend living with, but it's always *one* thing that takes them over the edge. It's not that they actually want to die.

Generally, they just want the pain to stop.

God...

Grant me the serenity,

To accept the things I cannot change;

The courage to change the things I can;

And the wisdom to know the difference.

Amen.

Why could people not just apply this prayer to everyday living? Maybe to all things life offered them? I often wondered. For me, it was second nature. As I thought about what may have taken Shellie over the edge, I drummed my fingers on the gear shift to the music. It seemed as though my hands were always busy doing something, and I rarely sat still. Just as I was finishing the current song on the play list, I looked up along the road in front of me. When I did, I *noticed* the brake lights of the car in front of me, but I forgot to *react.* I watched in horrific slow motion as the front of my BMW slammed into the rear of the twenty five year old Ford Taurus.

As I impacted the car and pushed it about five feet forward, I did not think about damaging the Taurus. I didn't wonder if anyone was hurt, or what may or may not have happened. I wondered what my current wreck count was.

Fifteen?

Thirty?

Seventy?

I had, over the course of the last year or so, rear ended at least five people. Each time, I needed a new hood, the front bumper repainted and new grilles. In past years I typically had a wreck about twice a year. Each time, I would rear end someone.

Disappointed, I got out of the car without even paying attention to the vehicle in front of me. I turned and looked at the front of the BMW, and as I suspected, it needed the standard repair. Hood, grilles, and bumper repaint. This was my third e46 platform BMW M3. I had driven this particular series of car for ten years, and it had become a trademark of mine. All I did was change colors.

I vowed to never have anything else.

I turned toward the car I had hit, and focused on the fifty-something year old woman as she exited the Taurus. She got out, turned to me, and placed her hands on her hips.

"What in the world were you doing? I can tell you what you *weren't* doing, and that's paying attention to driving. I watched you for the last three miles. Are you drunk?" her voice sounded like it was created by a rubber band which was stretched too tight and left in the California sun for a summer.

She was dressed like a bum, and it appeared her last few dollars were spent on cigarettes, one of which hung from her right hand. She stunk like a tobacco bonfire, and I was ready for her to vanish. Her hair didn't appear to have been washed for quite some time.

Nice look, lady.

Dreadlocks on a fifty year old white woman.

Perfect.

If she fell asleep smoking at least her hair wouldn't immediately go up in flames. Or would it? I stood and wondered if the grease in the dreadlocks would be an accelerant or a deterrent.

I looked at her hair with disgust, but offered a smile, "Ma'am, I am sorry for the damage to your car. Maybe we should pull over and discuss matters."

I suspect I looked like a liar.

"I have called the police," she sighed.

"That's what I was doing while you were looking at your car," she said as she blew smoke from her grotesquely tan nose.

Her lips were wrinkled and covered in deeply defined lines.

"Police?" I muttered.

"Why did you call the fucking police? This is something we can settle right here and now. I do not want to wait for the God damned police."

"Well, when you are involved in a wreck, you call the police. It's required," she said as she took yet another unnecessary pull from what appeared to be a cigarette butt.

I shoved my hands into my pockets and looked into her eyes.

"It is not *required*, it is recommended," I lied.

I smiled and shoved my hands deep into my pockets, "We can settle this right here and now, without the police. Then, we go about our way and everyone's happy."

She started to interrupt, but I continued with a little added embellishment, "You decide what the damage repairs to your car are worth, and I hand you cash. It's that simple. You decide, plain and simple. I haven't had my insulin shot this morning, and I need to get home as soon as possible. Truth be known, I am sure that's why I was daydreaming. What do you think?"

Seeming puzzled, she looked at me and spoke, "Let me get this straight, I give you an amount, and you pay me *caaaaaaaash?*"

The word *cash* lasted a lifetime. I waited as she attempted to finish her sentence for the rubber band in her throat to snap.

"Yes ma'am, cash," I said as I pointed to the side of the road.

So you can go buy shampoo and more cigarettes.

"But we either need to settle this or move to the side of the road. We are going to get hit. *Again*," I said in an effort to encourage her to make a decision.

I felt I really needed to leave before the police arrived.

People had gathered and were watching the show, asking to make sure we were not injured. She looked at the rear of her car, looked along the sides, and placed her hand on her chin. Turning to face me, she made her offer.

She raised one eyebrow, "Two hundred dollars."

She paused and tossed the cigarette butt in the street, stepping on it with her toe.

Satisfied with her response, I reached deep into my left front pocket and got my money clip out. As I turned away from her, I removed two one hundred dollar bills, making sure she couldn't see how much money I carried. Although I did not have a huge wad of cash at this point in time, it was not uncommon for me to carry several thousand dollars in my pocket. Just in case. For what reason I never really knew, but I just felt more secure with larger amounts of money. As I turned to face her, I extended my arm in an offering gesture.

"Ma'am, I appreciate the consideration. It's just simpler in this fashion, and we can both go our own way."

As she accepted the money and placed it into her palm, she looked down at my canvas sneakers and slowly up the height of my three hundred plus pound frame. After a quick study of my attire, she turned and began to make her way to the wrecked Taurus.

"You don't have insurance, do you?" she asked over her shoulder as she walked away.

As her hands fumbled with the two bills, counting them and recounting them as she walked, my blood began to boil.

Yes lady, they're both still there.

"Do I *look* like it?" I hollered, knowing I probably did not look like I had auto insurance.

"Lady, I have insurance," I shouted.

"I drive a sixty thousand dollar car, and it is insured. Let's just get out of here so I can get my insulin and we can prevent yet another accident, how does that sound?"

She continued to walk to her car and I turned to walk to mine. As I did, I looked at my shoes. Typical Fat Kid attire, canvas sneakers with the soles worn through. I opened the door and stuffed myself into the car. Getting in and out was a feat in itself, but once I was in I felt comfortable. I sighed deeply as I realized the cost of my repairs. I had done this too many times. Two thousand dollars. As I put the car in gear and began to drive away, I thought.

Do I have car insurance?

Frequently, I would hop in my car with no intended destination and drive. Sometimes, I may be gone a month or longer. As a result of these extended trips, I developed a pattern of not picking up my mail. I lived in a building of condominiums, and the mail was delivered to a common mail box area. This arrangement was similar to a post office with personal post office boxes. The boxes had numbers on them that corresponded with the house number of the residence they served.

One day, when attempting to pick up my mail, I opened the box. To my utter surprise, the box was void of any mail. A small yellow card was all that was in the box. On the card it said several things, but the primary message was clear.

"THIS MAILBOX HAS BEEN VACATED"

It went on to explain the mail was returned to the post office, and it could be picked up prior to a particular listed day. I checked the date on the card and the date on my phone. As fate would have it, I found my mail had been cancelled for two months.

I called the phone number on the card for the post office which would have been holding my mail and asked to speak to the postmaster. Within a few moments a very pleasant woman and I were speaking. After learning she was the postmaster, I asked several questions regarding procedure and policy, explained my extended trips, and made excuses for not retrieving my mail in a timely manner. Soon, I was offered an explanation of what may have happened.

The postmaster attempted to clear matters up with a detailed description of their procedure regarding the matter. When the mail collected to the point there was no longer room for any additional daily mail to be added, a notice would be placed in the box requiring removal of the existing mail. If within the allotted time frame listed on the card the mail wasn't removed, it would be returned to the post office. At which point in time the "VACATED" card would be added.

I offered my apology and agreed if I was out of town for an extended period of time in the future to place notice with the post office to hold my mail. We both admitted in a perfect world this should never happen again. I wouldn't abandon my mailbox without notice, and they wouldn't cancel my mail services and remove my mail. Niceties were exchanged, and I was informed my mail delivery would continue beginning the following day. As we finished the conversation on the phone, I made a note in the calendar of my smart phone to remind me to pick up the mail in two more months.

Two months later, as I drove to the coffee shop, my phone alarm went off reminding me to get the mail. After a short trip of coffee, lunch and other errands, I returned home. Upon my arrival, the mail delivery person was at my building, as was indicated by his mail truck outside the door.

Entering the building from the rear, I spotted the mail man. He was about fifty years old, gaunt, but in shape - as you would expect a mail man to be. He was a large man, and stood about six foot three. His skin was tan and leathery. As he gathered his things to go, I made an issue of opening my box and relaying to him my displeasure of his cancellation of my mail several months prior. He responded by telling me he was preparing to place yet *another* "VACATE" card in the box.

As I opened the box, I found a good two inches of spare room sufficient for *new* mail.

Making my position immediately clear, I brought it to his attention I had in fact talked to the postmaster. I continued with stating I assumed the postmaster to be his superior, and with a good two inches of mail room to spare, he did not have the authority or the need to cancel my mailbox. He, being a lowly delivery person should simply continue to smile and deliver the mail. And that is all.

His rebuttal was weak, but extremely offending, "Sir, you *need* to remove the mail from the box, or it will be cancelled. You can't allow the mail to collect in the box."

He seemed to get taller as he spoke.

And *that* is when I threatened the mail man.

"Oh, you're going to tell me what I *need* to do. *Really?* Well, let me tell *you* something. You need to get out of here before I whip your mailman ass. I will whip your ass all the way back to your fucking truck," I screamed.

As I stepped toward him he stepped backward, speaking to me as he left. In an elevated tone, but not screaming, he began a feeble attempt in defending his honor.

Extending his arm and holding his index finger in the air, he growled, "If you threaten me, I will call the police."

"I did threaten you. And go ahead, call the police. By the time they get here, this will all be over," I said as I began to lower my computer bag to the floor.

As he walked to his truck I turned back to the mailbox. The mailbox door remained open. Angrily, I removed the entire contents of the mail and dumped it into the trash - as if this were some form of satisfactory retribution for his being a complete incompetent ass. I smiled as I turned and walked to my car, thinking of him opening the box the next day. He would actually think I took the mail home with me.

I smiled again.

I entered my condo and remained there for the day, waiting on the police to arrive. No police. No phone calls from the postmaster, and no angry drunken mailman at my door wanting to try his luck at the Fat Kid. As I looked out the window for police who never arrived, I wondered how long it would have taken me to beat the mailman's ass. Thirty seconds? A minute? Certainly not two or three. I went to sleep that night extremely satisfied about the mail being in the trash. I didn't even look at one piece of it.

Now *that* was satisfying.

And as I pulled away from the accident, I wondered. Was it possible my insurance invoice for this period could have been in that pile of trash I threw away? As I fumbled for another tube of almonds, disappointment filled me. It frustrated me I had probably thrown away my insurance card, wrecked my car again, and someone would ruin perfectly good chocolate by inserting an almond in the center.

Entering the freeway, I tapped my hand on the gearshift. The Black Keys played over the stereo. As I used my tongue to clear the remaining almond matter from my teeth, the phone beeped. I picked it up and looking at the screen. Opening the email screen, I realized it was from Shellie. Relieved and filled with wonder, I opened the email. The "subject" line caught my eye. **SUBJECT : Getting worse**.

As I returned my focus to the road ahead of me, I knew what I had to do.

Help. This. Girl.

4

I LIKE THIS BOY

BRITNEY

Staring into my closet, I tried to decide what to wear. My mother had said we were going out to eat for my birthday, and we would be leaving at noon. I sifted through the clothes and looked at the price tags as I tried to decide what would be best to wear. The day was special, as it was my sixteenth birthday. I would be able drive now, and older boys only want a sixteen year old girl. Being fifteen years old is so childish. Basically, at sixteen years old, a girl becomes a lady. I needed to pick out clothes which would define who I am, and allow me to stand out as being a lady. Something to get me noticed.

Noticed and loved.

Typically, standing in my closet made me happy. Staring at my clothes always made me smile. I had more clothes and more *expensive* clothes than anyone else I know. No one had as many clothing options as I do. My parents could often be so stupid. Sometimes they tried to tell me *no* when I wanted to go shopping. They acted as if we spent too much money on clothes. Nothing could be farther from the truth. I truly wondered if they really expected me to wear my outfits twice. The thought of having someone see me wear something after I had already worn it once was just gross. If we were shopping as a family they never told me no; and when I believed they were acting selfish I routinely picked clothes which were far more expensive than others.

Spending money satisfied me to no end. When I purchased things I felt like nothing else mattered, like I was free. People respected me for who I was when I am bought things and they treated me with respect.

I started with the clothes on the end of my closet closest to my bed when an outfit to wear. When I was done wearing my outfits, they went to the cleaners. After they were returned from the cleaners, I would put them at the other end of the closet. The last time the closet was cleaned out I had seven trash bags of clothes I sent out to the trash. Cleaning out the closet is something I typically looked forward to because it meant the time to go shopping again had arrived. We always shopped whenever we wanted to, but after I cleared the closet of old clothes I got to spend as much money as I needed to try to fill it with new clothes again.

After getting dressed and posting a photo on Twitter, I went downstairs. I had carefully picked an outfit that didn't make me look fat. I weighed 110 pounds, but I appeared to be fat. When I posted pictures on Twitter people would tell me I looked good or that I seemed skinny, but they couldn't see me the way I was able to see myself. It was easy for me to seem or become sickeningly fat.

To keep myself looking thin I watched my diet and would exercise regularly.

I checked the bottom of my shoes before I went down the stairs, but when I reached the bottom I nervously looked again to make sure they didn't have any stickers on them. As I walked into the kitchen, it was apparent everyone had left. In wondering where they had gone, I looked out the window and saw my parents and little sister in the front of the house - standing by the entrance. They all stood and stared toward the garage, as if they were waiting on me.

They always complained I took too long to get ready. To create a woman who looked like this took considerable time. They were all so shallow, simple and unable to truly understand what it was like to be sixteen; to try to find someone to love you. It was such a competition with all the other girls.

Frustrated, I grabbed my purse and walked outside and into the driveway.

My father and mother stood together and my little sister was beside them. As I got closer I could see my father pointing toward the end of driveway, in the direction of the garage. I turned and looked to where he pointed, and that was when I saw it for the first time.

My father turned and smiled as he squinted through the lenses of his glasses, "Happy Birthday, Britney."

The glasses caused him look old and poor. I often wished he would get new glasses. I looked down at his shoes and shook my head. He had worn a pair of ridiculous Cole Haan shoes he always wore to work which had tassels. I wondered if he really expected me to be seen shopping with him if he wore those shoes.

Oh my God.

He grinned and turned to face the garage, "Britney, I have purchased for you. Happy birthday my dear."

He waved his hands toward the garage as if trying to push me along the driveway. As I walked toward my birthday gift I couldn't help but notice it was white.

White?

Seriously?

White?

As I approached the end of the car I noticed the round thing on the trunk - a blue and white BMW symbol. Clearly it was not a Mercedes.

Are you kidding me?

Who drives a BMW?

My father had purchased a white BMW for my birthday and expected me to be satisfied. It was disgusting in itself the car was white, but a white *BMW*? *Double gross*. Poor people drove BMW's and our family was not poor. As I stared at the ghastly car, my eyes began to swell and I felt as if I was going to cry. How could he expect drive to school on Monday and face everyone if I were driving a BMW?

And a white BMW at that?

I wanted to die.

As everyone stood at the end of the driveway and smiled I did my best not to cry. Frustrated, I reached into my purse and got my phone. After taking a photo of the car, I opened my Twitter and tweeted a picture for my friends to see. I felt it would be better if everyone saw it now and knew I was embarrassed.

I stared at my tweet.

Sooooo #NotAMercedes. Happy Birthday Britney.

I dropped my phone into my purse and turned to face my parents. My father reached into his pocket and pulled out the keys, dangling them from his fingers as if he were going to drop them in the driveway.

"Do you like?" he asked.

I stood and stared.

"Here take the keys. It is yours Britney," he smiled.

"It's white. And it's a BMW. I wanted a Mercedes, father," I explained as I walked toward him.

50

"You do not appreciate the gift?" he asked.

"Father, I appreciate the gift, yes. Thank you," I wiped my eyes and attempted to smile.

As he handed me the keys he held his arms out, opening them wide to give me a hug. Reluctantly, I hugged him. As we embraced I began to softly cry. My father was so inconsiderate and probably made me cry more than anyone else I knew. Realistically, more than everyone else combined. He just didn't understand. Being sixteen and being a girl was so impossible. Finding someone to love me was an unattainable feat. *How could he expect me to be happy?* Hugging him made me want to just die.

As I stepped away from him I took the keys from his hand and dropped them into my purse.

"Can we go now?" I pleaded.

"Do you wish to drive?" my father asked.

The previous night I had been up very late updating my Twitter, Facebook, and posting photos on Instagram, Snap Chat and Tumblr. After having updated videos on Vine and YouTube, it was almost 4:00 a.m. before I went to sleep.

"No father. I am tired, and just care to ride," I sighed as I attempted to wipe my eyes free of any tears.

He smiled and squinted through his stupid glasses, "Are you pleased?"

Frustrated, ready to leave, and tired, I lied, "Yes father, I am pleased."

Overall, I was pleased about the gift. As I stood and stared at it I became more disappointed with what it was. My sister, mother and father began walking toward the garage pointing toward the car as they walked. I stood and stared at it thinking to myself.

How could they actually expect me to make any form of progress in finding someone to love me if I were to be seen driving this car every day?

It was almost as if the white vehicle was some form of punishment. Like a scar on my face which would prevent someone from actually seeing me for who I truly was. A potential boyfriend would simply see the car and say *no* before they got a chance to actually understand me.

People could be so shallow. So inconsiderate. So fake. Fake people were so prevalent in my school. All I wanted out of life was for someone to love me truly for who I was. How could they expect it to ever happen if I was forced to drive the white BMW? Some of the girls in school drove similar cars, but they were prettier than I was. They are *always* pretty. They wore makeup. They didn't have as nice of a collection of clothes as I did and they didn't have my sense of fashion; but they were pretty. I could be pretty; but it took time for me to prepare myself. I had to wear makeup - which my father prohibited – and have my hair fixed properly. If I had enough time I felt I could be almost as pretty as the prettiest girls in my school - but not quite.

I felt I needed the car to be the one thing that put me over the top when compared to the other girls; something which might put me in a category all by myself.

A clear definition of who I was.

When we arrived at the mall I separated myself from my parents as best as I could. I tried to shop alone so I didn't have to listen to the complaints regarding the high prices of my clothing selections. While I looked at a dress and attempted to find the price tag I couldn't help but notice a boy looking at me from across the store. Quickly, I looked down at the dress; feeling a little bit embarrassed. As I fumbled for the tag I began to wonder why he may be looking at me. After a long moment of wondering, I looked up. To my surprise he was standing beside me in front of the rack of dresses.

"Hey," he said as he pushed his hands into his jeans pockets.

He was dressed in jeans, brown lace up boots, a white button down shirt, and wore an old weathered brown leather jacket. He was about six feet tall and thin, but appeared to be muscular – at least from what little I could see. His hair was long and had an unkempt look, but was stylish. He was white and by my standards, almost perfect. Cautiously, I looked around the store to make certain my parents didn't see me talking to a boy who was not Egyptian.

"Do you work here?" I asked.

After I spoke I felt rather foolish. Clearly he didn't work in the mall - dressed as he was and wearing his leather jacket inside the store. I didn't know what else to say and the stupid question was I could think of on such short notice. I talked to a lot of boys but almost all of my discussions were through the social media networks and didn't require any form of interaction in person. I generally felt comfortable with the boys on the Internet because I could be whoever I wanted to be; and take as long as I wanted to carefully prepare an answer to their questions. When I was on the Internet everyone paid attention to me – they cared about what I was doing and took time to commented on my postings. I had over a thousand followers on Twitter, 50,000 tweets and had almost reached the five thousand friend limit on Facebook.

He lifted his leather jacket and exposed his belt, "No, I am here looking for a new belt."

As he lifted his jacket I could see his wide brown belt.

"This one is brown, but I need a new black one," he smiled.

After he finished speaking he slowly looked over my entire body. As his eyes moved to my feet, he hesitated. I stood and wished he would simply speak and explain why he was looking at me. As I stood in wonder, I felt relief as I recalled I had worn my Jimmy Choo's.

I looked up and attempted to smile, "I like the belt you have."

After the words came out I felt like such a dork. He looked into my eyes while I spoke. He looked at me each time he spoke to me and seemed just as focused when I spoke to him. I liked this boy. I liked this boy a lot. He looked into my eyes each time he spoke. His gaze never faded from my eyes when he talked.

"I like it too. I need to get a new Brown one. Black one. I mean this one is brown. I need a black one. I have a brown one. Black one. I am going to buy a new black one," he stammered.

"I'm sorry, you make me nervous," he said.

His eyes remained focused on mine. He pushed his hands deeply into his pockets and he rocked back and forth on his feet as he spoke. I stood and wondered if he was nervous.

And why.

"You're just. Well, you're so beautiful. It doesn't even seem like you have on any make up. Yet just like you are standing here, you're so much more beautiful than any other girl I have ever seen in my life. I would like to know more about you. I am Marc. Marc with a "C". What's your name, gorgeous?"

Immediately, it felt like the temperature rose in the store by fifty degrees. It became insanely hot. I could almost feel myself getting sick from the heat. As I attempted to accept what he had said, my legs started to feel rubbery. I stood incapable of speaking and felt as if all the blood from my body was rushing toward my face. I turned both directions and looked for a sign of my parents.

My parents, especially my father, would kill me if they saw me talking to a white boy. My family was Egyptian and according to my parents I was to have no interest in anyone but Egyptian boys. White boys were off limits.

"I'm Britney," I grinned.

For some reason I could find nothing else to say. Unable to speak, I stood and admired him. He was so cute. His smile made me feel wanted. Appreciated. Beautiful. The way he stuttered when he tried to tell me about his belt just made him seem so real – so genuine. The boys at school seemed so phony and didn't really even give me the time of day and he seemed so different.

I glanced around the store again and looked for my parents; fearing they would see me before he decided to walk away.

"Where are you from, Britney?" he asked, still rocking back and forth on his feet.

"East Brunswick," I responded, "and you?"

"East Brunswack, huh? I'm in South Plainfield. Are you waiting on someone? You look like you're waiting for someone. You keep looking around, Britney."

He ran his right hand through his hair and immediately looked down at his watch. He seemed to be a little nervous, but there was no way he could have been nervous from talking to me. *Is that even possible? Nervous?* Certain he wasn't nervous, I continued to admire him as I attempted to find a flaw in his appearance or clothes. For what later seemed like an eternity, I became lost in his white teeth and good looks. I had never seen a boy who dressed similarly and I was pretty sure he didn't have to *do* anything to look as good as he did.

"Are you waiting on someone?" he asked again as he looked into my eyes.

"Oh, no. I am just nervous. I have never met anyone like you before. Uhhhhm, do you have Facebook?" I asked.

He looked down at his feet.

"No, I don't..."

"Twitter?" I interrupted.

I flipped my hair over my shoulder and turned to allow him to see my good side. My left side. My right side always seemed to make me look much fatter than I actually was and my left side made me look thin. As I looked over my left shoulder I waited for a response.

"Actually Britney, I don't use any of the social networking platforms or whatever they're called," he responded.

My jaw dropped. I stood and stared at him. I couldn't speak. Why wouldn't he have Facebook? Twitter? How could he function? Maybe his parents were strict. For what seemed like forever, I stood and stared. Incapable of comprehending how he could live in that fashion, I didn't speak for some time. I simply stood and stared. At some point a person behind me sneezed and startled me. A lady passed by and smiled. As I looked back over my left shoulder toward Marc, he smiled.

"I do not have Facebook. I do not have Twitter. I do not spend any time on Tumblr, post pictures, use Snapchat, Instagram, or spend time on YouTube. To me, that's a waste of my time. I look at my life as being far more important than that. I read, write poetry and spend time listening to music. I try to have some depth and not be like everyone else. Reading and writing poetry helps me," he paused and looked up at the ceiling.

"If someone wants to know where I am, who I am with, what I am

56

shopping for, where I am eating - or whatever - I want them to know because they actually *know* or because they are accompanying me. Oh, and I do not watch television or the news. It's always such bad things that they talk about. If they had a channel called the *good news*, I would watch it. But all the news is bad. Do you know what I mean, Britney?" he shrugged.

I liked the way he said my name when he spoke to me. At a loss for words, I nodded my head. My focus was stuck on his eyes the entire time. Nervously, he removed his hands from his pockets and looked at his watch again.

"The news is just full of bad things that happen. A bombing here - a shooting there. Someone cheated someone else out of money. A company lost millions by the hand of an embezzler. A massive wreck on 95. It's always something," he paused and raised his hand to his face.

"If they said…" he looked upward and paused.

He smiled and continued, "Well if they said, *construction is complete on 95, and it is three months early. Home sales are up in Morgantown. The economy is on the upswing, and unemployment is down to one percent across the nation, more after this commercial.* If that was ever on the news, I may watch it. I do read the newspaper before school, every day. I enjoy the newspaper because I can decide what to read and what to set aside."

I wanted to give him my phone number before my parents saw us speaking to each other.

Nervously, I spoke, "That is so cool. Definitely different, but cool. Uhhhhm, I hate to be forward, Marc, but would you like my number?"

"Yes, I would. I was going to ask you if you wanted to get something to eat," he said as he motioned to the door.

Frustrated with the fact I had my parents with me, I exhaled and stared at the floor, "No, I have to meet my family for lunch. It's my birthday today, so we're having lunch."

I shifted my body so he would stay on my left.

"How old are you, Britney?" he asked.

I should lie.

"Eighteen."

"Cool, me too," he said as he reached in his inner jacket pocket and got his phone.

"Okay," I started, "Nine Zero Eight Three Four Seven Seven One Four Seven"

"That's too many numbers," he sighed as he looked up from his phone.

"What do you have so far?" I asked.

He held out his phone and allowed me to see the number. Feeling silly, I touched the screen and deleted one of the sevens while he held the phone. With his free hand he reached over and touched my arm, sliding his hand along my arm until it stopped at my hand.

As he cupped my hand in his, he smiled, "Pleasure to meet you, Britney."

"I'm sorry Marc, I have to run and meet my family. Shoot me a text okay?"

Reluctantly, I slowly pulled my hand from his.

He raked his fingers through his hair again, turned, and walked toward the door which led to the parking lot. I stood and watched him walk away until he went through the door. As he exited, he held the door for a family as they entered. Smiling, he spoke to them as if he knew them.

A long moment passed.

My phone beeped. Excited, I reached into my purse and pulled it out. After swiping in the password, I looked at the screen. It was a number I didn't recognize.

Britney. I miss you already. I cannot wait to see you again. Happy Birthday, Marc.

I programmed the number in as *Marc.*

I liked this boy.

Alot.

5

FUCK OATMEAL

MICHELLE

By the time I realized the alarm was going off, it had been buzzing for three minutes. As I often did, I had fallen asleep after being up late on the internet. Scanning photos of tattoos I found interesting was a means of escape for me. It provided me the ability to dream. To dream of what was depicted by the tattoo itself and that one day I could, like the people in the photos, have the freedom to express myself through a tattoo I had designed myself. The time I spent admiring the photos allowed me to forget the rules and regulations of my typical Egyptian family for a short period of time.

Beginning when I was five years old, my family started traveling back and forth between the United States and Egypt. As with many Egyptian families, my family dreamed of living in the United States, working hard, raising a family and being successful. The problem in my opinion was with the last portion of the dream. *Being successful and raising a family*. I would prefer *successfully raising a family*. The burden in being an Egyptian high school kid in my neighborhood in New Jersey was grand. We were expected to be adults in almost all respects but we were treated as children and constantly reminded of the fact we were not an adult.

In seven months I would be attending Villanova University. Upon completion of my education there, I would continue on to Drexel University to attend medical school. I am, and not to my disliking, going to follow in my mother's footsteps and become a doctor. I imagine this was expected of me, but ultimately it was a conscious decision I had made. The thought of being a doctor satisfied me greatly. Helping people. Saving lives. Making a difference. Saving *something*. Doing what so many others cannot.

Not everyone has the capacity to go to school and become a medical doctor. I did and I intended to do so, and do it well. I did not have this desire simply because my family expected it. Without a doubt it was what I wanted to do. It defined me.

Me being me.

When I was around eight years of age my family moved to the United States full time. Following my immediate family moving here, most of our extended family relocated here in a very short period of time. We now resided in New Jersey full time. A few of our family members remained in Egypt and from time to time we would visit them as our schedule permits.

Living my life with an open mind, I tried to look at things realistically and without bias. I frequently found I may spend a significant amount of time looking at the many sides of a new topic which may be discussed - be it by my friends or my family - and *not* give an opinion. I often took a tremendous amount of time to think about the subject and looked at it from each possible point of view. Generally, I tried to view the subject as if I were every possible person who was or could be affected by the decision I may make or opinion I projected. I had always felt this open minded nature allowed me to make more educated decisions. Once again, it allowed me to be me. My free will, stubborn nature, and free spirit got me into a considerable amount of trouble with my parents throughout my childhood.

When I was ten years old, although we were *not* Catholic, my parents sent me to Catholic school in the belief it would instill discipline. I spent the majority of my spare time after school lying in my room crying. As all children do at some point in time, I wanted to run away or commit suicide. The logical side of my thinking prevented me from doing either. My first year was the only year I was required to attend the Catholic school - and one year was certainly enough.

Now, I was close to very few kids in my school. The kids I was close to were extremely close. The ones I was not close to were either kids I do not know, or kids I knew and choose not to be friends with. The kids in school who did not know me very well often described me as a bitch, and I found satisfaction in their verbal depiction of me. Their thoughts of me being a bitch generally meant if they did finally develop enough gall to approach me, they had already decided I was not as the other kids perceive me. Some of the kids might describe me as being conceited or uppity but nothing could be further from the truth.

I liked to think I had attractive qualities - my most attractive being my inner self. I believed my mind, spirit, soul, beliefs, principles, opinions, and general manner of living life were my true strengths. The outside of me, in my own opinion, was generally drab. I was average at best - nothing to neither balk at - nor praise. However, when people described this facet of me, they often characterized me as beautiful. When classmates described me as beautiful I was appreciative, and took their remarks into account. When boys said I was beautiful, I generally set the remark aside.

Boys cannot be trusted.

Boys have motives.

I varied from my Egyptian elders in many respects. All of the values my parents and relatives tried to adhere to weren't necessarily shared by me. Tattoos are one case, but a very important example. When I saw a person who had a tattoo I was often fascinated by it. I may wonder what it meant to them or the significance they saw in it. Often I found the tattoo to be beautiful, or an enhancement of the person's initial beauty. I was not so simple and shallow that I believed all tattoos on all people were beautiful or that they *always* provided some form of enhancement to one's beauty. I had dreamed of the day I would turn eighteen and be free to decide on my own. In doing so, I had made an appointment at a local tattoo parlor for my first tattoo to be obtained on that particular day. It would be a means of expressing myself and in my opinion enhance *my* beauty. It would allow me to be, in all respects, me.

On one typical evening in my typical Egyptian home, with my typical Egyptian parents and my typical Egyptian brother we had a typical Egyptian meal. The typical Egyptian discussion that followed was not, in any regard, what I had anticipated.

The discussion started about tattoos and all was going fairly well.

Tattoos are becoming mainstream. Tattoos are more prevalent on people in college and in professional sports. Tattoos are more frequently seen on professionals, and in professional atmospheres and careers. Tattoos are a great form of individual expression.

Unless.

Unless your Egyptian daughter wants to receive one. When your Egyptian daughter wants to receive one, tattoos become trash. They become a permanent means of not only being trash, but of *turning you into trash*. According to my parents, tattoos were not for Egyptian girls, regardless of their age.

End of story.

In their opinion, tattoo trash attached to my body.

In my opinion it was a means of expression and confirmation that I was an adult, and capable of making decisions on my own.

I was fascinated by tattoos and spent countless hours, sometimes nightly, on Tumblr looking at tattoo photographs of both men and women. I had planned on getting a tattoo since I was as young as twelve. A considerable amount of time, thought, and planning had gone into my anticipated tattoos; including design, meaning, and when I expected to obtain each one. This had not been a rash decision I made as a seventeen year old - to run and have a tribal winged piece tattooed on my lower back above the belt line.

To me, tattoos were a form of expression. If given enough thought they may suggest individuality in a person. They depicted creativity in a personality, made a statement, or expressed a strong belief. They could not, however, at least according to my parents, be attached to their now seventeen year old daughter after she turned eighteen.

For my entire childhood, I had looked at my eighteenth birthday as a line in the sand - a line I would step over on *that* day. An actual graduation if you will from being a child to being an adult. On that day, of all days, I would not be *perceived* as being an adult, I would *be* an adult.

In my mind, the day following my eighteenth birthday things would be different. I may not act differently or change anything, but I *could*. I would be able to think freely and make decisions without feeling the need or necessity to have an authoritative figure give me the nod of approval. To me, the chains that bound me for my entire life would effectively be removed. My shackles set aside, I would be free. It wasn't as much about the tattoo as it was about the freedom.

The freedom to decide.

Me, once again, being me

After the one-sided tattoo discussion, I believed I felt similar to the way a slave would have felt during the civil war. Not knowing if the day would ever come when I may be set free. Not knowing what the future holds. Not feeling I had the authority to make a decision without it being second guessed. Feeling as if I did make a decision, it may not be a decision after all. It may simply be a thought.

A thought.

A thought which *may* develop into a decision.

I would have to check with the person who was superior to me and find out if the thought I possessed was worthy of becoming a decision.

Thinking of all of these things caused me to feel ill. As the night wound down I didn't look at tattoo drawings or photos. Instead, I cried myself to sleep.

A prisoner sat in his cell.

He had been locked up for years, knowing the date all along of his eventual release, June 15, 2013. It had been printed in his legal documents he kept in his cell since his first day of incarceration. Since his arrival, the prisoner made a hash mark each day on the concrete wall in his cell to indicate another day removed from his sentence of confinement. The marked wall, 823 days later, stood behind him as he waited at his cell door for the authorities to arrive and release him. During his entire incarceration he had drawn, sketched and planned.

On the day he was released he would get a tattoo. Etched onto his skin would be a permanent reminder of the day he was freed from confinement. A new beginning. His tattoo representations were on a sheet of paper he kept neatly folded in his right pocket.

Yet.

On his scheduled day of release the authorities arrived with the key and unlocked the prisoner's cell. The prisoner, with a shaved head and neatly trimmed goatee, stood erect and proud. Tall, lean, and muscular he stood in the doorway. They handed the prisoner a sheet of paper. On the paper were written rules - rules which must be followed after his 'release'. Things he could do and things that he could not.

His 'freedom', in a sense, was nothing more than a thought in his head. A thought he would be incapable of implementing. He would be bound by these written instructions to comply with the requirements expressed within them. The man took the provided sheet, and peered down at the list:

__HOUSING__ - (location) Check with authorities for approval prior to commitment.

__HOUSING__ - (value, rent or lease agreement, regardless of location) Check with authorities for approval prior to commitment.

__CLOTHING__ - If using generally good taste, no restrictions. If poor taste is used, removal and replacement with alternated clothes is required. Taste is defined by the authorities.

__EDUCATION__ - Required. Housing and location must be approved by the authority.

__TATTOOS__ - Prohibited.

The prisoner turned and looked at the hash-marked wall behind him. He looked at the sheet of rules. He glanced up at the authoritative figures. He gazed at the sheet of rules and stared for a long moment. The prisoner thought. Pondered. He realized he could - after being provided the list of requirements - smile, nod, and sign the sheet of paper. Then, he could neatly fold his copy, place it in his pocket and exit the cell, walking free of the confines of the institution. And, after he was free from the watchful eye of the authoritative figures, he could simply say, "Fuck It. Fuck You. Fuck Prison. Fuck Authority. Fuck the Man. Fuck Hard-boiled Eggs, Fuck the System. Fuck Racism. Fuck the Government. Fuck Confinement. Fuck This. Fuck Oatmeal."

"Fuck NOT getting a tattoo."

The prisoner decided. He took the provided pen, and signed the sheet of paper. The man left the institution, avoided the authorities, and later that day walked to the local tattoo parlor. Standing at the door as he prepared to enter the man noticed a sign. The message was bold, clear and meaningful.

**Needles, flesh, pain, blood. But then
you take a step back and see a piece
of artwork. Creation from
destruction. That's what tattooing is.
That's how God created and saved
the world. That's what life is.
Keep calm and get inked - The Management**

The man entered the tattoo parlor and walked to the front counter to make an appointment. He unfolded the sheet of paper and showed it to the person scheduling the tattoos. He was told it would require a one and a half hour session. The man agreed, and made an appointment.

On the scheduled day, the man arrived on time. He stopped to read the sign again and smiled. The tattoo artist greeted the man as he entered and motioned to the rear of the parlor.

"There's an old barber chair back there that I just finished recovering. Take a seat and get comfortable. I will be just a minute. I'm Steve," the artist extended his arm, offering his hand in a friendly gesture.

"Call me Hoot," the man smiled as he grasped the artists hand and gave a firm hand shake.

The man walked to the rear of the parlor and found the restored barber's chair. In placing himself in the chair he found himself immediately comfortable. He began to relax and listen to the music. As the Five Finger Death Punch's "Coming Down" played over the speakers, the man remembered the video. It reminded him of some of the thoughts he had while he remained in his cell in prison. Thoughts of living, of dying and of recovering from the unhealthy thoughts.

He now realized the recovery would take time. This would be his new beginning. The man closed his eyes and became lost in the music.

"Hoot, you about ready? You alright?" the artist asked.

"Shit, I think I may have nodded off for a minute, Five Finger Death Punch. Hell I haven't heard that song for a bit," the man apologized as he opened his eyes.

"Good stuff, it sure is. I loved the video. Makes a man think, you know. Now, what are we doing today?" the artist asked as he sat in the chair beside the man.

The man reached into his right pocket and removed the yellowed sheet of paper, unfolded it, and handed it to the artist.

As he tapped his right inner forearm with his left hand, the man responded, "Here you go. I want it on my right forearm."

"Just like this?" the artist asked as he held the sheet of paper where the man could see the depiction.

"Exactly," the man responded.

The artist nodded his head. As the man watched, the artist sterilized the table and prepared the ink. Methodically, the artist retrieved the tattoo machine from a drawer. Holding the tattoo machine at arm's length, the artist looked at it admiringly. After removing a pair of purple rubber gloves from a drawer in the table, the artist carefully stretched them over his hands.

With his gloved hands, he removed a razor from a glass container on the top of the table.

Quietly, the artist took the man's right hand and extended his right arm. Without thought, he rubbed a soapy substance on the man's arm and began to shave the hair from his skin. Carefully, the artist traced the outline of the sketch with a pen, and pressed the paper to the man's skin. The man closes his eyes and leaned into the back of the reclined chair. The man closed his eyes as he heard a buzzing sound. As he became lost in the music and the buzzing, he felt as if he were being hypnotized.

"You ready, Hoot?" the artist asked.

The man, without opening his eyes or speaking, nodded his head.

As the needle began to dig into the man's arm he began to feel something he had never felt. The destruction of his flesh had begun. With each stroke of the needle the man felt as if something was being added - not to his skin - but to 'who' he was. The man, lying in the chair, was not asleep nor was he awake. He felt as if he was elsewhere. As the tattooing process continued the man felt as if he began to float. He felt as if he was rising above his past, his mistakes and his former self. He felt lighter. He began to feel freedom.

Freedom of incarceration, accusations, unanswered questions and of his entire past. The man began to feel lost in the feeling, lost in the buzzing, and lost in what was being added to his soul. He felt as if this was exactly what he had hoped for.

A new beginning.

The man lost concept of time and of being.

"Hoot, we're done. You want to take a look?" the artist asked sharply as he tapped the man on the shoulder.

The man opened his eyes, rotated his head to the right, and peered down at the newly applied tattoo. Unable to hide his satisfaction, the man smiled and looked up at the artist.

"Perfect," he breathed.

Carefully, the artist took the man's right hand and extended his arm. The artist admired his work as he cleaned the area of the tattoo. After retrieving gauze and medical tape from a drawer in the table the artist applied a bandage to the tattoo. As he taped the gauze he offered the man instructions, "You'll want to keep that on there for about an hour, and then you can remove it. After that, keep it uncovered. There's an instruction sheet at the counter on your way out."

"What do I owe you?" the man asked.

"Aren't you the guy that got sent to the joint on the bullshit gun charge?" the artist asked.

"Yes sir," the man responded.

"I bought a machinegun from the ATF. It was an entrapment case. The judge sentenced me to probation, but I decided to fight it to the U.S. Supreme Court. As a matter of law, I was not guilty. The Supreme Court didn't hear the case, and I was re-sentenced to go to prison. It was my choice to fight, my choice to risk prison time. But, I did my time. Now,

what do I owe you?" the man asked.

"Don't worry about it, Hoot," the artist said as he removed his gloves

As the artist tossed the gloves in the trash, the man offered a nod. Slowly, he turned and began to walk from the parlor. As he walked through the front door, he turned and read the sign again.

"Creation from destruction," he said as he acknowledged the sign one last time.

As he walked home, he felt as if his vision was better than before. His hearing. His sense of being. The man looked at his watch.

10:10 pm.

Sitting at home, the man looked at his watch and realized an hour had passed. He carefully removed the bandage and went to the bathroom. After discarding the bandage in the trash the man carefully cleaned the bandage with soapy water. He then applied lotion to the tattoo and rotated his forearm to meet his eye. Prideful, the man read his newly applied tattoo:

STAY HUMAN.

When the alarm went off the next day I awoke from the dream, stretched, and sat up in bed. As soon as I realized it was a school day, I reluctantly got up to get ready for the day. Staring into the closet, I remembered the disappointment I felt with my parents from the night before - my failed attempt at being an adult. Frustrated, I picked out my clothes for the day and got dressed.

I walked into the kitchen, clearly remembering the discussion with my family from the previous night. The more I thought about it, the more I *didn't* want to think about it. Filled with disgust, I opened the pantry. Although I had intended to prepare breakfast before school, I stood and stared into the cupboard. For some reason I no longer felt hungry. Discouraged, I closed the pantry, turned toward the refrigerator and grabbed a bottle of water.

As I slowly walked to the door, I considered my decision to not eat. *Fuck Oatmeal.*

6

SHE TOOK MY HEART

MARC

Growing up without a father was second nature to me. It was not, however, easy. A collision on his way home from college took his life. He was killed instantly. He wasn't wearing his leather jacket. My then pregnant mother cried for a year. Now, my first recollection of realizing I didn't have a father was when I was roughly four years old.

"Why don't I have a father?" I had asked my mother.

"You *do* have a father, Marc. He was killed in a car wreck. But. He is *still* your father," my mother responded.

She placed her hand on my shoulder when she spoke. I cried. I found a way to make everything make sense in my head. I had not cried since. Fourteen years had passed. No tears. I felt emotion. More than most, I imagine.

Yet.

No tears.

My mother completed college and went to work for a local hospital as a nurse. She had worked there my entire life helping others. She never remarried after the passing of my father. She loved one man. According to her, giving herself to someone else would not be fair to them, my father, or her. She could give herself but she could not give her love, for she had no heart. My father had her heart. Her love existed for one person only. Although he was gone, she remained *in* love with my father.

"I cannot love your father and love someone else at the same time," she had told me once. I do not recall my age at the time, but I was young. When I was a little older, maybe thirteen years old, we discussed the topic of love once again.

She placed her hand on my shoulder, "Marc, you don't *give* someone your love. They *take* it. Love is taken. And, when someone takes your love, you will know it. *Do you understand?*"

I did not understand. I simply nodded as if I did. She smiled. We had the same discussion often. The *taking of love*. Last year she placed her hand on my shoulder. She said nothing. I looked in her eyes. I was seventeen.

"Yes," I said.

"*Yes what, Marc,*" she asked.

"Yes, I understand," I smiled.

She smiled. We embraced. It was summer. My mother. My best friend. Her hand still resting on my shoulder, I looked up and smiled.

"Yes, mother, I understand," I said again.

She smiled.

Again.

Britney took my love. The day we met. A piece of me remained in Macy's. I walked through the store to leave. I held the door for a family who was walking in. I looked back into the store. I watched her through the glass as she walked away from where we were standing. And as she walked away a piece of me walked with her. She had taken my love.

Yet.

She was unaware.

I walked to the car. I thanked God for having an opportunity to meet Britney. Winter hung in the air. I zipped my coat, grateful for the warmth it offered me. The coat was my father's. A Christmas gift from his father, he believed it to be good luck. He was not wearing it at the time of his accident, and according to my mother, it may have prevented the accident all together.

When I was sixteen my mother gave the coat to me.

"I want you to have this," she said as she held it at arm's length, "It was your father's good luck charm."

"I know," I nodded.

"I've been waiting for this day. Thank you. I love you mother," I smiled.

"I love you back," she promised.

I wore the coat when I drove or I placed it in the seat beside me. No exceptions. The coat provided me with what it could not provide my father that day. Protection.

Outside Macy's, I sat in my car, bewildered. Something was missing. I stuck my hand in my pocket. *Nothing.* I stuck my hand in my other pocket. *Empty.* My inner coat pocket. *Void of substance.* I pulled the sleeve of my coat back and looked at my watch. I looked toward the store entrance and realized I had left it there. In the store.

My love.

My heart.

I had misplaced nothing. She had taken it. And with her my love would remain.

After returning home I asked my mother regarding her love for my father.

"How long had you known my father before you knew, truly *knew* you were in love with him," I asked.

Her mouth formed a smile, "Five minutes."

As we ate our spaghetti she continued to talk. Of love. Of relationships. And of being without. Being without a husband. My being without a father. And of having a family by most people's standards which was incomplete. I didn't really yearn to have a father *in* my life. I understood my mother. I *have* a father. I yearned to *be* a father. To be, to my children, what my father could not be for me.

Active.

Present.

Alive.

I opened my mouth. My tongue couldn't form words. Yet. I had so much to say. I took a bite of spaghetti. Time passed. When she stopped speaking her eyes were wet. She wasn't crying, but her eyes were full. Full of eighteen years of what someone had taken from her. I smiled and stood. I looked away. I ran my fingers through my hair. As I carried my plate to the sink she raised her hand to her face.

As she wiped eighteen years of love from her eyes, she spoke, "I love you Marc."

"And I love you back, mother," I responded.

She smiled.

Time passed. Britney filled my thoughts. Time *with* her passed at a pace much different than *without* her. We had been together for two months. When she was away, moments seemed like hours, hours seemed like days, and days resembled months. Together, a two hour evening easily passed in what appeared to be moments. I had not told her I loved her. I had, however, given every indication of my feelings for her through my actions.

She had my love.

I waited to see what she would do with it.

My mother's love for my father began to make sense. Love that *just was*.

"There's love that's *developed*," she had told me.

"And there's love that *just is*."

"Please explain," I asked.

She looked up toward the sky and inhaled a deep breath. As she looked down, she began to speak, "Well, Marc, I believe love can be *developed*. Two people meet. He thinks she is cute. She feels the same way. He asks her out on a date. She accepts. They go on a date, and nothing goes wrong. Because nothing goes wrong, when he asks again, she agrees. They go on a second date. *And nothing goes wrong.* And then, they go on a third date. And because nothing went wrong, they are now *dating*. Exclusive. Committed. And, time passes. To keep her convinced he cares for her, and because his family encourages him, he buys her a ring. They are now engaged. And time passes. They get married in June - because that's what everyone else does. And then because it's what married people do, they have children. And now they're a family. Because two people met, went on a date, *and nothing went wrong.* That, Marc, is love that is *developed*."

After a short pause she continued, "Then, there is love that *just is*. A love which can never be explained. This particular love, according to those who have it, can't ever be anything but what it is."

"Endless. Instead of sitting home and imagining the next *girls night out,* she sits at home and anxiously waits for his return from work -

because she can't fathom spending an evening without him. The person doesn't give you *reason* to live. That person *is* your life. *Love that just is,*" she smiled.

"And Marc, when they're gone - like your father - nothing on or of this earth can ever replace them. *Ever.* You choke. You try to breathe. You suffer. And time passes. It's difficult. They provide you with your every breath. Your heart resides in *their* chest and theirs resides in *you.* They *are* your heartbeat. And, because your heart dies with them and you remain, you suffer a life of loving *yourself* - with a heart inside of you which belongs to someone else. A heart incapable of loving others - because your heart loves only you."

And it made sense.

The statement I had heard so many times before.

My heart belongs to someone else.

I looked at my watch. 8:00. I realized sometimes things happen. I opened the refrigerator and removed a slice of lasagna from the covered dish. I ate it cold. I brushed my teeth. I looked at my watch. 8:10. I walked into my bedroom and changed my shirt. I glanced in the mirror and felt at peace with who I had become. Mentally. Physically. Emotionally. I looked at my watch. 8:15. I placed the dirty shirt in the laundry room. The doorbell rang. I ran my fingers through my hair as I walked to the door.

Maybe...

I opened the door and there she stood.

She was crying.

I felt sick.

"What's wrong?" I asked.

"My father," she responded.

"Come in, please," I offered.

Her face flush with sadness, she complied.

"I posted something on Twitter about you. Not much, just talking about you. How you make me feel," she wiped away her tears.

"Someone said something to someone who said something to someone else, and then someone's parent called my father and said I was dating a white boy," she sobbed.

She stood in my arms with *my* heart in her chest and sobbed. I held her. She hurt. I hurt with her. She placed her head on my shoulder. I ran my fingers through her silky smooth black hair. Tall, thin and curvaceous, she stared into my eyes.

"I'm sorry, Britney. But. Know. This. I cannot imagine a day without you in it," I sighed.

She smiled. We kissed.

Her beautiful brown eyes responded, "I'm scared."

"Of what?" I asked softly.

"I'm uhhm…" she hesitated.

Her mouth stayed open.

But.

No sound.

"I'm afraid I love you," she breathed.

My heart raced.

I smiled.

I reached toward the back of the chair and gripped the collar of my leather coat. Slowly, I wrapped her in it. For now, she'd be safe.

"Britney," I hesitated.

I placed my hands on each side of her face and looked into her eyes, "I love you, and I am *not* afraid."

I smiled and raised my chin slightly, "Together, we can get through anything. You're Egyptian, I'm American. You're Orthodox, I'm Catholic. But, we are both *human*. Your ethnicity or religion does not come into play. Not to me. How I *feel* does."

Britney looked at me and slowly grinned.

She pulled my coat tight against her body, "I feel the same way Marc, but I'm afraid my father doesn't. He will never accept you. But that doesn't change the way I feel. I love you. You love me. Let's just be together. Tonight and every night. I want every night to end with you in my arms."

I reached down and held her hand in mine. Slowly, I walked toward my bedroom as she followed closely behind, our hands still connected by our fingers. I looked at my watch. 8:30.

"When do you have to be home?" I asked.

"11:00," she responded.

We embraced. I held her. Time passed. We fell on the bed. And there we remained. I touched her face with my fingers. We kissed. She smiled. I took off my shirt and began to lie down beside her.

"I like looking at your body," she said.

"Thank you. I like looking at you, period," I responded.

She removed her shirt. She asked for help with her bra. We embraced. Our skins touched. I felt her heart beat against my chest. I felt my heart beating. Our heartbeats became one. *We* became one. *One heartbeat.* Time passed. I looked at my watch. 10:10. I stood. She remained on the bed, defining beauty.

"It's getting close to eleven, baby. You should probably get up," I said as I stood.

I walked through the room and looked for my shirt.

"Stand right there," she said, "don't move."

I stood still. She leaned over and reached to the side of the bed. Her arm emerged with her phone in hand. She held it at arm's length.

"Don't move," she said.

"I heard you," I smiled.

I stood. She took three photos.

"I wish I could paint a picture of you," I said.

"Do you paint?" she asked.

"No," I responded, "but I wish I could. I would paint a picture of you right now, lying there without your shirt. I could stand here Britney and admire you for all of what is forever. You make me want to cry. But. That part of me is broken."

"I know," she said, "I know."

"Take a picture of me and you can look at it whenever you want. You can practice, and one day, maybe you can paint it," she offered.

I agreed.

I picked up my leather jacket and reached into the pocket. And I smiled as I took a photo of the most beautiful woman in the world.

"You define beauty, Britney. And you do so by merely existing," I said.

"All you have to do to be this beautiful is simply be yourself."

"I wish I was as skinny as the rest of the girls. As pretty," she said.

Still standing shirtless in the same spot, I smiled, "You weigh 110 pounds, Britney. You are thin, almost too thin. We've discussed this. You are more beautiful than any other woman on this earth. *Ever.* And the more I know you the more beautiful you become. I love you."

"I love you," she responded.

"I love you back," I promised.

She smiled.

We got dressed.

With my heart in her chest, the most beautiful woman in the world walked through the door, out to her car, and went home to a father who did not understand. That night, out of a feeling of necessity, I wrapped myself in my leather coat and fell asleep.

A boy and a girl stood in a field of flowers. Dressed in a little black dress, she held is hand. Dressed in nothing but swim shorts, he smiled the smile of a boy in love. Their hands were empty - all they held was each other. A train slowly inched down the tracks as it approached an intersection a mile from where the couple stood.

"Come on, let's get on that train," he said as he tugged against her hand.

"How? It's moving," she replied.

He looked intently into the girls eyes and spoke.

"I've seen it in an old movie. It's easy. You run toward the train and then run in the same direction the train is moving - and simply jump in. Look..."

He pointed toward the train, "every second or third car has the door open. It's going west. Probably all the way to Los Angeles."

Through the flowers, they ran toward the train. As the train slowed they ran alongside. He jumped effortlessly into the car. On his hands and knees, he held his arm out the door and offered her a hand. As she ran along the train, she reached up and grasped his hand. Without effort, he pulled her inside the moving car.

Together, hand in hand, they looked out the door of the train car into the field of flowers and smiled.

"Are you cold?" she asked.

"No, not at all," he responded.

"Are you?"

"No, I feel perfect. I love you."

She smiled and leaned toward the boy, her face approaching his.

"I love you back," he responded as he leaning toward her.

Their lips touched.

As he wrapped his arms around the girl, they embraced, kissing for miles. As the train passed through the fields of flowers various colors and shapes could be seen through the train door. The couple continued to kiss. With her heart protected by him, and his protected by her, they gazed into each other's eyes.

Two people, in a world all alone, sat on the train and loved each other.

Naturally.

Completely.

Without effort.

The boy leaned against the inner wall of the train car and admired the beauty of the girl. The girl, against the opposite wall, sat and smiled, but did not notice the boy looking at her. She ran her hands through her hair and looked out the train door toward the fields of flowers as the train passed through them. She, filled with a love that would last a lifetime, was content.

For once in her life, she sat, satisfied with who she had become.

The train slowed. The boy looked at his watch. The watch had no hands. The boy looked away and noticed a leather briefcase in the corner of the car of the train. Slowly he stood and walked to the briefcase and picked it up. As the girl watched the flowers pass through the train door he carried the briefcase to where he was sitting. Carefully, he placed the briefcase onto the floor, opened it, and peered inside. A hand written note sat on top of a leather divider. The boy picked up the note and read it to himself.

TO THE PERSON WHO FINDS THIS CASE:
I HAVE WORKED A LIFETIME,
AND HAVE NO ONE TO LOVE.
PLEASE USE THE CONTENTS OF THIS CASE -
LOVING THE PERSON WHO
LOVES YOU THE MOST.

The girl turned from the flowers and noticed the boy with the case.
"What is it, Marc?" the girl asked.

The boy, without speaking, handed her the note as he lifted the leather divider. Hundred dollar bills, tightly bound and marked by $10,000 bands filled the case. A key on a necklace was sat on top of the money. Slowly, the boy closed the case and checked the key against the locks. The key operated the two locks of the case with ease. The boy placed the key around his neck. The boy opened the case and began to count. Left to right. Top to bottom. Carefully, he lifted the stacks of bills and checked the depth of the stacks.

"It appears to be about $900,000, if this is marked correctly. Nine times two. Eighteen times five. Yes, nine hundred thousand dollars. Did you read the note?" he asked.

With the case still open, the boy stood and walked toward her.
"Yes, I did," she responded as she handed him the note.

The boy took the note and places it in the case. Slowly, the boy closed the case. After removing the key from his neck, the boy placed the key around the neck of the girl. The key hung between her breasts, hidden by the black dress she wore.

As he embraced the girl, the boy looked into the girl's eyes. They kissed.

"I love you," the boy said.

The boy looked into the girl's eyes and ran his fingers along her face. As she closed her eyes, his hand slid to the side of her head and through her hair.

"I love you back," the girl responded as she opened her eyes.

Time passed. The train stopped. The couple stood together and peered outside the train door. On the left, a sandy beach. On the right, a hill with a large sign on the side. The sign is one they recognized, and clearly marked their new location.

HOLLYWOOD.

Smiling, they stepped off of the train with the briefcase and begin to walk toward the beach.

I turned and looked at my watch. 6:05 am. I rubbed the sleep from my eyes and stood from the bed. Slowly, I walked into the kitchen. After I read the newspaper and finished my coffee, I sat and smiled. One way or another I intended to spend the rest of my life with Britney.

We had what it would take to survive anything.

Love that just is.

7

CUPS

DAVID

Some days when I woke up I immediately felt as if I should to go back to sleep and forget who I was. Yet on other days I felt like jumping out of bed and rushing through the day, eager to see what life would offer me. This particular day was the latter. I woke up refreshed and ready to meet the day. It was sunny, Saturday, and my parents were gone shopping. The day couldn't have been any better. Being home alone could be so satisfying. I had planned on getting some exercise, taking a shower, and going to *Cups* for a frozen yogurt.

The day would be just grand.

Throughout the morning I found it increasingly difficult to contain my excitement for the frozen yogurt I would later receive. I loved the yogurt and adored the atmosphere of the establishment. As I surveyed my room for defects, I wondered who may be at the yogurt shop when I arrived. It was Saturday and on Saturday mornings I would often see Michelle and her friend Brianna there. If they were there, I imagined I would speak to Michelle. Her eyes were so pretty. I had always felt the eyes didn't lie. If someone smiled at me and their eyes smiled with them, they were truly smiling inside. *The eyes don't lie.* And Michelle's eyes smiled with her.

As I made my bed, John Coltrane played. On weekends the wrinkles in my bed were more noticeable. Because I got up later, the sun was up and my room much brighter than normal – much more than school days. On weekdays when I got up to make my bed it was much earlier in the morning, and dark. In attempting to free the blanket of wrinkles, the sunshine caused them to stand out like little valleys of imperfect fabric. After a little more stretching and pulling than a normal day, I was off to *Cups* for a yogurt.

As I drove my car into the parking lot of *Cups* I noticed a Camaro parked in front. I hoped it was Michelle's but I couldn't remember what color her car was. *I must have a brain tumor. A brain tumor would cause problems with my memory. Sadly, I have a brain tumor, and at such a young age.* As I walked into the store I raised my hands and felt my head. It appeared normal and not at all enlarged. *I should be a scientist. A fabric scientist. I could invent a wrinkle-free fabric.*

If I didn't die of a tumor first, I felt I could invent the perfect fabric. Wrinkle-free.

For my bed.

And legs.

As I made a mental note of my future in fine fabrics, I grabbed the door handle and pulled the door open.

Upon entering, I saw her in the corner seated at the table where she normally sat. She was there with Brianna as she always was, laughing and talking. There were two boys from school with them, but I didn't immediately recognize them. Although their faces seemed familiar, I could not recall their names. No differently than the color of Michelle's car, I had once again forgotten.

Twice in one day.

Accelerated aging. Probably a chromosomal disorder. Or some form of deficiency. And at such an early age.

Alternating glances between Michelle and the display of toppings, I walked toward the counter to prepare my yogurt. I stood, staring down at the empty cup and wondered if I would forget anything else. I considered the effect of memory loss. *What if I forget something really important, like how to park? Or drive. Oh my God. What if, while driving home, I forget how to turn the steering wheel? Just completely forgot, driving straight the entire afternoon. Where would I end up?*

The thought scared me. Depending on which direction I turned when I left the store, I could end up in Canada or maybe Florida. As I stood and fueled my worry, I realized if I *couldn't* turn I would simply back into the car behind me and sit there in reverse like a fool. Incapable of turning the steering wheel, I would inevitably remain in the lot dumbfounded until the police arrived. Subsequently I would be arrested and questioned for hours on end. Later, I would be improperly diagnosed as having some form of mental retardation. Later, they would determine my problems were brought on by a brain tumor the size of a tangerine.

I shook my head to clear my thoughts and filled my yogurt cup with vanilla yogurt. As I turned and walked to the area where the toppings were located, I became indecisive. *Peanut butter cup pieces. Almonds. Gummie bears.* I stared down at the toppings, spooned in some almonds, peanut butter cups, and eventually picked out only red gummie bears; leaving the orange and yellow ones for someone else.

Someone foolish enough to eat them.

"That'll be $6.90. Are you the guy that always picks out the red ones?" the cashier asked as she pointed into my cup.

Her hair was blonde and she wore an unzipped hoodie. She was cute but her eyes were not as pretty as Michelle's. Michelle's eyes were so much more beautiful. As I realized what she asked I felt somewhat guilty. At a loss for words, I stood and wondered if they had a corporate policy regarding picking out the red gummies. I suspected it shouldn't be any different than picking out the bigger chunks of the peanut butter cup pieces, and I had never been questioned about them.

Incidentally, on previous days I had never been asked about the gummies either. I imagined she could call the police.

Police scare me - they remind me of my father.

Think, David, think.

"Yes, I am. I am allergic to the other colors," I lied.

She looked up from my yogurt cup and smiled, "You're funny. Funny *and* cute. What's your name again?"

I liked receiving compliments from girls. It didn't offend me the way it may offend a boy if another boy complimented them. Girls are just girls. At times I considered myself as a girl but typically after a few minutes I would become very confused and just stop thinking about anything.

"Thank you," I said as I retrieved my wallet.

"And I suppose you know, but I was joking. I find the other colors less satisfying than the red ones. And I don't like all the mixed up colors in my yogurt. I just get the red gummies every other Saturday or so. I hope it's not a huge deal," I shrugged.

I handed her a ten dollar bill. While she placed the money in the drawer, I left my cup on the counter and tugged at both sides of my jeans.

"$3.10 is your change. I guess you're not going to tell me your name," she frowned and bent at the waist as if to reveal more cleavage than she was already showing.

The skin between her breasts was freckled considerably more so than normal. *Probably skin cancer.* She obviously hadn't made it a point to apply sunscreen between her boobs. As I stared at her freckled boobs, I decided we would both die young; she of cancer and I of a tumor.

"David. It's David. I am sorry I got carried away with all of the gummie talk," I blurted.

I looked down at my yogurt cup. In the time I had wasted staring at her soon to be cancer infested breasts, it had begun to melt. I was certain in a matter of minutes Michelle would be gone and the gummies would be swimming in a pool of liquid yogurt.

"Nice to meet you, David, I am Cloe," she offered her hand when she spoke.

"Nice to meet you Cloe," I said as I shook her hand.

Her skin felt cold.

She's deteriorating from the inside out. From cancer. So sad. And at such a young age.

"I'm going to eat this before it melts. I will talk to you before I go, I promise," I grinned.

As I turned toward the seating area I was relieved to see the boys were gone from where Michelle and Brianna were sitting. Shyly I walked in their direction. While they weren't watching I looked down and made sure I was wrinkle free. Mentally, I chose the table beside the girls and pulled out the chair to seat myself.

Michelle looked up and smiled, "David, right? You're alone? Sit here with us, we're about to leave."

When she smiled her eyes smiled with her. Brianna, without smiling, immediately got up and walked toward the restroom.

"So how are you doing in making your decision for college, Michelle?" I poked a gummie in my mouth as I asked her.

Eating around strangers typically made me so much more comfortable than normal. I often wondered if it was because I occupied my mind to chew; and chewing made me think less of what they may be thinking about me.

"I'm going to Nova, and then Drexel. I decided a few weeks ago," she said excitedly.

Incapable of containing my excitement, I screamed, "Villanova?"

Excited about Michelle's successes and future at Villanova, I eagerly grabbed my spoon and without making a perfect bite or even looking down at the cup, shoveled a spoon full of yogurt into my mouth.

"Tell me more," I said over my mouth full of yogurt.

"Well, I am going to be a doctor and I was accepted into their program," she continued to smile and ran the fingers of her left hand into her hair.

Half way through her hair, her hand got stuck. She rolled her eyes and tugged at her hair, freeing her hand. We both laughed.

"That's so exciting. What's your friends name again?"

Although I knew the answer, I asked anyway. I wanted her to think Brianna wasn't as important to me as she was. For some reason the thought at least made sense in my mildly tumor infested head.

"Brianna. We come here almost every Saturday. Well, actually, we come here almost every day," she chuckled.

"My parents get disappointed if I come here too much. They complain of the cost," I said as I looked into my yogurt cup.

I stared into my cup, making certain the bite I was preparing had only peanut butter pieces and one gummie. Carefully, I spooned a perfect bite into my mouth, being careful not to drip on the table.

"Get out of here! My mother just did the same thing to me the other day. She told me I had to have some shrinkage," she turned toward Brianna as she returned from the restroom.

"What does that even mean?" I asked.

"I have no idea," she laughed.

Brianna walked to the table, turned and faced Michelle, then placed her hands on her hips.

"Michelle, are you ready to go?" she asked in a frustrated tone.

My heart sank. I preferred to sit and have a conversation with Michelle. We had seen each other in school for years, but rarely got a chance to speak to each other for any period of time. I was white and gay, and she was Egyptian. We wouldn't typically be friends, but at *Cups* we sure could be. As I sat and secretly wished Brianna was in the bathroom throwing up or sick with diarrhea, Brianna stared at Michelle. I wished something would happen.

Something.

Something which would cause Brianna to go away.

I sat and wished she would have stayed home. Or that she busy doing something else – something that didn't include her standing in front of me staring at Michelle rudely. It seemed as if she was never separated from Michelle. I wondered as I looked at her if she and Michelle would grow apart as college got underway.

I decided we *all* would grow apart and I began to feel terrible for wishing Brianna had diarrhea. I quietly sat and wished she would just sit down. Frustrated at Brianna's continued existence, I looked up at

Michelle and waited anxiously for her answer.

"No, go ahead. I am going to sit here with David and talk, Okay?" Michelle responded.

Oh thank God.

I tugged on the thighs of my jeans as I quickly turned to view Brianna's reaction.

"Bye," Brianna snapped.

And she turned and walked away.

My head quickly spun to face Michelle and see how she reacted to Brianna's bitchy departure. Michelle shook her head and tossed her forehead backward as she rolled her eyes. Together we watched as Brianna walked away. I took a bite of my yogurt and then another, careful both times not to drip. I sat and attempted to think of something meaningful to offer, but was unsuccessful. I felt bad for Brianna but I was glad Michelle decided to stay. I felt this would possibly make for the best Saturday *ever.* I looked at Michelle admiringly and decided to take a chance.

"Do you like John Coltrane?" I asked.

Although I doubted she had ever heard of him, I asked anyway. I felt as if she had heard of him - and she liked him - we could remain friends *forever.*

"Are you kidding me," she responded as she raised one eyebrow.

"*A Love Supreme. Giant Steps. My Favourite…*"

Before she could answer, I completed her sentence, "*My Favourite Things.*"

"I love Coltrane," she smiled.

"John Coltrane is like magic. I get so lost in his music. When I listen to it, nothing else matters. I can get so wrapped up in listening I even forget where I am or what else, if anything, matters. Sometimes I forget to even breathe. Bad days turn good. Bad thoughts go away. When I listen to his music, well, I just," I hesitated and smiled.

"I just become whoever I want to. I just float. Or something. I don't know. Now I sound like an idiot. I am sorry," I rattled.

There was so much more I wished to say, but I hesitated and gave her a chance to speak.

"No, I know exactly what you mean. The other night I was arguing with my mother about a tattoo I wanted to get when I turn eighteen. She said I couldn't get the tattoo," she paused.

"End. Of. Story." she placed emphasis on each word as she spoke.

"I went up to my room and listened to *My Favourite Things.* It didn't fix it but it sure let me fall asleep," she sighed.

"I think it's just fabulous you like Coltrane. Not about the tattoo, that's not fabulous at all. Now, what happened, exactly?" I asked as I took a few more quick bites of my yogurt.

Oh my God, an almond.

I sat, chewing my almond infused yogurt, and smiled. Whoever decided to offer toppings for frozen yogurt was a genius - especially the almond toppings. As she sat and pondered responding, I clenched my cup of heaven filled with crunchy almond surprises.

She looked down at the table and spoke softly.

"Well, I told my parents when I turned eighteen I intended to get a tattoo. I had already made an appointment to do so on my birthday. I struggled with telling them *anything* because," she hesitated and raised her hands to her face.

"Well, you know. I was going to be *eighteen.* Free to make choices. Or at least so I thought. But I decided to be forthright and tell them. It just didn't go very well. They said if I got a tattoo, they were basically done with me. I would no longer be their daughter. I was so shocked. And now? Well I am trying to decide what to do. What's right. What's wrong. You know what I mean?" she said as she looked up from the table.

Her eyes were magic. She stuck her hand in her hair again. It didn't get stuck this time.

"Well, my father told me now that I am eighteen, I am a man. He is of the opinion that the instant you turn eighteen you are an adult. Just bingo. Poof. An adult. I don't believe there is some form of transformation the day we turn eighteen, but I do think it's the age we *should* be given the freedom to make decisions on our own. I think we should proceed with caution. Maybe ask a lot of questions. Maybe be careful not to do stupid things or make ridiculous decisions. My father was a Marine and he believes *if you can fight and die for this country at eighteen, you are an adult*," I hesitated and rolled my eyes drastically.

"So, *my* parents want me to be an adult. Like *now*," I chuckled.

"I wish your parents were my parents," she said.

"Believe me, you don't," I pressed the palms of my hands to my temples and made an awful face.

My head felt frozen from the yogurt.

"What's wrong, David? Brain freeze?"

"What do you know about brain tumors, Michelle?" I rubbed my temples with the tips of my fingers.

"It's a brain freeze from eating the yogurt so fast, you idiot. You've been eating it like a starving hostage," she laughed.

She shook her head and smiled. Her eyes followed.

I spooned the remaining loose almonds from my cup.

98

"I just love this place," I said.

I would tell her later of my tumor. Being gay was enough for one day, and I intended to tell her. Maybe.

"I do too," she smiled as she spoke.

Her smile was infectious. I smiled in return.

She smiled a lot and I liked it. She made me comfortable - immediately comfortable. She reminded me of Dr. Baritz, which made perfect sense because Michelle was *going* to be a doctor. Maybe doctors possessed a quality which caused them to be more caring than other people. It could be quite possible they were more understanding or more *able* to understand people. More kind. More considerate. More compassionate. Michelle was all of those things. I looked over the table, pulled at my jeans one more time, and smiled.

I stood from the table and stared at the trash receptacle. Leaving my trash on the table was not an option.

"I am going to toss this in the trash and get a glass of water. You want anything?" I asked as I stood.

"Thank you. Yes, a cup of water. When you get back I have a question," she smiled again as she spoke.

She didn't have her hand in her hair this time. She did, however, have her chin in her hand.

I placed the trash in the receptacle and walked to the counter to get our water. When I returned, I handed Michelle her water and placed mine on the table. I smiled and handed her the straw, still covered with its paper protective cover. As I begin to sit, I pulled at the thighs of my pants so my jeans wouldn't wrinkle under my legs as I sat down.

As I sat and admired Michelle for who she was as well as her appearance, I raised my cup of water and took a slow drink. My cup differed from hers in that it had no lid. I believed lids on cold drinks to be disgusting. A lid required the drink to be sipped through a straw. The thought of a straw in my mouth made me cringe. As a result, I never drank from a straw or used lids.

As I lowered my cup to the table, she looked toward me and smiled, "So David, are you gay?"

"Yes, Michelle, I am," I responded without hesitation.

I couldn't believe my ears. I couldn't believe anything. I had actually told someone besides Dr. Baritz that I was gay. In a sense Michelle was a doctor, but not actually. Just sort of. Well not really, but she was more of a doctor than I was. I had so much more to say but I left it at that. I sat and waited excitedly to hear what she had to say. As my heart began beat faster than normal I realized I was not nervous or sweating like I was in Dr. Baritz's office.

"Does it bother you?" I asked.

"Does it bother you that I am a girl?" Michelle asked in an almost offended tone, her eyes opened wider than before.

Her response excited me.

"Heavens no," I responded.

"Well David, I look at it this way. I was born a girl. Cloe was born a girl. My brother was born a boy. I was born heterosexual. You *are* homosexual. I haven't decided if it's necessarily a decision you *make* or if it is the way God made you. Were you born that way or did you consciously or subconsciously decide? I struggle with that. We can talk about it more later," she took a shallow breath and continued.

She reached into her purse and pulled out her phone, "I want to show you something."

After she looked at her phone for a moment she smiled and carefully handed it to me.

"Look at that picture, David. Look at it good," she said as I took the phone from her grasp.

I looked at the screen of the phone. The picture on the screen was a black and white photograph with no caption. In the photo, which was taken in an operating room, there was a white man lying on an operating table. He was wearing a KKK Clansman robe which was covered in blood. There was a black doctor whose hands were covering a gaping wound, obviously in an effort to stop the bleeding. The look on his face was one of urgency. The operating room was full of black nurses, black doctors and a white Clansman. Although there was not a series of photographs, the message was clearly made - every one of the black staff was rushing to save the man's life. A man who would rather hang those helping him than allow them to live. I could not stop looking at the photograph. I was moved. With a broken voice, Michelle began to speak. I placed my hand on my chest and checked my heart.

Still beating.

"David this particular picture basically defines all my beliefs about medicine, life and humanity in general. How much more beautiful does it get? They're black, and rushing to save this guy's life. And he's in the KKK. Tolerance. Respect. Grace. It's so beautiful."

She stood and continued to speak, "That picture will forever be dear to my heart. And that's the thing about medicine. The doors to a hospital, to a doctor's office, or at least to *my* Doctor's office are an equalizer. It doesn't matter if you can pay, it doesn't matter where you are from or *what* you are. Because I will have already sworn I will do whatever I can to help you or to save your life."

As her voice faltered from emotion she rubbed her eyes and

continued, "The practice of medicine is a place where, theoretically all prejudices *disappear*. And as a doctor we help people because our hearts want us to. This picture is so beautifully human. It's like the epitome of humanity. I love it and it hits me hard."

I swallowed a lump in my throat and attempted to force a smile, "Thank you, Michelle, for sharing that with me. You are an amazing woman and will be a great doctor."

My entire body buzzed from the intensity of seeing the photograph and hearing her speaking with such authority and purpose. She truly *believed* in what she was saying.

"So, the long answer? No I do not care if you are gay. You're human. That's all that matters," she opened her arms to give me a hug.

Doctor Baritz didn't give hugs. Dr. Michelle did. I stood, wrapped my arms around her and hugged her with all my might. As my jeans surely wrinkled, we embraced for what seemed like forever. She tapped my back with her fingers. And I decided. This girl was going to help me. She would help me. I had to tell my father I was gay. Before Michelle went away to college she could figure out a way to help.

Help me be me.

8

SHOW SOME RESPECT

MARC

Treat people with respect, and people will admire you for being respectful.

Always be respectful.

My mother drilled these things into my head from the time I was old enough to understand her speak. I found them to be true. I lived my life in a manner of always being respectful. I didn't necessarily *respect* everyone, but I *treated* everyone with respect.

Always.

Treat everyone you encounter as if today is their last day on earth. The life you live will be your reward.

"Dude, have you had sex with her?" Adrian asked as he hit me in the arm with the palm of his hand.

"Our relationship is private, you guys know that. Now, stop," I responded.

"C'mon, Marc. Just tell us something. You've never really had a girlfriend. Give us *something*," Marcus begged.

"Listen. I told you guys already. I will tell you *about* her. Who she is. What she's like. But it's not fair to her or to us to give anyone intimate details about what we do. Don't ask again. It's a matter of respect," I responded in a stern tone.

We sat and ate our lunch. Joey and Adrian were the closest friends I had ever had. Marcus moved into the city one year prior, and quickly became part of our group as soon as he arrived.

We ate lunch together daily.

I took another bite of my apple.

I thought of Britney.

"Dude, cut that shit. It's fucking long," Marcus remarked.

"No, I'm not cutting it. I like it this way," I responded.

I felt my hair gave me comfort and had become somewhat of a trademark.

I desperately wanted the day to end. Britney and I had planned to see each other after school. I looked at my watch. 11:50. Having Britney in my life and experiencing her exist made it difficult to *not* have her beside me every moment of the day. Her absence caused me to yearn for her presence.

"I'm going to the bathroom. Be back in a second," I sighed.

"Me too," Joey said as he stood.

We walked away from the table.

Joey and I were close friends. His father had always treated me as if I were one of his own children. He wasn't a replacement for my father, but it was pleasurable to be around his family. He was Catholic and had seven brothers and not one sister.

I didn't envy Joey. I often wondered, however, how many brothers or sisters I may have had if my father lived. What may have happened differently.

"Sorry if we made you mad back there bro," Joey said as he tilted his head my direction.

"No problem, Joey. It's just. Well. You know. I respect her. And I have to treat her with respect. Always. You can't love someone if you do not respect them," I responded.

"I'm ready for this year to be over aren't you, bro?" Joey asked as we walked out of the bathroom.

"Yeah, I suppose so. In some ways I would never like it to end. You know, we all lose each other when school ends. We all go our separate ways. It is the beginning of a new life. Some of us might come back here during the summers to see our families. But if you think we will all be back here at the same time, or during the same period of time, you're crazy. Things will change. *We* will change. We will meet new friends, find new places to hang out, and different things will become important to us," I ran my hands through my hair as I responded.

Thinking of losing my friends made me feel somewhat uncomfortable.

I turned to face Joey as we walked, and continued speaking, "The friends we have *now*? They will be the best friends of our life. The memories we have *now*? They will be our most fond. I guarantee you, Joey. We will soon begin our next phase of life. Being responsible. Responsible for ourselves. Responsible to our relationships. And ultimately, we'll begin a new family. Begin a new generation. An extension of ourselves. Become responsible fathers. And things change. Priorities change. We tell ourselves they won't. We want to hold on to this," I motioned to the room in front of us.

"But we can't. Life begins. And *these* friendships Joey, they will fade," I sighed.

"Dude, you are so fucking deep. But I totally don't agree," he said as he shook his head.

I shook my head.

"Joey," I stopped walking and hesitated.

"Ask yourself this. Your mother or your father? Are they still friends with their high school classmates? I am sure they're not. Think about it. Things change. And we are going to lose this. All of it. Time will pass. And. It'll all be gone," I said with outstretched arms.

"You say that a lot, *time will pass, time passes*, you know?"

"I got it from my mother, you know that. She says it a lot. And it's true. Time passes. Things change. It's really the only assurance we have. And I suppose it's about all we know for sure. *Time will pass* and things *will* change."

As we stepped to the edge of the table the others looked up and stopped talking. It appeared we had interrupted them from some form of a conversation – more than likely one about sex. I pulled my hand from my pocket and looked at my watch. 12:00.

"Well, you guys about ready?" Adrian asked.

I grabbed my leather jacket and pulled it over my shoulders.

"Yes, I've got to text Britney before class. I'm ready," I reached into my inner coat pocket and got my phone.

"Well, holler at me tonight, Marc," Joey grinned.

"See ya."

"See, ya."

"Alright."

As I walked down the hallway I sent Britney a text message. She immediately responded with a smiley face. As I made my way to class, I considered what Joey and I had discussed. *Time will pass, and things will change.* Change was as inevitable as the tide. Things do change. I placed my hand on my chest.

Baboom…baboom…baboom.

As I walked away from the lunch room, I watched two kids arguing in the hallway. The argument quickly turned into shoving. Almost immediately all of the other kids began to gather around, hoping to see a fight. I'd never quite understood fighting, nor did I care to. I had come to believe we become the sum of our experiences in life.

In my opinion people aren't really individuals; we are assembled from a little bit of everyone we encounter in life. I had carefully spent my life exposing myself to all of what was good. As a result, I was a good person. By choice, I had not intentionally exposed myself to any of what life offered which was bad. My lack of diversity in life and lack of these types of exposures worried me sometimes. I would often lay and wonder what I might do or how I may react if I were ever exposed to something I did not have some form of previous experience dealing with. A fight, for instance. I wanted the diversity life offered, but I did not want the exposure. Being good and surrounding myself with what was good provided me with comfort. I was assembled of a thousand pieces of what was good. As a result, I was and felt I always would be good.

The evening finally arrived, and with the evening, came Britney. As we snuggled on the bed together it was as if I were living my life for her and her alone. As if I was taking each breath to keep her alive. If for some reason I were to die, I felt she would certainly die with me. As Britney's heart beat in my chest, I thought of my mother. How and why had my mother made it this long without my father? If this love - *love that just is* - is truly the once-in-a-lifetime love only a select few find, and with it love comes dependency, how could she *live* without him?

I felt she did it for *me*. If she wasn't pregnant, I believed things would have been different. She had lived a life for something she loved and sacrificed her love for my father to love me. My mother's love for me kept her alive.

As I held Britney, I absorbed my mother's love and smiled.

Lying on the bed with her elbow bent and her head resting in her hand, Britney turned and smiled.

"What are you thinking about, Marc?"

As she spoke, her hair hung perfectly across her face.

"Loving you, Britney," I responded as I looked into her brown eyes.

"What about it?" she smiled.

"You, Britney. You. Us. It's just. Every stupid thing that made me happy. Every pointless thing which I thought defined me. It completely shattered when you entered my life. I have thoroughly realized after meeting you and having you in my life, going back to the person I was before you is unimaginable," I sighed.

I attempted to continue, but the lump which formed in my throat prevented it.

"Why would you want to live a life without me? Don't you still think I am pretty?" she asked as she began to sit up.

She looked worried.

I reached over and touched her face lightly, "Britney, I love you. It has nothing to do with the way you look. You *do* look pretty. You are gorgeous. Again, you define beauty. You truly do. It's just. I know if for whatever reason I no longer had you, nothing that gave me a false sense of happiness before you could ever come close to filling the void you would leave in my heart. In the entirety of my soul. Without you I would be empty and it scares me, because I've never felt this way about anyone before. I never thought I would let anyone get close enough to me to make such an impact to begin with."

"It makes perfect sense. I love you, Marc. I truly do. You are all I ever want and all I would ever need," she said as she leaned forward to kiss me.

I tilted my head to hers and placed my hands on the sides of her face. Cradling her face in my hand, we kissed. As we embraced, I felt as if yet more of her was being absorbed into me. Into my inner being. My skin began to tingle. We continued to kiss.

Her lips were so forgiving, so soft. I became lost in the kiss.

As she looked directly into my eyes, she slowly pulled her lips from mine, "I love kissing you, Marc."

Her gaze made me feel weak.

I ran my hands through her hair and gazed into her eyes, "And I love kissing you, baby."

As she turned her head to meet mine, she spoke softly, "So, what scares you? You said you were scared. Or, that this scared you."

I thought for a moment about what I had said. *Without you, I would be empty, and it scares me, because I've never felt this way about anyone before.* As I tried to make every word count, I responded.

"With you, Britney, I am as weak as everyone else I ever looked down upon before you came into my life. To be honest, I am probably much worse. Because I know I love you with a ferocity that most people will never have the capacity to feel for another person. I need you, and this necessity causes me to be vulnerable. The vulnerability makes me weak. I am weak for you. And to be honest, it feels great. The thought of *not* having you is what scares me."

Her eyes began to swell with tears.

She stared into my eyes.

A tear fell out of her eye and rolled down her cheek. As I reached to brush it away she grabbed my hand by my wrist and pulled it to her chest. Softly, she placed my palm against her breast. As my hand cupped her flesh, another tear fell.

"Do you feel that Marc? The heart beating?" she asked.

"Yes, I do," I smiled.

"Marc, it's yours. Remember that. And don't be afraid. You and I will always be together. I love you."

She leaned into me and offered her lips.

"I love you back."

With my hand still on her chest, we kissed.

I awoke confused.

For a moment I was incapable of separating reality from dream. I looked at my watch. 2:10. Britney lay beside me, asleep. I looked at my watch again. 2:10. I looked toward my bedroom window. Darkness. I looked down at Britney. I placed my hand on her shoulder. I shook her lightly and whispered into her ear.

"Baby. We fell asleep, wake up. Baby. We fell asleep, wake up."

Confused, she looked up and spoke.

"What time is it," she asked as she rubbed her eyes.

"It's two a.m.," I responded as I sat up.

"Oh my God. Where's my phone? My father is going to kill me!" she screamed.

"Just tell him…"

"You don't understand, I can't tell him anything. I love you. I have to go. I love you," she leaned toward me and kissed me.

"I have to go," she said as she turned and ran to the door.

As I stood in the doorway of my room and watched her hurry out, I responded, "I love you back."

I stood in my doorway for a long period of time. I ran my hands through my hair. Time passed. My mind filled with thoughts of Britney, I stood. I felt empty - as if my next breath was dependent upon someone else's being. This feeling of necessity for another filled me with emptiness.

I checked my watch. 2:15.

Without you I would be empty and it scares me, because I've never felt this way about anyone before.

9

FATHER KNOWS BEST

BRITNEY'S FATHER

As a parent, I had always made decisions that should have been instrumental in assuring my children would grow up understanding the difference between what was right and what was wrong. Children do not always understand the reason for the decisions we make, but they should believe we make them with their best interest in our hearts.

My daughter Britney was no exception to what has become a typical American teenager. She was disrespectful, lacked appreciation, and had a low level of understanding of what life and family offered her. She spent far too much time on her telephone and had far too many friends keeping track of her progress in life and in school.

When George called, I knew almost immediately that his concern with my daughter would be regarding a matter of respect. Her lack of respect became apparent when she was about twelve years old. We had continued to give her what we felt she needed, and we provided her with a quality life. Her car, her clothes and her electronic devices were second to none. She did not appreciate or respect what we provided her. As a child I grew up with nothing. She had everything and no appreciation of what it was, or the degree of work which went into obtaining those things.

George expressed concern and asked we meet to discuss Britney.

When I asked that he explain what the matter specifically pertained to, he didn't give me a definitive answer. His only reply, *we need to meet and talk as soon as you are able* caused me to fear what may be ahead.

I agreed, got into my Mercedes, and drove to meet him immediately.

When I arrived at the bar he was already drinking. I ordered a Scotch and a cigar and we began to talk of work, family, and life in general. George worked as an attorney and had a banner year with his firm. His two sons were children to be proud of, and always treated adults as they should, with respect. We hadn't been at the bar for long, and as I smoked my cigar he began to talk about his sons.

"My boys are good boys, you know this," he said boldly.

I agreed. He continued to explain of kids in school today, and the sharing of photos on internet sites. Kids will take photographs, and place them on a Twitter website and other children comment about the photo, he explained. He made clear how the children today use this website as if it were a form of contest. In an effort to see how many of the other children may make comments on their photographs, they sit in wait. In his opinion, today's children used this Twitter website as a form of a popularity contest. So far everything he said made sense, but did not pertain to my daughter.

George continued speaking of his sons, and how they shared photographs of each other to other boys and to other girls. He explained it was common for children to take a photograph and use their telephone to text a copy of the photo to other classmates. The kids, he explained, forwarded these photos as they felt necessary to spread the word of what they deemed important or newsworthy. Children, according to George, had become more apt to share photographs of others than of themselves.

The expression on his face changed when he removed his phone from his inner coat pocket.

"I have a photograph of your daughter that is disturbing and you need to see it."

His face expressed embarrassment and worry. After agreeing to remain and talk after seeing the photograph, he handed me his phone. I took a long pull from my cigar and a drink of my Scotch. I looked at the screen of the phone. Naked, my daughter lay on a bed, and the bed was not hers. It was apparent she had intentionally posed naked for the camera. My mind immediately filled with embarrassment and rage. I placed the phone into my inner coat pocket and stood.

"How many people have seen this?" I asked.

He raised his eyebrows and shrugged his shoulders. He explained the photo had been sent to his son from another classmate. Only one of his sons had received the photograph. I explained I expected him to punish his sons for having the photograph, and he should forbid them to discuss it. He agreed, and requested I return the telephone. I disagreed and suggested he accept $500 for a new telephone to which he eventually agreed.

Filled with disappointment, I finished my Scotch and left the bar.

As I returned home, but before I spoke with Britney, I logged into the home server and blocked Britney from any internet access except her email, which she needed for her school work. All other internet was eliminated from her use.

As soon as she returned home from school I had a lengthy discussion with her about respect, and about boys.

"Men, especially the white boys at your school, are pigs. I want to know who took this photograph. When, where, and why!" I demanded.

After her initial denial of the photograph even being her, we discussed the boy she had been sneaking around and seeing. According to her, she had his phone number and had been seeing him, but did not have his email address.

After a short discussion, she was forbidden from contacting him in any manner ever again. She was forbidden from use of her telephone for one year, and forbidden from any internet usage for one year. Other than her attendance in school, she was forbidden from being seen in public. Until I decided otherwise, she was also forbidden from having any friends come to the house to visit. I made perfectly clear any disobedience or disregard for these rules and she would no longer be considered a member of my family.

It is important our children, especially in the United States, be given specific rules to live by. The freedoms practiced by many families and passed on to the children in America should not be applied to *all* families. I believed most of the American beliefs to be immoral. The American population had lost touch with providing discipline and moral values to their children. The children grew up, did not have sufficient careers, and lacked discipline in merely living life. My children, God help me, would not adopt the mediocre standards and principles of the typical American and become like so many other undisciplined children of the country.

In my early years, I had nothing. My family had very little and we grew up in a disciplined home. I learned the value of an education, of hard work and of respect. These values allowed me to provide my family with a good way of life in America, and I worked hard to obtain everything we had as a family. I did not reach this point in time in my life to allow a child to embarrass me by posing nude for photographs.

I did not discuss the matter with my wife. I considered talking to the police the next day and having the boy arrested. After much consideration, I decided against any police involvement, for fear of the police sharing the photograph.

The disrespect in this generation of children is going to be the death of family values, the death of disciplined young adults, and the death of respect for their elders. I fell asleep ashamed of my daughter and filled with disappointment.

Children in America do not understand.

My children will grow up with respect.

So help me God.

10

BROKEN PEOPLE

FAT KID

There always seemed to be unknown people in my life who would expose themselves to me throughout the course of my day. I supposed I may expose myself to them, but either way, they would appear. Time after time I was forced to witness their existence and be reminded of the fact they never actually did anything.

A week might pass and I wouldn't see them, but inevitably I would see them again.

And they are always doing *nothing.*

I would go to the grocery store and look up from my shopping.

There is that fucking guy again. The guy who I always see, and he's never actually doing anything. This guy is always wherever I go. And he's just wandering around, doing nothing.

What the fuck does this guy do for a living?

Doesn't he have a job?

I seemed to see these types of people in my process of perfecting nothingness. I wondered what it was they did for a living. Were they broke? Or did they inherit a fortune and live on the interest checks? A pimp? A drug dealer? Arms smuggler? Pornography?

As I pulled into the parking lot, Pavel looked in my direction and nodded his head sharply.

I waved toward him and smiled.

Pavel was five foot seven-ish, 160 pounds, athletic build, and always wore a dark blue track suit. He preferred the blue shiny type from the early 1990's with white stripes down the arms and legs. His jacket, as always, was unzipped to the waist; exposing a ribbed tank top - a.k.a. *wife beater*. Pavel was Bulgarian, and was a part of a larger group of Bulgarians who met at the coffee shop daily.

To do nothing.

The group had always treated me with the utmost respect and kindness. We spoke, sometimes at length, *about nothing.* I often wondered what they did for a living, but I never asked and they never offered. Years prior, I decided it must be trafficking of some sort. Drugs. Firearms. Stolen art. People. Stolen vehicles. Something of the sort. Often, as I spoke to Pavel or the group, I would have to allow them to complete a sentence, think about it for a moment, and try to decide what exactly had been said.

Although they spoke English, their accents were so strong it was as if they spoke Englarian - a mixture of both the English and Bulgarian languages. It was not uncommon for any member of the group to toss in a few Bulgarian words into an otherwise English sentence.

Interesting.

They always kept it interesting.

I parked the car, shouldered my laptop, and got out to start my day. As I walked toward the outside patio area of the coffee shop, I pushed the key fob button to lock the car. The beeping sound of the car alarm got Pavel's attention. As he turned to face the noise, he nodded his head and spoke.

"Vaaht Keed. Come. Seet. Spend time vith us on this vabulous day, no?"

I thought. I digested. After realizing for certain what he said, I responded.

"Sure, let me get a coffee, and I will be right out."

Then, the lies began, "I have a ton of shit to do today, so I can only stay for a bit, okay?"

Pavel nodded.

I nodded.

Upon entering the coffee shop, I was immediately pleased there was not a line. I scanned the area for the presence of the Nightmare, who seemed to be elsewhere, at least for now. Maybe today would truly be, as Pavel had said, *vabulous.*

"Hey, Kid. The usual?" the doll faced cashier asked.

I nodded my head as I reached into my left pocket. As I fished for my money clip she marked a cup with the intended concoction and handed it to the barista. I looked down at my money clip and laughed. *One hundred dollar bills.* This being the first stop of my day meant all I had available in my money clip was the cash I placed into it to start my day. I handed Doll Face a hundred dollar bill.

As she laughed she extended her arm to hand it back to me.

"I'm sorry, we can't accept this," she explained.

I clenched my teeth and inhaled a shallow breath through my nose.

"You *can* accept it. You won't. You have change, I know you do. Look, you do fifty thousand worth of business a day at minimum. Simple mathematics. Let's see, you're open from 6:00 am until 11:00 pm. That's seventeen hours. Fifty grand divided by seventeen," I looked at the ceiling.

"Three grand. Roughly three grand an hour, on average. That's fifty bucks a minute. Sounds about right, especially when you're busy," I shook my head.

Gingerly, I waved the back of my hand in the direction of her hand as she held the money, as if shooing a fly. As a line began to form behind me, I started to sweat.

"Kid, I'm sorry, we can't take it," she explained as she attempted to hand it to me again.

"Look. What's your name again?" I asked as I looked for her name tag.

I nodded my head once toward her name tag, "Uhhm, Gretchen. I have no other option. I have no credit cards. I use cash. Cash is king. Break the hundred dollar bill and give me the change. Fives, ones. Fuck, Gretchen, give me rolls of quarters. *I don't fucking care*."

Incompetent and incapable of thinking on her own, she stared. As she stood holding the bill with her arm extended, she smiled and waited.

From the receiving end of the counter, the barista barked, "KID, AMERICANO AT THE BAR!"

I snatched my hundred dollar bill from her fingers, walked to the counter, got my coffee, and waddled toward the door. As I began to exit, I noticed the Bulgarian mafia had formed on the outside patio area with Pavel. I turned and offered Doll Face a smile, holding my coffee high in the air for her to see. She showed no sign of amusement.

I walked outside and approached the Bulgarians. As I placed my laptop on the ground beside their table, I looked at Pavel and nodded.

"Vaaht Keed. You know, I mean, you know everyone," he said as he began to point toward the people who surrounded the table.

"Ivan......Svetli.......Svetlani......Yuri.......Demo."

As he pointed, they each stood, shook my hand, and nodded their respective heads.

I nodded my head in return. Pavel, Svetli, Svetlani, Yuri, and Demo could have easily been quintuplets. They were all the same height, all the same build, and all wore the same one inch long over-the-entire-head haircut. The identical track suits acted as garnishment. Ivan, however, was a different story.

"Vaaht Keed. Vaaaht dah fuck. Vaaht you do today, Vaaht Keed?" Pavel asked.

The entire crowd looked toward Pavel as he spoke. Upon his completion of the question, they turned and stared at me.

I contemplated my answer.

"Well, I'm getting ready to get on my laptop and begin responding to emails on my Internet site. On my blog," I responded.

I took a drink of my coffee. Everyone shifted their eyes toward Pavel.

"Vaaht dis blog? Vaaht for you blog? For vaaht?" Pavel asked.

Again, the entire crowd turned my direction and waited for a response. I digested the question, making certain I fully understood what he had said before I spoke.

"Well, it's a blog for anyone who wants to talk about whatever may be bothering them. It has become a place for primarily teens and young adults who are having issues with just living life. They have me give them advice. Right now I'm talking to a suicidal girl, a pregnant fifteen year old girl, and a kid with parents who can't find time to attend his school functions. One is suicidal, one is worried, and one is depressed," I responded as I admired the six identical track suits.

Again, upon the completion of my last sentence, the entire crowd shifted their eyes to Pavel.

Pavel didn't disappoint them.

"Keed, Vaaht money does this cost for some people? Vaaht zaay pay you for advice?" he asked.

The crowd, once again, shifted to me. I studied Ivan for a moment. Six foot six. Probably 240 pounds. Not an ounce of fat. He stood military erect, waiting for my response. Slowly, I took a drink of coffee. I wondered where this conversation was headed. I focused on Ivan and responded.

"Well, they don't pay anything. It's free. I just do it to help them. Sometimes people need help, and they can't get it elsewhere. So, I offer free advice. *For free*."

The crowd stared at me. This time their eyes didn't shift to Pavel. They stared at me as if they wanted more. A different answer. An explanation. *Something.* I sat, not knowing what else to say. Feeling somewhat nervous, I took another drink of my coffee and dug into my left pocket for a piece of chocolate. They stared. I peeled back the wrapper. I took a bite. They stared.

Pavel began to speak.

Their gaze shifted.

Thank God.

"Kid, vhee talk. Vhee vonder. Vhee talk. Vhee vonder. Vaaht dah fuck. Vaaht dah fuck Keed do for the money? You drive Beemer. You never working. You come. You use laptops. You stay all day. Vaaht dah fuck you do for the money, Keed?" Pavel asked, his hands buried deeply in his track suit pockets.

The entire mafia, upon Pavel's completion of the question, shifted

124

their eyes toward me. Intently they stared, waiting for an explanation of some sort.

And at that moment it dawned on me.

I was one of *those* people.

The people I detested. The jobless people I seemed to see all of the time. The people who made me *wonder*. I pondered my answer, finished my chocolate, and decided I would go fishing. In some respects, I lied.

Some.

"I import weapons. I am a weapons smuggler," I said in a very matter of fact tone as I took the last remaining swig of my coffee.

Immediately, all heads spun in Pavel's direction.

"Vell, Vell, Vell. Vhee must talk. Not for now. But vhee talk. Zoon. Keed, have nice day."

I stood and smiled.

I picked up my laptop, shouldered it, and nodding to each of the men as I spoke my departures.

"Pavel, Svetli, Svetlani, Ivan, Yuri, Demo," I grinned.

As I walked away I stuffed my chocolate wrapper into my left pocket. As I did, I could hear them speaking in Bulgarian. Turning to walk away, I wondered about the availability of a Rosetta Stone in Bulgarian.

Walking to the door with my hands in my pockets, I decided to try my luck at tossing my trash in the trash can. It was a huge steel can which sat at the entrance of the coffee shop. Modern looking, cylindrical and black; it appeared exactly like a huge 250 pound dildo. It was shaped like a futuristic cock-like space ship, about twenty inches in diameter and four feet tall. The opening at the top of the rounded tip was about the size of a grapefruit. *Everyone* made fun of it. Standing fifteen feet away, I crushed my candy bar wrapper into a tight wad, and tossed it.

Without contacting any portion of the trash can, it fell inside. I turned and looked for witnesses. Not a soul enjoyed this magnificent feat.

It satisfied me nonetheless.

Today would, in fact, be *vabulous.*

Once inside, I found a seat. I retrieved my laptop from the case, opened it, and logged onto the Internet. I knew better than to attempt to buy another coffee from Doll Face, so I went to the counter and asked for an ice water. Doll Face Gretchen graciously granted my request, and filled with disappointment I walked to the table. Once logged into my email account, two emails immediately grasped my attention. One was from Michelle and the other from Shellie. Shocked at my not knowing I had received these emails, I unsuccessfully attempted to find my phone. As I expected, I had left it in my car. I opened the email from Shellie.

Kid,

My parents are livid. They have prohibited me from use of the phone, social media networks, and from going out in public. I am afraid that I cannot make it any longer. Neither of my parents will allow me to even try to discuss things with them or try to explain. I no longer have friends. My life is over. Contact me as soon as you can, please.

Shellie

The date and time on the email confirmed it was about two hours old. I considered my potential response, knowing email was the only means of communicating. I opened Michelle's email as I processed Shellie's message in my thoughts.

Kid,

Why I'm deciding to tell you this right now I don't know, but whatever. You can read it when you get a chance. Regarding Shellie, your suicidal girl - if I met her somewhere and she told me her story, a spark would go off in my heart and I'd just want to give her love. I've done it a million times. But sometimes I wonder if I do this because I have a selfless love for everyone, or if it's just because broken people attract broken people. That's a personal theory/belief. That broken people attract broken people. And not in a sexual sense, but just that they are drawn to each other. But if that's the case, then there's a problem. Because broken people shouldn't be helping broken people in that way. If you're whole, you're safe. There's no room for anything foreign to creep in. And I like to think of myself as strong, but am I really? I don't lie to myself. There are times where I have thoughts I thought I had gotten past. I guess that means although I am strong, I am not quite whole.

Three years ago, it was like my body was a shell, dragging my soul behind itself on a 100 foot rope. Now it's maybe 3 feet behind me. I am so close, I'm trying. I wake up every day smiling and happy to be alive, but there's still that little drag. The parts of me that still haven't learned how to be alive. I'm not saying that's exactly the case with you. But ask yourself...are you whole? You may very well be, but only you can answer that...so just be careful and know your limits I guess. I don't want to undermine your capabilities but you're still human like the rest of us. Make sure you're taking care of yourself first. I don't doubt that you can do her some good. But every once in a while just detach yourself and take a look at it all from the outside. If all is well, proceed.

I'm losing logical flow so I will shut up here... and umm, I don't really have a conclusion, because I don't even know what I'm trying to say. But I think I mentioned everything I wanted to. It's just, when you said you weren't planning to tell me, I thought maybe it was because you didn't want to hear what I had to say. Which is why I'm telling you anyways, since you probably won't ask. Haha. I'm annoying. And this doesn't need to be a conversation if you don't want it to be. But those are just my thoughts.

Michelle

Broken people attract broken people. I thought about her statement. I never really looked at it in that fashion, but it made perfect sense. And therein was my problem. Michelle was right. She was seventeen years old, and teaching me about life. *Broken people shouldn't be helping broken people in that way...If you're whole, you're safe. There's no room for anything foreign to creep in.*

I sat. I thought. I looked around the coffee shop. I devoured two chocolate bars. *I've been broken for longer than Michelle has been alive.* She didn't realize the extent of my broken nature, and it wasn't important she do so. But what she said rang true. It hit home. *If you're whole, you're safe, there's no room for anything foreign to creep in.* And there I sat, broken. My entire adult life after *the incident*, I hadn't done anything except try to help those people who I deemed incapable. Now, I wondered.

Was I worthy?

Was I capable?

My not being whole allowed these people, their thoughts, their feelings and their problems - *things foreign* - to *creep in.*

I felt as if I was drowning, and Michelle was my floatation device. Feeling somewhat confused, I got up, grabbed my keys, and began walking toward my car. I truly *needed* a coffee. Half way there, I stopped and stared at the Bulgarian mafia's summit meeting. I reached into my pocket and pulled out my money clip.

"Pavel, do you have change for a hundred dollar bill? I need a coffee, and they can't break a hundred," I explained.

Pavel nodded toward Ivan. I shifted my gaze. Ivan reached into his track suit pocket and retrieved a rubber banded wad of cash the diameter of a can of Dr. Pepper. Carefully, he unrolled it and dug through what appeared to be ten thousand dollars of hundred dollar bills to reach the twenty dollar bills buried inside.

I glanced at Pavel.

Pavel nodded.

I looked at Ivan.

Ivan nodded, and handed me five twenty dollar bills. I handed Ivan a one hundred dollar bill. Ivan nodded at me. I nodded at Ivan.

I nodded at Pavel.

What in the fuck do these guys do for money?

As they spoke in Bulgarian, I walked to the passenger door of the car and unlocked it. A quick glance into the car window and I saw the phone on the driver's seat.

As I walked back inside, my phone and five twenties in tow, I sent Michelle a text requesting she call me as soon as she was able. I was struggling with being broken. Not being whole. I stood inside the door, confused. *Broken people attract broken people*. Maybe *formerly broken* people attract broken people. Maybe those who *were* broken at some point in time felt a compulsion to help other broken people later in life. Like Alcoholics Anonymous. The principles of AA worked because of the common bond. Everyone who was recovering from Alcoholism, or felt they had recovered felt possessed the same thoughts and feelings as their respective counterpart. The people in AA were certainly all broken yet they were a support group.

They supported each other.

Broken people helping broken people.

"Hey, Kid. We can break your hundred dollar bill now," Doll Face exclaimed as she smiled from one of her oversized ears to the other.

I considered handing her a twenty and quickly decided *fuck it*. Just *fuck it*. I walked to the register, reached past the five loose twenties in my pocket, got my money clip in my hand, and pulled a hundred dollar bill from it.

I handed it to her.

She rang up my typical Americano.

"$3.17, Kid. Let's see," she said as she reached into the register.

She carefully extracted a fist full of bills and began counting.

"Five, ten, fifteen, twenty, twenty-five, thirty, thirty-five, forty, forty-five, forty-six, forty-seven, forty-eight, forty-nine, and one makes fifty," She placed the fifty dollars down, and began counting again, "fifty-one, fifty-two, fifty-three, fifty-four, fifty-five…"

I couldn't take it. Not for another second.

"Hand me the money, Gretchen. Just fucking hand it to me," I ordered as I scooped the fifty dollar pile of bills from the counter.

I extended my hand for the remaining cash.

"I'm sorry Kid, I have to count it. It's corporate policy. We have to count it to keep our register…"

Before she could say another word, I reached over the counter, grabbed the wad of cash from her hand and turned to the barista. As Gretchen attempted to see over the register, her mouth agape, I shoved the wad of bills into my left pocket. As I walked to the counter to get my coffee, I heard my phone beep.

Michelle, I hoped.

I grabbed the coffee, tipped it up, and drank about half of it in one gulp. I had developed a drink I became content with. Four shots of espresso, hot water, and two inches of cold cream poured over the top. It came to me fresh and luke-warm. This allowed me to immediately enjoy it and not be required to wait for it to cool down. The staff just called it the *Kid.*

As I took another sip, I walked to the table and looked down at my phone. Opening the text screen, I realized I had a text from Michelle.

MICHELLE: Busy. I will call in you in twenty.

I placed the phone on the table, re-opened the email screen, and noticed I had received an email from the 15 year old pregnant girl. In remembering her lure, I laughed out loud as I opened the email.

My parents my boyfriend and me have discussed what you said and we have decided what to do we got with the doctor and we signed the papers and the family signed them too and now we have a family to adopt the baby I am happy my parents are happy and me and my boyfriend are going to get married as soon as we graduate the family is really happy about the baby my baby well it is their baby and about the adoption thank you for good advice

I stared at the email. It aggravated me to no end when kids texted and used portions of words, or made up words. I texted frequently, but did so as if I were typing a thesis. I wondered how people who texted with acronyms and *text speak* would type a letter. Case in point.

I thought about my response, knowing this one was in the bag so to speak, and responded. I thought about my response, knowing this one was in the bag so to speak, and responded.

Iamsohappythatallwentwellsorryiaminahurryandihavenotimeforspaces idothinkadoption,consideringallthings,wastheonlyviableoption.rememb er,birthcontrolisagreatthingforteens.bewell

I clicked the *send* button and laughed. I used no spaces but took time to use periods and commas. I suspected she would need to get Mr. *Just The Tip* to interpret it for her.

I recalled her previous statement of abortion being the only option. Now considering a needy family was going to be able to have a child they may not be able to otherwise have made me feel as if I had done *one* thing right in this last year. Full of pride, I took another drink of coffee. Fearing I may fall below 319 pounds before I went home, and being low on chocolate, I got up and pulled my scale from the bag. As I tossed it on the floor, I wondered. Eagerly, I tapped with my toe. After zeroing itself, I got on.

317.

I got off. After it zeroed itself again, I got back on.

317.

FUCK, fuck, fucking fuck. I tossed the scale back in the bag, and went to the register.

"Give me three donuts, Gretchen," I reached into my pocket and grabbed my wad of cash.

"The glazed donuts?" she asked.

I stared at her ears. Her head was so small, yet her ears were monstrous.

"What?" I asked.

I had heard her, but for some reason said *what.*

"The glazed donuts?" she asked again.

I looked into the pastry case. The establishment only offered one style of donut. Glazed. I looked at her. I started to scream, but refrained.

"You only offer one type of Donut, Dumbo. The *glazed* one, I want the glazed one. Times three."

As soon as I spoke, I realized what I had said. I felt terrible and hoped she didn't notice.

"*What* did you say?" she asked.

"Glazed, Gretchen. I said I want the glazed," I smiled.

Her face covered in a confused look, she reached in the case and pulled the three donuts out.

"I do not want a plate or a bag, Gretchen. Just put them in my hand," I requested.

I held my hand out, palm up. I hated wasting things and required the staff provide my pastries without plates or paper bags. Additionally, I did not use a cardboard sleeve on my coffee cup. Her face covered in uncertainty, she turned and looked at the barista as if she wanted confirmation or approval. I doubted it was covered in the corporate policy manual. The barista, just like the Bulgarian mafia, nodded. Reluctantly, Gretchen dropped the donuts into my hand.

"That will be $6.47," she said as she wiped her hands free of donut matter.

I handed her a wad of bills, clearly in excess of seven dollars. She, as if handed foreign currency, looked at the cash in bewilderment. She counted seven dollars, and placed them in the register.

She attempted to hand me the remaining bills and change.

"Put it in the tip jar, Gretchen," I said.

I smiled as I stuffed half a donut in my mouth. As I turned to walk back to my seat I overheard her whisper to the barista, *Kid actually left a tip.*

Sitting in my seat, I was relieved to have a donut. I shoved the remaining half donut into my mouth and took a drink of coffee. I ate donuts the way the 110 pound Asian ate hot dogs at the Nathan's Hot Dog Eating Championship. Bite. Drink. Swallow. Bite. Drink. Swallow. As if I was in a donut gobbling contest, I continued. The thought of being thin and having people approach me scared me. Thinking of my weight plummeting and waking up thin one day, I began to eat even faster. Bite. Drink. Swallow. Bite. Drink. Swallow. As I was preparing to swallow the last half donut in my mouth, my phone rang.

I looked at the screen. As I suspected, it was Michelle.

I answered.

"Hey, Kid, what's up?" she asked.

"Well, I will go with the easy one first. The pregnant girl in Kansas signed adoption papers. Her child is going to be adopted and become part of a family somewhere. She didn't give too many details. But that's the gist of it. Oh, and *broken people helping broken people.* Your email regarding Shellie. You made some comments that hit a little too close to home. And I want to talk about that. Shellie emailed me and she appears to be at rock bottom. Her parents have her confined to the house, have taken her phone, and are prohibiting her from using Facebook. For her and her type of personality we both know that's a huge thing for her to come to terms with."

As I started to take a breath Michelle began talking.

"Well, that's good about the pregnant girl. It sure beats abortion.

Abortion may be *someone's* right, but it doesn't make *it* right. Not always, that's for sure. That makes me happy. And I was just saying," she paused and breathed into the phone.

"I don't know. Really I just wanted you to take a look at yourself. To step back away from your life for a minute and look at it. Take a look in from the outside. Look at yourself from a different vantage point and be honest with what you see. Does that make sense?" she asked.

It did. It made perfect sense. Michelle and I had talked for some time about my *running*, as she called it. Running from everything in life I didn't necessarily want to deal with. I had, at one point in time, traveled through nine states in seven weeks. Accomplishing nothing, I was just running from my day-to-day life of being me. I was done being me for a while. I wanted to be someone else. Michelle called me out. And, as always, she was right. After seven weeks on the road, I turned around and came home. And at home I remained.

"Yes, Michelle, it makes perfect sense. I was looking at it differently. I was taking it, as I always do, as a personal stab at me. At how I am living my life, how I am incapable in your eyes."

I picked up my coffee cup to take a drink. *Empty.* I held it in the air and waved it toward Gretchen until I had her attention. I pointed at my phone with my free hand. She looked confused. I turned the cup upside down. Nothing dripped from the cup. I pointed at my phone. Finally she acknowledged my hand signals and nodded her head in confirmation of my desire.

She looked at the barista.

The barista nodded and grabbed a cup.

What is with all the fucking nodding today?

"Kid," Michelle began.

"Let me finish," I said.

"Just let me finish."

"Bob Dylan wrote a song, *Everything is Broken*. I often think of that song, and not so much the lyrics, when I think about people. We're all, in some respects, broken. When we realize it - when we truly accept it - it allows us to, in being conscious of it, possibly make adjustments in our lives to combat the fault," I smiled and nodded my head as it began to make perfect sense.

"We can attempt to correct it. It's knowing *what* is broken that's almighty important. Knowing or admitting being broken doesn't help if we aren't conscious of just what the underlying problem is. I am conscious of *my* faults, *my* character defects, and *my* shortcomings. I do what I do, not to mask it or separate myself from the realization, but to make my life less *painless*. I'm selfish, Michelle," I stopped talking and waited to see what she had to offer.

I noticed the barista delivering my coffee. He walked up and handed it to me. As I reached into my pocket to get money to pay, he waved his hands from side-to-side.

I held up the coffee and nodded.

He nodded, turned, and walked away.

"Kid, why doesn't *admitting* being broken fix anything," she asked.

"Well," I paused and thought.

I loved using analogies, so I started with one.

"Look at it like a car. You have a broken car. Knowing that it is broken doesn't allow it to be repaired accurately. Having it diagnosed, and knowing *what* is broken allows a timely and accurate repair. And one that will in fact fix it. *Sir, your car is broken*, versus, *sir, your car is broken, and it needs a radiator to be repaired*. Does that make sense?"

I asked.

"Yes, it does," she answered.

"Also, that gets us about half way to my overall point. The knowing *what* it is. Then, there's addressing it. Generally speaking, it helps to discuss your area of concern with someone else who may have the same problem or problems you do. A common bond. The feeling the person you are speaking with has been there before. It's what makes AA work for drunks. Everyone in AA has had the same problem. The stories told in those meetings are the same year after year, just told by different people. They find comfort in the fact they aren't alone in their faults or in their mistakes," I thought of another analogy of sorts and continued.

"For instance, in the veterans diagnosed with Post Traumatic Stress Disorder or PTSD I have spoken with; I have found these things to be true. They come home from the war and have a difficult time functioning. Upon returning home, some have PTSD, and some don't. It has been determined recently there is something in the brain, the way we're wired at birth, which makes you either a candidate for developing PTSD or not. At any rate, some of the veterans with PTSD sit at home and are afraid to come out in public. If they do, a sudden certain movement, a smell or a noise can cause their mind to return to a place they mentally fear. So they often sit at home and do nothing. They may hide the fact they were ever even in the military. They cover their tattoos. They put away their boots and their BDU's, and try to do their best to recover. When they finally do find out what's wrong and admit it, they only find comfort in talking to other veterans who have had the same types of incidents or problems."

I began to think of *the incident* and felt my spine begin to tingle.

"The bottom line is this: A rape victim who has PTSD *has PTSD*. It's the *same*. But you won't find someone returning from Fallujah talking to a rape victim in hope of finding a common bond."

I paused, feeling rather uneasy and weak. I began to shake. I reached into my pocket and got a chocolate bar. Alternating chocolate, coffee, chocolate, and coffee I ate it quickly and allowed Michelle to speak.

"Kid, yes. It makes perfect sense. We find comfort in others who are *like us*. The Egyptian kids at my school hang out with the Egyptian kids. The kids who are into sports and the kids who compete in debate, they hang out with the kids in sports and debate. I think having someone with the exact same fault or faults as you may allow you to *feel* as if you're normal. At least while you're in their presence."

"Just like *you* try to, Kid. Now, back to Shellie and broken people and people who are the same talking to people who are the same," Michelle babbled.

"Jesus, Michelle. Take a fucking breath. I really wanted to ask if you had anyone in your school like Shellie; someone who really relied on social networking for a means of feeling alive. Someone, in the absence of having their electronic Facebook friends, would have nothing or no one?" I took another drink of my coffee and waited.

"Oh my God yes, tons of them. There are so many kids here that are social misfits. They are afraid of being rejected, so they don't expose themselves to anyone in public. They're shy, and I feel sorry for them. They stay on their phones all day and night. They Tweet, Instagram photos, they post things on Pinterest and Facebook and they try to get recognition for being pretty, being smart, being intelligent or being thin from their social networking friends. It's so sad," she sighed.

I cleaned the chocolate from my teeth with my tongue.

"What if someone took one of those kids you're talking about and eliminated the social networking from their life? What would happen?" I asked although I felt as if I already knew the answer.

"Kid, they'd just die. It has become such a necessity, such a way of life for these kids. It's incomprehensible. At least some of them would probably be suicidal. Can you imagine if when you were in school, your parents took every friend you had? What if they said you couldn't have any of them any longer? For these kids, the *electronic* friends as you call them, that's all they have. I want to send you a pic of a girl that I was going to ask you about anyway. This is important. And it's so funny you asked this question, and about Shellie. This friend of mine is having similar issues, and I am so worried about her. She is a mess. She's OCD about everything, has zero self-esteem, and she thinks she's fat and she's so *not* fat. She self-harms. She has eating disorders. She broke up with her boyfriend. Her parents don't really pay any attention to her. She looks at herself as not being worthy of being on this earth. I want you to *read* her. You know, look at her photo and read her, okay?"

Before I had a chance to respond, Michelle asked again.

"Okay?"

"Sure, send it. I'll hang up and call you back in two or three minutes," I responded.

I hung up the phone and waited, finishing my coffee as I did. The phone almost instantly beeped. I opened the text message, and there was a photo from Michelle. It was not a girl. It was a handsome boy. He had short hair, an athletic build, and he appeared to be troubled. I studied the photo. I could read this kid like a book. I sent Michelle a text, explaining I got a photo of a boy and not a girl. The phone rang instantly. It was Michelle.

"Buns. I can't find a pic of her on my phone. I sent the other my mistake while I was sorting through my phone. I will send you one of her tonight. I just want to know if I should be worried about her. I took a few recent candid photos of her, I just can't find them. But the boy? He's a friend. Did you read him?" she asked.

"Is he gay?" she asked.

"What? *Is he gay*?" I couldn't believe she had asked the question. Not of *this* kid.

"Yes, Kid, is he gay?"

"No, he's not gay. Why?" I asked.

"Are you sure?"

"As sure as I am fat. Yes, Michelle. I am a hundred percent certain, why?" I asked as I wondered who the kid was.

"I *knew* it," she squealed.

"Well, I met him about a month ago and he's so nice. Kind of weird, but nice. He thinks he's gay."

"Well, I will tell you what I *know* and what I *think*. I know this. His father is a prick and has spent this kid's entire childhood telling him he will never accomplish anything. That he will never amount to anything. Additionally, his father will never give any form of recognition when the kid *does* accomplish anything. The kid suffers from *fear of failure*. Shit," I paused and stared at the ceiling.

"It's uhm, *atychiphobia*. That's what I know. People who suffer from fear of failure often place themselves in situations in life that they *know* they can succeed at. They settle for mediocrity instead of setting higher goals. It ends up being a *lifetime* of mediocrity if they don't get help. Parents who humiliate their kids, constantly undermining them, or who are extremely unsupportive, create children like this. This kid in my opinion has made himself - at least in his mind - gay. He subconsciously has a fear of failing in a relationship. That's what I think. Bad thing is this; he believes it. The gay part. It's a subconscious self-preservation thing. Wow. But he's *not gay*. Not one bit. I know that," I studied the photo on my phone as I spoke.

"Well Kid, you made my day. I have to get back to my competition. I snuck away for a bit. I'm going to be in such trouble if I get caught. I will send you a pic of my friend as soon as I can, okay? I am worried about her. I really am."

"Okay, Michelle, do that," I responded.

"Bye, and don't forget Shellie," she said.

Shit, don't forget Shellie.

I laid my phone down and started typing my response to Shellie's email.

Suicidal people, generally speaking, don't actually want to die. They want to stop hurting. Shellie was in pain. Considering all of our previous discussions and Michelle's input, Shellie was feeling as if she had no one. She was in pain. I knew I needed to be brief and make her feel I truly cared about her.

Shellie,

I am sorry for the punishment that your parents have imposed on you. I know it may feel like it is more weight than you want on your shoulders right now, but in the big picture of life, it's something you can manage. You have demonstrated more ability to manage events and catastrophes better than anyone else I have ever encountered. You impress me every time we speak. I feel in the short period of time that we have been emailing each other that we have become extremely close. It makes me proud to call you a friend. Let's start a more frequent emailing process to try and break up the monotony of the day. I receive my email, as you know, on my phone as well. Look forward to hearing from you.

I miss you.

Kid

I looked down and reread it. I felt as if it were lacking. Suicide is so difficult. Don't say too much. Don't say too little. People who are suicidal often feel as if no one would miss them if they were gone. I knew she'd feel this way, especially now. All of her friends were probably on Twitter or Facebook. She felt abandoned, I was sure. I logged off, closed my laptop, and placed it in my bag. I shouldered the bag and looked outside. The mafia had left. Scanning the lot for the Nightmare's car produced nothing.

Splendid.

Short of suicidal girls, this was an otherwise perfect day. I scanned the store to make certain the Nightmare wasn't hiding. *Nothing.* I was the only patron. I smiled and started to walk out. The barista was sweeping the floor. As I opened the door he made eye contact and nodded his head.

I nodded in return.

I wondered.

Is it me, or…

As I slowly pulled the car out of the parking lot at an angle, I attempted to prevent the undercarriage from scraping the exit ramp. As a man exited traffic and began to pull into the store, he noticed I was blocking the ramp. As he sat in traffic waiting to enter, I felt terrible. Cars were backing up behind him and drivers began to honk. Slowly, I exited a little more, making room for him to enter. In appreciation for my effort to make room, he nodded his head. *Vabulous.*

11

SHOES NOT REQUIRED

BRITNEY

When I was young I dreamt of being older. I had always thought older meant better. Not of *having* things, but of *doing* things and of being a family. Laughing, going, doing, loving, and just simply being. As I grew older, I dreamt of having someone love me. From the time I was roughly eleven years old I had not felt as if I received any form of love from my parents. I felt I was merely something or someone they needed to process through varying stages.

My parents were determined to process a child through the factory of life.

Place on conveyor. Elementary school. Middle school. High school. College. Career. Get married. Have children. Remove from conveyor when process is complete.

They rarely seemed concerned with what I wanted or how I felt. I had never been asked by my parents how I was feeling. Not once. As I lay alone, they slept. Further proof they had no concern for my feelings. I couldn't help but wonder if after I was gone, and they were left to live a life without me, if the skin color of my boyfriend would matter.

You may have no after school activities. No friends can come over.

I'm sorry, you have to be a doctor; we do not want an attorney in the family. We don't want you to see that boy. Give us your phone. There will be no use of social networking. You will have no tattoos. Don't wear makeup in public.

I lay smothered in an unbearable pain; a pain which could not be described or imagined. Those who hadn't experienced this level of suffering had no ability to understand how deeply it would cut. The degree of pain I felt was more than I or anyone could ever be expected to live with. Not one single soul could have ever lived to describe it.

It would be impossible.

I was alone. I would forever be alone.

I feared it would not stop. The pain had become heavy, and the pressure continued to crush me. And no one cared. No one was there to help me. No one bothered to ask. And the pain progressed to a point it pushed me further into the hell in which I resided.

I had no phone or friends to call. Now, not one person expressed love for me, and no one tried to stop me.

Because no one cared.

Sitting at my desk frustrated, I began to cry. Nothing mattered. My father had blocked me from all Internet activities short of emailing. After I completed my last email, I logged off the computer. I removed some paper from my printer and stared at the pen I held in my hand and wept.

Filled with pain and feeling empty, I began to write. As the words escaped my mind, I felt relieved. The more I wrote, the less pressure I felt. It was as if the closer I came to the end, the clearer it became – the end was the only answer. Proof not only the end was near, but reinforcement of the end being my only escape from the overwhelming pain. No one was willing to help me. No one cared enough to provide me with what I needed to end this pain. A simple hug. A kiss. Some form of expressed love. The one person who truly loved me was gone and my father would not allow him to return into my life.

Ever.

The words flowed from my mind through the pen and formed into sentences on the paper. As I wrote, I read. The pain was almost over. It would end soon.

Mother and Father,

Without a doubt, you will find this letter after you find my body. I guess when you do, consider what I have written. Take a moment to actually examine what I have said. Don't just read it, please take time to understand and ultimately apply it. What would you have done, knowing now the pain had been this severe, to stop this? I ask whatever the answer may be that you provide it to my sister. Treat her every day as if she may be in this pain tomorrow, because if you don't pay better attention to her needs, she will be. Don't buy her a car. Give her a hug. Don't tell her who she can't go on a date with. Ask her to bring whoever he may be home to meet you. Don't tell her where to go to college and what profession to choose, ask her how she feels and what she prefers.

Don't try to buy her happiness.

Instead, give her love.

When I was young I was your pride and joy - your daughter. And I can't help but ask - as I remove the bed sheets from my bed - where those feelings went. At what point in time did I become expendable? As I twist my bed sheets into a rope, I wonder if a simple 'Britney, how was school today?' was too much to expect?

The pain has become unbearable.

You will not listen. You do not care enough to. I plead. I ask. And nothing changes. And, while you are at work earning money to buy my little sister a car for her sixteenth birthday, I am hanging by my neck in the garage, waiting for you to come home from work so you can find me.

Let this letter be read. By all that are able. Because if this can save one life, let that life be saved.

Tell Marc I love him.

And find comfort in knowing...

The pain has ended.

Britney

I listened as my parents left for work. I took a shower, walked into my closet and picked out a dress. I considered wearing shoes, and decided against it. For someone to find me with one shoe on and one off would be awful. I placed the clothes on my bed. After carefully putting on my otherwise prohibited makeup, I got dressed. I looked in the mirror.

I was beautiful.

I looked thin.

I wished I hadn't felt the level of pain I wallowed in.

I twisted my sheet into a rope, and draped it over my shoulders. I looked into the mirror as I tied it around my neck, making sure it wouldn't come undone when I jumped. After I placed the note I had written on my dresser I walked down the stairs, my bed sheet rope following close behind.

Bare foot, tired, and alone, I walked to the garage.

Once in the garage, I looked for my father's ladder. Carefully, I placed the ladder where my mother parks her car, knowing she would be home first. I climbed toward the top of the ladder with the other end of my bed sheet rope in my hand. Before I reached the top of the ladder, I tossed the knotted end of the bed sheet over wooden structure above me. I carefully tied the end of the bed sheet to the rafters and attempted to look down at the floor.

The length of the bed sheet was so short it held my head up at an uncomfortable angle. Frustrated, I decided to climb a little further and make it less tight.

As I stood on the ladder I started to pray. I questioned if praying prior to committing suicide would fall on deaf ears. Would God understand the pain? It mattered not. I could not continue to take this level of pain. Now, more than ever, it had become unimaginable.

As I began to try to kick the ladder, it wobbled and slowly became stable again. *I can't jump, this is too high.*

I decided I wanted to just fall.

Slowly.

Softly.

Simply.

I kicked the ladder and caused it to wobble again. As the stability of the step left my feet, I heard an angel call my name from the heavens. As the rope became taught, I lost my sight and hearing. Eerily, I began to recall my childhood as if it was a dream; and I hung from my neck until everything faded to darkness.

And the angel called my name.

12

DUDE, YOU'RE CREEPING ME OUT

MICHELLE

Life asked so many questions but never provided us with the answers. We were required to find them on our own. I had been on this earth almost eighteen years. In my eighteen years, I had made many observations and determined a few things. As I progressed through my years, I maintained and modified several notes. I compiled a list of these findings and planned on continuing as I grew older and observed more of what life had to offer me. To date, I had developed a list of twenty-two things I had learned.

Things I've Learned in 18 Years of Life

1) True love is not something *found*, rather [sic] something encountered. You can't go out and look for it. The person you marry and the person you love could easily be two different people. So have a beautiful life while waiting for God to bring along your once-in-a-lifetime love. Don't allow yourself to settle for anything less than them. Stop worrying about who you're going to marry because God's already on the front porch watching your grandchildren play.

2) God WILL give you more than you can handle, so you can learn to lean on him in times of need. He won't tempt you more than you can handle, though. So don't lose hope. Hope anchors the soul.

3) Remember who you are and where you came from. Remember that you are not from this earth. You are a child of heaven, you're invaluable, you are beautiful. Carry yourself that way.

4) Don't put your faith in humanity, humanity is inherently flawed. We are all imperfect people created and loved by a perfect God. Perfect. So put your faith in Him.

5) I fail daily, and that is why I succeed.

6) Time passes, and nothing and everything changes. Don't live life half asleep. Don't drag your soul through the days. Feel everything you do. Be there physically and mentally. Do things that make you feel this way as well.

7) Live for beauty. We all need beauty, get it where you can find it. Clothing, paintings, sculptures, music, tattoos, nature, literature, makeup. It's all art and it's what makes us human. Same as feeling the things we do. Stay human.

8) If someone makes you think, keep them. If someone makes you feel, keep them.

9) There is nothing the human brain cannot do. You can change anything about yourself that you want to. Fight for it. It's all a mental game.

10) God didn't break our chains for us to be bound again. Alcohol, drugs, depression, addiction, toxic relationships, monotony and repetition, they bind us. Break those chains. Destroy your past and give yourself new life like God has given you.

11) This is your life. Your struggle, your happiness, your sorrow, and your success. You do not need to justify yourself to anyone. You owe no one an explanation for the choices that you make and the position you are in. In the same vein, respect yourself by not comparing your journey to anyone else's.

12) There is no wrong way to feel.

13) Knowledge is everywhere, keep your eyes open. Look at how diverse and wonderful this world is. Are you going to miss out on beautiful people, places, experiences, and ideas because you are close-minded? I sure hope not.

14) Selfless actions always benefit you more than the recipient.

15) There is really no room for regret in this life. Everything happens for a reason. If you can't find that reason, accept there is one and move on.

16) There is room, however, for guilt. Resolve everything when it first comes up. That's not only having integrity, but also taking care of your emotional well-being.

17) If the question is 'Am I strong enough for this?' The answer is always, 'Yes, but not on your own.'

18) Mental health and sanity above all.

19) We love because He first loved us. The capacity to love is the ultimate gift, the ultimate passion, euphoria, and satisfaction. We have all of that because He first loved us. If you think about it in those terms, it is easy to love Him. Just by thinking of how much He loves us.

20) From destruction comes creation. Beauty will rise from the ashes.

21) Many things can cause depression. Such as knowing you aren't becoming the person you have the potential to become. Choose happiness and change. The sooner the better, and the easier.

22) Half of happiness is as simple as eating right and exercising. You are one big chemical reaction. So are your emotions. Give your body the right reactants to work with and you'll be satisfied with the products.

Usually, I did my best thinking while lying in my bed. As I lay there, thinking about what Kid said regarding David, I looked at the list. Number five certainly applied to David. If Kid was correct, and I suspected he was, David had a deep fear of failure. So deep he developed a homosexual inner being to prevent his outer shell from failing at a relationship. The thought of someone building a shield or shelter with such conviction fascinated me. I struggled with his being conscious of what he was doing in developing his homosexual character.

I started thinking about what Kid and I had talked about.

Broken people attract broken people.

I thought of Kid. We met by chance on the Internet. A one in a 220 million chance, from what Kid calculated. I suspect he was right. He was generally right in what he said regarding statistics. He had proven to be a genuine person and a great friend, always willing to listen when I wanted to talk. I had spent many nights on the phone with him, talking for hours and hours on end. Most of the time when we spoke on the phone, I hid in my closet so my parents wouldn't hear us talking. To them, the thought of me meeting someone over the Internet would be beyond what was acceptable. My act of talking to him on the phone alone would make my desire for tattoos look like nothing.

Kid had demons he wouldn't speak of, but they were apparent. I spent considerable time piecing together his life and trying to figure out exactly who he was. I never assumed or thought he lied to me, but it was obvious he only gave me bits and pieces of his life. The small fragments he chose to. He allowed me to learn the things he wanted me to know, and didn't offer me the parts he didn't want me to know. I attempted on many occasions to try to gain information about him on the Internet, but generally failed at finding much. I didn't even know his real name and through attempts to track his phone number, I found it was a pay-by-month phone with no name attached to it. He had lived most of his life as a private person, and wanted to keep it that way. Keeping his name a secret was probably yet another way to keep his life with me on a less personal level.

One of the things which fascinated me about him was the fact that he gained 140 pounds to shelter himself from people. He was so scared of people failing him he gained weight to prevent them from ever wanting to meet him. He became unattractive to the eye so people would look past *who* he actually was. We all have a degree of fear of failure within us, some maybe worse than others. Kid wasn't excluded from this. He just wanted to live his life without failing, or without people perceiving him as a failure.

Quite possible he was truly afraid of *people failing him.*

Immediately after we met, I asked Kid about *the incident* as he called it. He quickly changed the subject and explained he would tell me some other time. I asked him again, on no less than three more occasions, all of which got me the same answer. *I will tell you some other time.* I had determined *the incident* was what caused him to stop drinking and quit using drugs. It was obvious this was also when he turned his life around and decided to start helping people. Although I wasn't certain, I think it was immediately following this point in time when he decided to gain weight and to force people to leave him alone.

During my initial excitement of meeting him, I told my cousins about him. At this point in time, I had known Kid for about three months. My cousins went crazy. Immediately, they began to question his motives for speaking to me.

"Don't give him your real name," Tiarra said.

"He will find out your address and rob you," Marianna screamed.

"He knows my name and where I go to school. He doesn't want *anything* from me. All he wants to do is talk to me and get my opinion about issues he has with teens. I am a sounding board for him, a means of checking his work if you will. A teen text book," I explained.

"Oh my God, you are so stupid," Tiarra said, looking at me as if I were an utter idiot.

"I met a guy on the Internet, and he fucked me over so bad. He lied to me, manipulated me, and used me for money. Block his number. Call the cops. He's going to steal from you. I know it," she continued.

Egyptian families are tight knit and tend to mind each other's business, even when they shouldn't. The incident with meeting Kid became a weekly discussion with my cousins. They constantly wanted to know what he was asking and what he was doing. They feared eventually he would request naked photos, bank account numbers, and my address. Each time I told them he had yet to request these things, they explained, "It's only a matter of time."

I thoroughly enjoyed each time my cousins and I met; knowing the questions would be the same, and I could give an answer which wasn't what they wanted to hear. Their expectations of him being a pedophile or a thief were unfounded, but I was incapable of changing their minds.

Although I was able to talk to my cousins about Kid, I couldn't talk to my brother or my parents about him. Their ability to understand the situation was non-existent. I would be advised by my parents to cease all discussions and communications with him. Then I would be forced to decide whether to listen to my parents and grant their request, or go against it and keep a line of communication open. I decided them not knowing was what was best.

I had told Brianna about him, and her response was, "That's just weird. Bye."

Writing things down when they came to mind made me more

capable of understanding the thoughts in general. I decided to make a list of similarities between Kid and David. I made a list on paper, Kid on the left and David on the right. As I made the list the similarities were shocking. Kid used his weight as a shelter or shield against others. He said it kept people from approaching him. I believed it was to keep him from getting close to people emotionally, and from later failing. David was OCD. He weighed himself constantly, making sure he was at his target weight. If he wasn't at his target weight, he would exercise and modify his diet until he was. He counted objects. He looked at any and all things mathematically speaking. He compiled lists in his head and built statistics. He based his decisions through the course of a day on his expectation of the success of the decision based on the statistics he had compiled in his mind regarding the situation.

Kid did the same types of things. Kid weighed himself, and if he fell below his lower threshold weight, he ate to gain weight. Kid feared elevators, planes, and riding in someone else's car. David used his homosexuality as a shield to keep women away, and Kid used his obesity to keep *everyone* away. As I thought of things to add to the list, I eventually gave up, aggravated.

I felt I had had learned what I suspected all along, but never took time to consider.

Kid feared failure. That was why all of his dealings with people were over the Internet. It's why he only had one actual friend, Shawn. It's why he didn't have a job. It's was why he was fat. And it was probably why he gave me little or no information about his past. He feared I would judge him for whatever he had done, or who he had been, and I would abandon him. This abandonment would be perceived by him as failure. The more I considered my thoughts, the more sense it made. His abrasive attitude, sarcastic nature, cussing, and calling people names was a way for him to keep everyone from even *wanting* to get to know him.

No different than the obesity.

I wanted to talk to David about his homosexuality, and I wanted to talk to Kid about everything, so I sent both of them a text message. I rolled over on my bed and looked at my list of what I had learned in life. Numbers fifteen and sixteen stood out. There is really no room for regret in this life. *Everything happens for a reason. If you can't find that reason, accept there is one and move on.* And, *there is room, however, for guilt. Resolve everything when it first comes up. That's not only having integrity, but also taking care of your emotional wellbeing.* I began to believe there must be something in Kid's past that he regretted or couldn't accept as being the way it should be.

I knew I would get to the bottom of this as soon as he texted me.

Waiting had never suited me well. I was about as impatient as a person can be. Waiting for them two to text me made me even more impatient. Frustrated, I grabbed my purse and my phone. After I folded the list and placed it in my purse, I stood and walked toward the door. I decided going to *Cups* was probably my best bet, because if David could meet to talk we would have to meet somewhere other than my home. My parents weren't particularly fond of me talking to white boys, and especially not a white homosexual boy.

Driving to *Cups*, I remembered when I first started to drive. I had begun driving to school, and my parents at the time were becoming less and less interested with my day to day activities. At the time, I had become more distant from them in general. Several things weighed on my decision to become distant. A combination of me wanting desperately to be my own person, combined with my desire to determine if there was someone out there who actually, unconditionally, cared for me. My feeling of necessity to separate myself from everyone else and become my own person was growing daily during that time. My parents' schedules and their belief their daughter *was* growing older made them less attentive to my needs.

In time, we became more distant than I ever believed we could be.

Filled with these types of feelings I drove to school daily. As my life progressed, and I became more active in school, my parents became less active in their desire to understand who I was and what I was doing. Feelings of abandonment filled me. I felt I was no longer loved. Frequently, as I drove to school or drove home, I would consider taking the steering wheel and yanking it -thrusting myself into oncoming traffic. I had convinced myself this would be a simple way to end the pain I was feeling at the time.

One day I realized the feelings were something which would pass in time. I prayed for the ability to live with the pain. The ability came. Making it through those days was never easy, but every day I prayed to make it another day. And the next day, I would pray for one more. I couldn't necessarily place my finger on a particular date that it got better or went away, but one day it did. One day I drove to school and I did not have those feelings, and then another day. Before the end of the school year I had gone for months without possessing those feelings. I was grateful I never drove into oncoming traffic, but I wondered how many other kids had feelings similar to mine. I decided of all of the kids I knew I was probably the most responsible, mature and reasonable thinking. If I maintained those feelings, I suspected other kids had them as well.

At the time I asked a few kids, and it wasn't received well. I dismissed the lack of participation to the conversation as being due to embarrassment and finally stopped asking people altogether.

As I sat at the traffic light, I realized as it turned from green to red that I had probably been sitting there - zoned out - thinking of the time in my life when I harbored suicidal thoughts. As I waited for the light to turn green *again* I thought of how many other people on the road must be zoning out. Not paying attention or thinking of things they should or shouldn't be thinking about. Eventually the light turned green and I was back to driving.

As I pulled into *Cups*, I didn't see David's car, which didn't surprise me as he hadn't texted me yet. Filled with an excitement to tell David he was heterosexual, I entered *Cups*.

I loved the yogurt, but the entire theme puzzled me. *Cups* was like a *Hooter's* which sold frozen yogurt instead of chicken wings. The girls who worked there wore hoodies, unzipped - and their breasts hung out. In the summer they shed their hoodies and wore tank tops - and their breasts hung out. Great marketing scheme, I imagined, as they were always busy.

Kid and I had talked at length about codependent women - women who sacrificed themselves at almost any cost – for a relationship. I had learned these women would do almost anything for a little attention and praise from a man. I couldn't help but wonder if girls who worked in atmospheres like the yogurt shop were codependent? Were they working half naked for wages alone? Was it just another job? Or were they working half naked for wages while they hoped to be noticed, sacrificing themselves and showing their bodies in hopes of luring a man? The answers interested me and saddened me both. The thought of so many women on this earth knowingly sacrificing every bit of moral fiber they *should* have, simply to have someone give them attention and praise, was sad. I wanted to tell the girl behind the counter to zip up her hoodie and go get a job at Barnes and Noble.

I got a cup and prepared my yogurt. This was one place I enjoyed treating myself to. Brianna and I come here quite frequently. I think I enjoyed it far more than she did. In fact, I think she could care less where we went. She enjoyed spending time with me, regardless of where we were spending it. I enjoyed it because it was a treat - a guilty pleasure. Almost like ice cream without the calories. Maintaining a body I was comfortable with was a constant fight, and although my exercising and diet worked well, I was never quite satisfied with the results. Daily, after school, I was at the gym working frantically on some ridiculous machine. I attempted to shed calories, and in turn, shed size and weight. I didn't necessarily have a target weight or size, but wanted to be comfortable in my own skin. I wasn't there yet, but my goal was not missed from lack of exercise or proper diet.

In a sense, I looked at *Cups* as a reward for all of my hard work.

I took my yogurt cup to the register to get it weighed. Cloe stood on the other side of the counter and grinned. *Could she be skinnier or have larger boobs?* She looked good in a disproportionate kind of Barbie Doll way. Probably five foot seven, a hundred five or ten pounds, and boobs the size of oversized swollen grapefruits.

"That will be $5.23, Michelle. Oh, and that David guy you have been talking to in here lately, is he your boyfriend? He is just freaking cute," she said as she bent down to scratch her calf.

When she did, one of her boobs fell out of the hoodie. *Out.* Like out, out. Out in the freaking open. *Are you kidding me?* As I stared at her massive teenage boob, I decided maybe she didn't belong at Barnes and Noble. Looking at her provided me some odd form of satisfaction in knowing I looked the way I did.

"No, he's just a close friend," I said as I reached into my purse, still staring at her monstrous tit.

I wanted to point and explain part of her was hanging there for the world to see. *How could she not know?* As she straightened her posture back to a standing position, her boob hung there; defying, to some degree, the very laws of gravity.

She smiled and reached for her boob, "Well, he's just adorable."

As she spoke, and even without looking, she reached down and cupped her boob in her hand. As if she knew it was there and exposed all along, she stuffed it carefully back into her hoodie. She didn't mention it, nor did she change her facial expression. Maybe this was something which happened frequently and I had never had the opportunity to witness it. I graciously paid for my yogurt and sat down satisfied, at least for an evening, of *who* I was.

I enjoyed being in public far more than being at home, and yearned to be in college, where I felt I would be free. Free of my family. Free of relatives. Free of being bound to rules, regulations and expectations. For the most part, I stayed in my room while I was at home and I acted as though my family didn't exist. I never saw them if I didn't have to. I felt, for the first time in my life, that if I never saw them again I would survive. Feeling like this, at least initially, was troubling. I had become comfortable lately with these feelings. I did have hope after college, or maybe during college, these types of feelings would change. I secretly wished I would develop a new fondness for my family while I was away. Either way, I had become comfortable living with those feelings or having things change. I loved my family, and that would never change. I didn't, however, love being around them or spending time with them.

In public I was able to be myself. I typically didn't worry about being judged nor did I feel the need to meet the expectations of others. In public, no one had expectations of me. I was accepted by those around me for being who I was and my actions were never questioned.

Michelle, why did....Michelle, are you wearing makeup, Michelle what are you wearing, Michelle, what did you decide about your college, regarding...Michelle, what happened at school the other day, Michelle, you are spending too much money on...Michelle, do you really think you need to do.

Truly knowing I could be in the presence of others and not be criticized, ridiculed, and/or questioned regarding life and my way of living it was priceless.

In my more recent years of living, I developed a trait of being critical of others – both male and female. I secretly used to pick people apart - their clothing, mannerisms, comments and beliefs. Recently, I had begun to pick them apart in the presence of my friends who may be within eye or earshot. It had become a part of who I was to be critical of others. All of my friends had come to expect it, and I would be critical of all people who I encountered. I could not help but wonder whether or not this was a reaction to me feeling as if I was being held under some form of microscope. These people, under *my* microscope, were under a great degree of scrutiny. Whatever portions of them they allowed me to see, I would be critical of. Some people appeared - by my observations - to be valuable to me. I set those people aside. Group number one. I intended to keep them. Others had so few qualities which I preferred;

I set them aside as group number two. This group was on the side of failure - failure of my personal testing for my expressed purposes of value, enjoyment, or satisfaction.

In general, people have many layers. Determining who they were was similar to peeling an onion. Each portion in itself didn't define the person; but when combined, the layers created a whole.

Who they were.

With Kid, each layer I peeled back interested me. I found him to be a complex person – yet a person who chose to live a simple life. For me to be critical of him and find something he didn't already know would be nearly impossible. Kid was his own worst critic. He was conscious of his shortcomings and character defects. He did at times need a little direction or another point of view on some matters. For the most part, however, he was aware of his faults whether he admitted it or not.

David on the other hand had proven to be nothing short of an accident waiting to happen. The revelation of his heterosexuality excited me - not for reasons of developing a relationship but for the satisfaction of exposing it and the possibly helping him accept it. A new beginning, if he would accept it. David was intelligent, had an open view on life, and was quite a vivid person. His intelligence, good looks and personality would afford him almost any girl he wanted; and I was anxious to open this layer of his personality and hold it under his nose.

I derived a great degree of personal satisfaction from helping and healing people of whatever it was that caused them harm or discomfort. This was either totally or in part what caused me to migrate to the medical field. The thought of exposing David to himself and having him at some point in time agree I was correct would potentially provide me with satisfaction for a lifetime.

I am a selfless person and live a selfless life. In this regard, however, I am selfish.

As I finished my yogurt and stood to place my cup into the trash I heard a scream. I had not noticed anyone entering the store, so the scream itself startled me greatly. When I looked up I realized the store had filled with people while I was daydreaming about David and Kid.

"Michelle!" screamed David at the top of his lungs.

The entire store looked at him and then turned to at me. He stood, in Khaki pants and a dress shirt, with his arms outstretched and parallel with the floor. He was headed my direction and doing so at a very rapid pace.

"Dude, slow down," I said as he got within ten feet of me.

Knowing his fondness for hugs, I held my arms out to give him a hug. As we embraced he laid his head on my shoulder. Eventually, he leaned away from my body, pressed his hands against my shoulders, and took a deep breath.

"So I got your text and I thought, *I bet Michelle is going to Cups.* So, hoping you'd be here, I drove here as a surprise. Well, not a surprise, but a surprise *of sorts*. I'm so happy to see you," he said as he released my shoulders.

As he stood in front of me and smiled. He tugged on his pants, making his *pants pulling face* as he tugged at them.

In an hour long period of time, subconsciously, David pulled or tugged at his pants twenty times – roughly every two or three minutes. When he performed the task, he made an awful face, as if he were playing tug-of-war and was about to be pulled into the mud pit. I never asked him why because I was sure he was self-conscious about it. At first I thought it was cute, but as time passed it became a very odd character defect. Not necessarily annoying, but odd.

I smiled and motioned toward an empty chair, "I'm happy to see you as well, David. Sit down, we need to talk."

"I need to throw this away, and when I get back we can talk," I reached toward the table and grabbed the empty yogurt cup.

"No, let me get that. I need to get a yogurt anyway," he said as he reached for the cup.

He took my cup and carefully placed it in the trash receptacle. When David placed things in the trash he didn't push them into the receptacle. He opened the trap door with one hand, and reached inside carefully with the other and placed the trash into the receptacle. It was as if he were throwing away a container of explosives. In watching him, I wondered how many of these idiosyncrasies were a result of his fear of failure. The thought of potentially getting to the bottom of these defects caused me to smile.

David, upon returning with his cup of yogurt, began shoving it into his mouth as fast as he could. He was always careful and never really made a mess, but he generally ate as fast as he could possibly force food into his mouth. Inevitably he would develop a headache and act as if this was the very first time it had happened. Since we had met at *Cups* the first time we had probably met there no less than fifteen more times.

Each time, the same thing happened. David was a yogurt eating maniac.

Staring into my eyes and smiling, he continued to shovel the yogurt into his mouth. In between bites of yogurt, he finally spoke.

"So, what's going on, doctor college stuff? Do you have Villanova news?" he asked.

"No David, something else. You remember my friend, Kid, right?"

"Oh, yes. The big guy who's kind of clairvoyant?" he responded as he raised both eyebrows.

He shoveled another spoon of yogurt into his mouth and waited for my response.

"Yes, that's him. Okay, I have to tell you some things he told me today but it's a lot to take in. It's…"

Before I finished speaking, he interrupted.

As he slapped his hands against his cheeks, his eyes widened, "Is it clairvoyant stuff?"

"Yes, it…"

"This is so exciting," he interrupted.

He removed his hands from his cheeks and clapped them together as he spoke.

Annoyed, I spoke in a stern tone, "David, stop! Let me tell you what he said. You can nod or shake your head, and that's all. No speaking. Okay?"

He nodded as soon as I finished talking.

"I gave him a picture of you and asked him to *read you*. He about…"

"Oh my God, what did he say!!?" he interrupted as he slapped his palms into his cheeks once again.

"David, stop. Please. This will take forever. Shake or nod, okay?"

He nodded.

"I gave him a picture of you and asked him to read it. Read *you*. He read you and said a lot. Primarily, he said you were somewhat OCD and your father was a very strict man. He said that probably - ever since you were young - your father had attempted to convince you that you were never going to amount to anything," I paused.

David nodded repeatedly.

"Additionally he said this caused *fear of failure* which could, and obviously has, created all kinds of other issues. He gave me the clinical name for fear of failure, but I do not recall what it was, and for the sake of this conversation it is not important."

"Then," I paused, intending to drop the bomb.

I took a deep breath and blurted everything out at once, "He said he was certain you were not homosexual, and in fact when I asked him a second time he laughed and said he was a hundred percent sure and that you are definitely not homosexual and fear of failure had caused you to tell yourself you are because you are concerned greatly, probably subconsciously, that you would fail in a relationship and that your father would be critical of that."

I took a deep breath, and waited.

David didn't nod or shake his head. His eyes followed my eyes as if he were in a trance.

"David. David!!! DAVID!! Are you still here?"

He continued to stare into my eyes into my eyes with his mouth partially open. With his elbows resting on the table, and his chin in his hands, he gawked without speaking.

"Dude!" I screamed.

"Oh. Yes, I am sorry, can I speak?" he asked.

"Yes, please do," I responded.

"Well, I have been wondering about this lately. The homosexual part of me, that is. Because to be brutally honest Michelle, since we met I have become more and more attracted to you and the attraction has not been a friendly attraction. I have actually," he paused for a moment and made a strange distorted face.

"I have actually fantasized about you. Not sexually, but as a

167

girlfriend-boyfriend type thing."

I sat and stared at him in disbelief. *Was this really going to be easy? Was he aware or second guessing his homosexuality for the last month or two, and saying nothing to me?* I was somewhat disappointed there was less excitement to this revelation and felt as if someone let the air out of my sails so to speak. I looked down at the table and rubbed my forehead with my fingertips.

I looked up from the table, "David, you've been second guessing your homosexuality for the last month or two and you haven't said anything?"

He nodded his head.

I started to say something, and stopped. I considered he more than likely did exactly what Kid said. He probably began to feel somewhat attracted to me and made no outward sign of it for fear of me rejecting him, and ultimately, him failing. He would rather have me a friend at some level than lose me altogether. I sat, satisfied Kid was right. As I sat, I began to look at David differently. Not as if I was attracted to him, but as if he was actually a boy who may be interested in me. Slowly this began to make me fractionally uncomfortable.

I began to fidget in my seat.

The phone ringing broke my concentration. As I grabbed it and began to silence the ringer, I realized it was Kid.

"David, it's Kid, I have to take this, okay? I will make it quick," I shrugged.

"Okay, Michelle, that's fine," he said with his face still resting in his palms.

"Hey, Kid, I have a ton of questions for you but I am with David right now, can I call you back in thirty?" I asked.

"Yes, Michelle, that's fine. Did you confront him about his homosexuality?" Kid laughed.

I looked at David and smiled. David, with his face still pressed into his hands and his eyes fixed on mine, immediately smiled back. He was beginning to creep me out.

"Yes, I did, and it went really well," I responded.

"Okay..." Kid prolonged the pronunciation of the word, as if he wanted to hear more.

"Be sure to send me the pic of your crazy friend, remember?"

"Oh, yeah, I will as soon as we're done here, okay? I promise," I said apologetically.

"Okay, talk to you soon."

"Ok, thirty minutes."

"Sorry David," I said.

He continued to stare at me with his face resting in his palms and his elbows on the table. His face had fallen to a point where he was almost resting his chin on the table. His eyes were glued to mine. I moved my head from side to side. His eyes followed.

He was *really* beginning to creep me out. I decided to make an excuse and see how he responded.

"I really need to go home and get a picture for Kid. I have a friend who is dealing with some serious issues and he needs a picture of her. I am going to have him read her, and I only have a picture on my computer at home. He's been asking me to send it to him for days, so I really need to go do that. Can we take this up tomorrow? I am so sorry," I sighed.

"Sure Michelle, I understand. This was really unexpected entirely, but such a delight," David said as he stood.

He immediately tugged on the thighs of his pants. As his face

169

contorted, I rolled my eyes. In turning away from him, I looked toward the table. His yogurt cup sat at the edge, empty. He had shoveled the entire cup into his mouth as we were talking.

In ten minutes.

What a nut.

"Give me a hug, David," I said.

"Do you think Coltrane hugged people?" he asked as he wrapped his arms around me.

"I'm sure he did, David. I am sure he did," I responded as I pushed myself away from him.

Dude, you're creeping me out.

"Okay. I am so sorry, but I have to go do this," I said as I grabbed my purse.

"That's okay Michelle. Go do what you have to do. I am going to throw this away, go to the bathroom, and say hi to Cloe before I go," he said as he picked up his yogurt cup.

"Okay. I will see you tomorrow or whatever, okay?"

"Okay, Bye Michelle."

With my purse over my shoulder and my phone in hand, I walked toward the exit. David and his lack of homosexuality had me thoroughly confused.

As I passed the cashier, Cloe waved. Her upper body shook when she did, and her boob partially fell out and hung on the zipper of her hoodie for the world to see. I waved in return. As I turned to face the door, I grabbed the door handle and rolled my eyes.

Maybe that little bitch does need to go find a job at Barnes and Noble, before her boob falls out again.

170

13

HEART ATTACK

FAT KID

I stood in line at the grocery store with twelve things in my hand. Twelve chocolate bars - enough to get me by for the day - maybe a day and a half depending on my activity. I would have willingly bought fifty, but the line to the twelve items or less aisle was short; and the lines in the other available aisles were ten people deep. In the twelve or less aisle I had carefully chosen, there were only three people in front of me.

And the line was at a standstill.

Is it just my lack of patience, or do they always place the mentally challenged checkers in the aisles that take twelve items or less?

As I stood in line the three people ahead of me didn't budge. The checker was working in slow motion, sliding items across the infrared scanner, and it wasn't scanning them. She was attempting unsuccessfully for the fourth or fifth time to get a round bottle of dairy creamer to scan. This was becoming ridiculous. I was ten minutes into this ordeal and there was zero measured progress.

The man directly ahead of me was thin and in his early thirties. He wore a baseball cap, black Dickie's style work pants, slip on sneakers and a khaki shirt. His hair hung well below his cap; almost to his shoulder. His eyes told me he was either drunk or completely mentally lost. I've always said the eyes don't lie, and his were no exception. All of a sudden, as we silently stood in line, he decided to spin in circles.

He literally began pirouetting in place on one foot. The two elderly women in front of him, one of which was trying desperately to purchase a bottle of creamer, turned around and watched him each time he rotated. The woman closest to him turned and smiled. This, more or less, egged him on. Fueled by the little encouragement he was receiving, he began to spin more frequently and faster. With a sack of baby carrots in one hand and a jar of peanut butter in the other, his hair stretched outward from the cap as he spun endlessly in place. He and his spinning were effectively working on the one nerve I had left.

"Dude, stop. You're fucking freaking me out. Seriously, just stop," I said in an almost whisper as politely as I could muster.

As he spun past me he muttered, "Fuck off, fat ass."

"Seriously, *fat ass*? You're going to come at me with *fat ass*?"

I slipped the chocolate bars into my left pocket, took two steps back, and spread my stance a little. I didn't want this guy falling into the elderly ladies when I busted him in the eye with my ham sized fist.

I motioned with my right hand in the same manner you would call kids in from the outfield in baseball practice, "Come here for a minute, I want to talk to you."

"No!" he responded loudly.

He planted one foot and stopped. Almost immediately he started spinning the other direction. I decided this lobotomy patient was not worth my potential trip to jail, so I tried another means of stopping him from working my nerves.

"Look, the lady with the creamer is done. You're next," I said as I pointed toward the checker.

"So?" he responded flatly.

He planted his feet again, stopped, and made an effort to change directions - all at once. In his mentally deranged state, at least at this juncture, he was incapable of performing the instantaneous change in direction without losing his balance. Upon stopping and shifting his body weight, his upper body and his lower body were going in two different directions. It proved to be too much for him and he proceeded to plummet toward the tile floor. As he began to fall he dropped his cute little sack of carrots and the jar of peanut butter soon followed.

The carrots fell flat on the floor.

The peanut butter fell and rolled across the floor stopping a foot in front of my size twelve Converse sneaker. Feeling very satisfied with the result of his botched disco-spin, I smiled and looked downward.

Jiffy. Creamy. And in a plastic jar.

Perfect.

He broke his fall the instant his hands were free of his soon to be purchased snacks. Oddly, he immediately bounced up into a standing position, as if it were a break dance move he had invented. I looked at him, glanced down at the peanut butter, and slowly shifted my gaze to him again. My mouth formed a shitty grin. With my eyes focused on him, I kicked the peanut butter as hard as I could. The jar stayed about two inches above the freshly waxed tile floor for a hundred feet or so and then slid for the remaining fifty feet to the produce section, where it hit a display of oranges.

Standing and staring as if in shock, he glared at me for a short second. He blinked and turned to face the produce aisle. Sheepishly, he looked down at the sack of fallen carrots. It was obvious he was planning his getaway. In one fluid motion he snatched the carrots from the floor and took off across the store in a dead sprint toward the jar of peanut butter.

I shook my head and looked toward the cashier.

Splendid, she's caught up.

I stepped to the aisle and pulled the chocolate bars from my pants pocket. After tossing them onto the conveyor, she began to slide them one at a time across the scanner. As she did, she asked me about the peanut butter punt.

"What happened?" she asked without looking up.

My focus was fixed on her hands. She was attempting to get one of the bent bars to go through the scanner. Looking at the banana shaped chocolate bar, I imagined it became distorted in my pocket when I was booting the mentally challenged ballerina's peanut butter. I looked up from her incompetent hands to answer her question.

"My capacity to put up with any more bullshit was exceeded by his ability to dish it out," I smiled.

"Huh?" she looked at me as if I had answered her in Latin.

"Try one of the others," I said angrily I picked up one of the undamaged bars and handed it to her.

As her hand continued to wave back and forth over the scanner with a mutilated candy bar in her grip, my temper reached its all time limit for foolish behavior.

"Try one of the other ones. Try one of the ones you already got to go through," I said again as I pointed at a perfectly flat, unmolested candy bar.

"What happened?" she asked in a monotone voice.

I stared at her hand as she thoughtlessly waved the smashed bar over the scanner repeatedly. I clenched my teeth and shook my head slowly.

"I kicked the asshat's fucking peanut butter. Look, try one of *these*,"

I said as I grabbed one of the already scanned bars and waved it in front of her face.

She accepted the bar and successfully scanned it the proper amount of times.

"$16.10, please," she requested in her monotone voice.

I shook my head and handed her a hundred dollar bill. She held it up to the light and checked for the watermark. After placing it in the register she began to count my change.

"And ninety cents makes seventeen, three makes twenty, and twenty, forty, sixty, eighty make a hundred," she smiled.

I stood, staring her in the eyes as she counted my change. As she attempted to place the candy bars in a plastic bag, I grabbed the bag and the bars out of her hand and tossed the bag on the conveyor in front of her. Frustrated with mankind in general, I turned and walked out of the store. As I walked I wondered if she acted stupid toward *everyone* or just to a select few. Making my way across the lot, I hoped the remainder of the day would be without incident.

As I approached the car my phone beeped, indicating an email message. Almost certain it would be Shellie, I reached into my back pocket and retrieved my phone. The message was from Michelle and the subject was *Many Things*. Michelle, if nothing else, kept me on my toes. I decided to read it after I got to the coffee shop. I grinned and slid my phone back into my back pocket, imagining what the message may contain.

Sitting at the stoplight and waiting for the left turn arrow, I began feeling uncomfortable. I removed my phone from my back pocket and tossed it into the passenger seat. It didn't help the situation. I felt hot. I felt cold. I turned the temperature control down to 55 degrees. Although it was 60 degrees outside and early spring, the air conditioner began to blow in full force. I felt as if I was having a heart attack. Staring up at the street light, I wiped the sweat from my forehead and pressed my wet palms onto the thighs of my pants.

I'm going to fuck around and actually die two hundred yards before I get my coffee.

Perfect.

The car honking behind me brought me to my senses and I proceeded to inch my way to the coffee shop. As I entered the approach slowly to prevent bottoming out the car, time stood still. An odd tingling over my entire body began to wash over me.

I'm having a heart attack.

Fuck.

Once safely positioned in the parking stall, I sat and took slow deep breaths. I surveyed the empty lot. As I sat in the car with the air conditioning blowing on my face, I began to feel fractionally better. If I was going to die I wanted to die driving or possibly in a location where I would fall out of my chair and onto the floor. My fat ass on the floor would be dying perfection. I wanted people to have to step over my dead body. I did not want to die in my car where no one would immediately notice. I wanted people to scream.

Oh my God, is he dead?!

I wanted to lie there, dead as absolute fuck, and have everyone walk around me or step over me until the ambulance arrived. Dying in line at the coffee shop would be so much better. If there's satisfaction in dying, to die in line at the register would be extremely satisfying. As I kept my driver's license hidden in my car, the ambulance attendants would check my money clip and find nothing to identify me.

Does anyone know this guy? I imagined the paramedic screaming to the patrons as he zipped the body bag closed.

The entire coffee shop would respond in unison, *Yeeesss.*

Satisfied they had found the answer to the fat man riddle, the paramedics would then ask, *What's his name, he doesn't have ID in his pocket.*

Everyone would look at the person beside them and mouth the words *Fat Kid.*

Confused, the paramedics would ask again, *Anyone? Does anyone know his actual name?*

Fat Kid, that's all we know would be the universal response.

A police search of my phone would turn up no name.

Death perfection.

The thought satisfied me greatly.

I absorbed the air conditioning for an immeasurable amount of time and the uncomfortable feeling in my chest didn't pass. My body continued to tingle and I was covered in sweat. I turned and faced the front door. I really preferred this would come to fruition in the coffee shop. Waiting in line. I wanted my death to be a mess - a memorable mess. In a perfect world, I had always dreamt of someone pushing me from the roof of my condominium onto the sidewalk below during rush hour - in my opinion a very satisfying way to die. A huge pile of dead flesh right there on the sidewalk. Cars stopped and people screaming frantically. Incapable of immediately comprehending what had happened, they'd peer down at the pile of bloody blubber and then up toward the roof.

In the absence of the swan dive off of the high rise I would settle for the line at the coffee shop. I looked up and toward the store. The inside of the store was as empty as the lot.

Damn the luck.

I reached behind me, grabbed my laptop, and got out of the car. Shouldering my bag, I began to walk across the lot. I locked my car. As I heard the sound of the car alarm beep, I smiled. Tingling and sweating, I continued walking slowly down the sidewalk to the entrance. I focused on my sneakers, making certain my feet were still carrying me at a reasonable pace. Standing at the front door, I looked down at the trash receptacle and smiled. As I passed through the door, I reached back and dropped my car keys into the trash.

This would be an ending worth noting.

I pulled the door open and walked to the register.

Doll face greeted me at the register, "Hey Kid, the usual?"

She must have pinned her ears back, she actually looks cute.

"Yes, Gretchen," I responded as I handed her a twenty.

"Keep the change," I said as I turned and walked to my seat.

Stunned, she held the money in her hand and stared.

I smiled.

She smiled in return.

Slowly, I got my computer out and opened it. After powering up my laptop, I removed my scale and placed it on the floor. I tapped it with my toe and waited. As I stepped on I was immediately relieved with the display. 320. I picked up the scale and smiled; satisfied I was as fat as I could possibly be for my untimely but imminent death. I wiped the sweat from my brow and waited for my coffee.

I felt as if my mind was out of my body, my soul acting as a hovering halo to my outer self. I felt peaceful.

"KID, AMERICANO AT THE BAR," the barista barked.

Having strategically placed myself close to the pick-up counter, I took the few steps to the bar, grabbed my coffee, tipped it up, and downed half of it. As I turned and stepped toward the table, I felt at peace with this being the last cup of coffee I would ever consume. Consciously, I decided to savor the second half.

I sat down and placed my coffee on the table. Anxiously, I logged into my email account. Several meaningless messages were present, but the two most recent emails stood out - one from Shellie and one from Michelle. Somewhat nervously, I opened Shellie's first.

Kid,
You were sweet. Thank you.
Shellie

I stared at the email. I *was* sweet.

Past tense.

She could have said *Kid, you are sweet.*

Fuck.

In her mind, she had reached the turning point. I knew I had to get in touch with her and do so quickly. I felt helpless. I had no phone number - nothing but an email address. I looked at the date and time of the email. It was only a few minutes old. I had probably received it while I was in line. I needed to respond, but I needed to keep it short. I knew she would lose interest if she opened a rambling email. My entire body tingling and chest aching, I stared at the screen and tried to clear my mind as I typed.

Shellie,
The pain will end. I know this first hand. But it takes time.

179

Contact me as soon as you get this message, I can help.
I love you,
Kid

I read it, reread it, and pushed send.

There was nothing else I could do. I felt helpless and empty. I began to recall my girlfriend who had died when I was younger. Oddly enough, she was named Shellie as well. The poem she left me changed my life. I carried it in my wallet for over a decade. When I put the poem away, I put my wallet away with it. I had not carried a wallet since. We tend to make adjustments in our lives to get by, to survive. Sometimes we don't actually heal. We make changes. We deny. We mask. We cover up. We hide things. I could not change the fact Shellie committed suicide while I was away no more than I could change the fact she left me the poem. Eventually, I put the poem away to separate Shellie and the thoughts of her from my day-to-day life. I quit carrying a wallet because the wallet reminded me of the poem, and the poem reminded me I was helpless.

I had felt as if I had been incapable of providing whatever may have been necessary to save Shellie from the pain she was feeling. I believed my incompetence or inability to recognize such pain was certainly the reason she chose to commit suicide. Ultimately, the pain eventually exceeded her capacity to cope with it. I hurt, and I still hurt today. The pain never ended. I ran from it and denied the fact it even existed, but it remained. It would never leave me. I ran from person to person attempting to save *someone*, thinking all along *this person will be the one who allows the pain go away.*

And the pain never stops.

It burns from within me and consumes me. Living with the pain had not become *part* of who I was; *it had become me.* Since the day of receiving the poem, it had controlled my life. Try as I might, I wallowed in the guilt of Shellie's suicide no less than once a week ever since.

I opened Michelle's email. It had a few paragraphs and two attached photos. I scanned the typed text but felt unable to focus. Eventually the small thumbnails of the photos at the bottom of the page grasped my attention. Confused, I scrolled down and stared. I clicked on one of the photos and stared at the enlarged picture.

My heart raced.

I swallowed a lump in my throat, feeling as if I had swallowed a tennis ball. Immediately filled with a level and type of emotion I couldn't identify, I immediately typed a response to her email.

MICHELLE RIGHT NOW. THIS IS AN EMERGENCY. 911. NO MATTER WHAT YOURE DOING, STOP. CALL ME.

I clicked send.

Frantically, I searched for my phone. It was not on the table, nor in my bag. Not in my pocket. *Where is my fucking phone?* Standing and furious, I searched for my car keys. I was clearly losing my mind. *Breathe, Kid, breathe.*

Breathe in, breathe out, and don't do anything stupid between breaths.

I emptied my pockets onto the table. I grabbed my bag and dumped the contents onto the floor. Frantically searching both piles produced keys or phone. And it hit me. My keys were in the fucking trash can. And my phone was in the front seat of my God damned car.

I ran outside as fast as I could. I picked up the metal trash can, turned it upside down and dumped the contents onto the concrete. Three days of trash fell from the can onto the sidewalk. A mound of coffee cups and

McDonalds sacks was all I could see. *No fucking car keys*. Furious and almost out of time, I bent down, bear hugged the trash can, and stood. Through the empty lot with trash can held over my head, I ran as fast as I could toward my car.

About ten feet from the car, I heaved the can like a missile at my passenger side window. The window shattered and the alarm sounded. As the alarm wailed, I reached into the passenger seat and grabbed my phone.

14

HEROINE

MICHELLE

Sitting in class could be so boring. I was beyond ready for the year to end and for the people to fade away. As I sat in class, ready for the new chapter in my life to begin, my mind faded to thoughts of college. I wanted to begin defining who I was and start developing what it was I was going to become; a doctor. The thought of being in the medical profession satisfied me deeply. It seemed more of a dream than anything. I wanted it, and I was accepted into a program in school to obtain it, but it still seemed so unattainable to me. The excitement of finally becoming that person was more than I could imagine. When I thought of it in a serious manner I found it difficult to do so without feeling, and sometimes even showing, tremendous emotion.

As I sat and daydreamed I heard my phone buzzing. Due to the length of the repeated buzzing, it was obvious someone was attempting to call me. Eventually the buzzing stopped. I decided after class I would check and see who called. I tried to decide who would call and wondered what the reason may be. Everyone I knew was aware I was in school.

No one called me during the day, ever. I had sent Kid an email earlier in morning after I found the pictures on my computer, but he never called me during the day. He would typically text first, and ask me to call him later. I began to scroll through names in my head of people who would possibly call me. I thought of no one who would - unless there was an emergency. My phone began to buzz again - a short buzz - clearly a text message.

As I continued to wonder, it began to buzz again constantly. Someone was calling, and I decided it must be an emergency. I stood, grabbed my purse, and walked to the teacher's desk.

"Mr. Nelson, I have an emergency. I'm sorry, I have to go to the restroom," I shrugged, attempting to look embarrassed.

"Go ahead Michelle," he said without looking up from his desk.

I walked down the hallway and into the bathroom. I didn't dare pull out my phone in the hall way. My phone had been taken by staff on countless occasions for not following school policy. As I walked through the door to the bathroom, I pulled my phone from my purse. In looking at the screen, I realized there were three voicemails. A quick check of the call log indicated Kid called three times – within minutes of each other. Almost frantic, I opened the text message screen. I walked into a toilet partition, closed the door, and sat on the toilet.

No less than a dozen unopened messages had been received from Kid. I opened the first message.

KID: MICHELLE EMERGENCY 911 CALL IMMEDIATELY NO MATTER WHAT YOU'RE DOING A LIFE IS AT STAKE

My heart started to race, and I hurriedly pushed the buttons to call Kid. I was shaking, and my body began to immediately with emotion. It rang once and he answered.

"Michelle, don't say a fucking word, just listen," he said sternly.

"The picture. The picture of the girl. Who is she, do you know her?"

His tone was different. He wasn't screaming, but his voice sounded direct and urgent. It was very matter of fact and crisp - similar to a police officer during an interrogation.

"What girl? Kid, I'm lost. I'm sorry, but you're scaring me. What's going on?"

As I stood, I realized I was shaking from head to toe.

"Michelle listen, Goddamn it. You need to pay fucking attention. The girl in the pictures you emailed me. Who, *specifically*, is she? Do you *know* her?"

Oh, he means Britney.

"Yes, I go to school with her. She's a friend, she lives down the street. She's the one who was in a similar situation to Shellie, the suicidal girl on your blog. What's wrong? Is it bad?"

I was afraid he had seen something bad when he looked into her eyes and *read* her. I stood and continued to shake, fearful of how he was acting, and what he may have seen.

In a very matter-of-fact tone, he spoke, "Michelle, once again, *fucking listen.* Pay attention and focus for me. Is she at school today? Your friend? Is she there?"

I thought. Normally, she sat in the corner of the class, by the window facing the parking lot. As far as I could remember, she wasn't in class.

"Uhhm, no she isn't, why?" I responded nervously.

As if he were a military officer barking out orders to command troops on the battle ground, Kid spoke clearly and crisply.

"Michelle, be quiet for a fucking moment and listen. Just listen. This is almighty fucking important. I need you to do something. Pay attention. The girl in the picture. She is the suicide girl I have been telling you about, Shellie. She wrote me an email a few minutes ago.

185

I am afraid she is going to kill herself this morning. As in *right now.* I need to leave school and go as fast as you can to her house. See if you can find her. Do not call police; if she hears sirens she may kill herself immediately."

Confused, I stood and tried to make sense of what he said. He was clearly confused about the photo's I had sent, and the other email he received.

"Kid, you're confused. The girl in the pic is Britney. She lives down the street, she's my friend. She goes to school with me. It's *not* Shellie, what's wrong with you? You're scaring me," I sniffed as I began to softly cry.

"Mother fucker!" he shouted.

Again, in a stern but calm voice, he began to explain.

"God damn it Michelle, listen. Shellie was Britney all along. Ironically, she emailed me seeking help, and it just so happened she was friends with you. A one in two billion chance, but it's true. Britney changed her name when she emailed me – to Shellie. She probably didn't want me to find out who she was, hell she probably initially learned of me from you. So, she changed her name to Shellie," he paused and took an audible breath.

Puzzled and probably in shock, I stood and nodded my head.

"Please, Michelle. Right now. You need to go. She may be dying. Stay off your phone. Don't text or call, and don't wreck your car. And please, don't call police until after you arrive. Find her Michelle. You must find her. You have to find her and stop this."

Kid appeared frantic and sounded as if he were in tears.

I pulled into the driveway with no recollection of leaving the school or even driving. I slammed the gear shifter in park and jumped out of the car – not certain of where to go. Naturally, I ran to the front door of the house and checked the handle. It was locked. I beat on the door, screaming Britney's name. I turned from the porch and ran to the side garage door to see if her car was in the garage. I looked through the window, and over the top of her parked car I saw her on top of a ladder.

The images played in my mind as if they were in slow motion. I watched as Britney stood on top of a ladder, a light blue cloth rope tied around her neck, and kicked her legs. Frantically, I tried to open the door, but it was locked as well. I beat on the door and screamed her name. I watched as she fell from the ladder and hung in mid-air by the makeshift rope. I kicked the door as hard as I could, over and over. The door made cracking sounds but didn't open.

I don't ask for much, God. Please help me. A girl is dying here.

Scared and crying, I stepped away from the door, ran toward it as fast as I could and kicked it, right beside the door handle. The door made a crunching sound and flew open.

As I ran around the back of her car, she hung by her neck, motionless. The ladder continued to rock back and forth. I grabbed her ankles and attempted to lift her, but her legs simply bent. As I frantically screamed her name, I stabilized the ladder, moved it to her side, and grabbed Britney's waist in my arms.

Give me the strength of a dozen men, Lord.

I began to climb each rung of the ladder with her in my arms. My legs burning, I pressed harder and harder until I had all of her weight against me. I looked up and noticed the cloth rope was loose. I sat her down on a step of the ladder and balanced her there.

She was limp.

I have to get the rope off.

187

If I get it off, she'll be fine.

Hysterically, I removed the rope from her neck as I screamed her name. Standing on the ladder below her, I grabbed her body in my arms and tried to carry her down the ladder. Somehow the ladder immediately collapsed, and we both fell to the floor.

I shook my head and regained my senses from the fall. Britney lay flat on the floor beside me, lifeless. I shook her and screamed her name. She did not respond. Scared, I stood and ran to the car. I grabbed my phone from my purse and called Kid, running into the garage as his phone was ringing.

"Did you find her?" Kid asked excitedly.

"Kid, she was hanging. Oh my God. I got her on the floor, Kid. I got her on the floor. She's on the floor, Kid. She's not hanging. Not on the floor. We fell. She's on the floor," my voice was strangely quiet and cracking.

I began sobbing uncontrollably.

"Michelle! Hang up. Perform CPR. Call 911. Get paramedics there right now!"

I hung up and called 911. Britney remained lifeless on the floor. I couldn't tell if she was breathing. If she was, she wasn't doing it very well.

As the 911 operator talked, I heard nothing. Sitting beside her with my hands in her hair, I continued talking to Britney, begging her to never leave me.

I touched her cold pale face and fixed her hair.

I prayed for God to give me the strength to perform his will.

I heard the ambulances in the distance. The sound of the sirens got louder and louder.

Not today, God. Don't take her today.

Police officers were the first ones in the garage, and the paramedics were right behind them. In a matter of minutes, paramedics, police officers and firemen filled the garage. Someone opened the big garage doors and there were people everywhere. Confused, I sat beside her and hummed.

Someone handed me my phone. The 911 operator was gone. They covered Britney's face and hooked a machine to her.

I cried and cried, until the crying turned to sobs. Everyone was talking at once.

A police officer tapped me on the shoulder, "Ma'am, what relation are you to the victim?"

Victim?

I looked up and attempted to stand, "I'm her friend. I found her hanging by the bed sheet that's tied to the roof of the garage."

I pointed to the bed sheet hanging from the garage roof.

"Ma'am, specifically what time did you find her?" he asked in a monotone voice.

He stood erect and held a small note pad in one hand and a pen in the other.

Was this really happening?

Finally standing, I looked up as they were moving Britney out of the garage and toward the ambulance. She was on a stretcher. As I turned and started walking toward her, I faintly heard the officer's voice barking incomprehensibly.

Clutching my phone in my hand, I walked toward the ambulance, immediately behind the paramedics. I could hear my car still running in the driveway. I was halfway down the length of the driveway as they began loading her inside the ambulance.

"Ma'am, we're going to need you to answer some more questions," the officer said as I reached the ambulance.

I turned and looked over my shoulder. Right now my focus was Britney, and not answering meaningless questions.

"Ma'am, to the best of your knowledge, had the victim been depressed? Had she at any time directly expressed thoughts of suicide that you are or were aware of?"

He tapped his pen against his pad in wait.

I turned away and faced the ambulance.

"Ma'am, I need…" his voice began to echo in my head, but made no sense.

As I reached for the rear door of the ambulance, they were securing the stretcher to the floor.

As I began to pull myself into the ambulance, the officer placed his hand on my shoulder.

"Ma'am. Ma'am. Ma'am!" the officer shouted.

"*Fuck you.* And fuck your retarded questions. I'm going with *them*," I said as I attempted to climb into the ambulance.

"You can ask me all the retarded questions you want at the hospital," I barked as I pulled my shoulder away from his grasp.

"Ma'am I'm sorry. You aren't allowed back here," one of the paramedics said.

"Fuck you," I said as I shoved my phone in my back pocket.

I grabbed a metal handle on the inside of the ambulance and hoisted myself in. Both paramedics looked at each other and raised their eyebrows.

"She's my friend, I found her, and I am riding with you to the hospital. You want me out, throw me out," I said as I wiped tears from my face.

Someone shut the back doors to the ambulance and it began to roll forward. One of the paramedics began connecting an I.V., electrodes and numerous wires to Britney. Her face was covered in a plastic mask. The other paramedic glanced in my direction and spoke.

"You've got a lot of guts getting her off the ladder and performing CPR. That took tremendous drive, young lady. It speaks volumes of what type of person you are inside. Not many girls would have maintained a level head through all of that. You did well. What's your name?" he said in a very soft appreciative tone.

"Michelle," I sniffed.

"You did well, Michelle," he nodded.

Oh shit. Kid.

I needed to call Kid. I reached into my back pocket, removed my phone, and called Kid. I held the phone to my cheek and waited for it to start ringing. As soon as the paramedic noticed me on the phone, he shook his head from side to side slowly.

"Ma'am you can't use that in here. The machines," he said as he pointed around the ambulance toward the numerous devices.

I nodded my head as Kid's phone continued to ring in my ear.

"We're in the ambulance and headed to the hospital," I blurted as soon as he answered.

As I began to talk, the reality of the situation hit me and I began to cry uncontrollably. As tears were dripping from my chin, Kid began to talk.

"Michelle, you did great. Did you give her CPR?" he asked quietly.

I nodded my head, and realized I wasn't speaking.

"Yes," I responded.

"Is she alive?" Kid's voice was soft and kind.

I shrugged my shoulders and thought. I had no idea. I assumed she was dead but I hoped that she was alive. She wasn't moving. I looked toward the paramedic, moved the phone from my face, and asked the question.

"Sir, is she breathing?"

"She's alive, ma'am," the other paramedic answered.

"Is she breathing?"

As I asked the question, I realized it was not what Kid had asked.

"Ma'am she's alive. We're trying to keep her that way. We'll need you to get off the phone, please," the first paramedic asked.

"Kid, she's alive, yes. They're telling me I have to get off the phone. I will call you from the hospital, okay?"

"Okay. Be well, Michelle."

I hung up and pulled the phone from my face. It was dripping water from my crying. I wiped the screen on my pants and looked down at my combat boots. I wiped the tears from my face with the back of my hand. As I leaned over and pushed the phone into my back pocket, I noticed for the first time that the second attendant had a tattoo on his forearm.

U.S.M.C.

He had probably spent his early years in Iraq, doing what he could to help fight for what he believed was right. Or at least what he was ordered to fight for. He had fought for the United States to remain United. And now he was fighting for Britney's life. I realized as I looked at him I was going to spend my entire life doing versions of what he was doing right now. After college, I would be doing it every day; saving lives. A feeling of warmth enveloped me. I prayed. I looked at the attendant with the tattoo and smiled.

"She's going to be alright, isn't she?" I asked.

He looked up as he wiped the sweat from his forehead with his forearm. Without speaking, he narrowed his gaze and looked down at Britney.

She's going to be alright, isn't she?

15

ARE THOSE ROCKS IN YOUR POCKET?

MARCUS

Girls had always thought I was pretty cool. I've never had a problem pulling good looking girls. All the chicks I hung out with wanted me and they never friend-zoned me. It was pretty cool, because I normally got to pick and choose the ones I wanted to be with, and the others just had to live without me until it was their turn.

Going to school at South Plainfield was a lot cooler than going to school in Buffalo. We moved to South Plainfield almost two years ago, and I liked it in South Plainfield much more. There were a lot more chicks to choose from, and they were almost all hot. And my friends were cool too. There were basically four of us that hung out together, Adrian, Marc, Joey, and I.

We were together all the time.

We ate lunch together every day, pretty much. One day while we were eating I began to think of summer and the school year finally ending. Three more months and summer would arrive. Summer beat the shit out of going to school for sure. School could be so boring, but lunch wasn't bad, something I kind of looked forward to.

Marc had a banging hot new girlfriend but he never brought her around any of us. This particular day at lunch, Adrian started before I had a chance.

"Dude, have you had sex with her?" Adrian asked Marc.

"Our relationship is private, you guys know that. Now, stop," Marc said.

Marc started moving around in his seat, trying to get comfortable. I figured eventually we'd probably get some stories about this hot little bitch he was seeing. Maybe he'd say something if we hit him hard enough, I thought.

"C'mon, Marc. Just tell us something. You've never really had a girlfriend. Give us something," I said.

Marc started looking at his watch like it was time to leave.

This pussy isn't going to tell us anything about this girl. I can't believe he is going to deprive us of this bitch.

Really, Marc?

Dude. Tell us something. She's a bitch. Bro's before hoes.

"Listen, I told you guys. I will tell you about her, who she is, what she's like. But, it is not fair to her or to us to give anyone intimate details about what we do. Do not ask again. It's a matter of respect," Marc said angrily.

Marc started messing with his hair and acting mad. I felt like I should make him feel better. We weren't attacking him; just really attacking the bitch he was dating.

"Dude, cut that shit, it's fucking long," I said.

"No, I am not cutting it. I like it this way," Marc responded as he took a bite from his apple.

Marc and Joey got up to go to the bathroom and left Adrian and I sitting at the table. Frustrated with Marc's lack of willingness to give up sexual details, I sat and stared as they walked away. As they turned down the hallway toward the bathroom, I looked over and noticed Marc left his coat at the table.

"Dude, hand me Marc's coat," I said to Adrian.

"What?" Adrian responded.

"Hand me Marc's coat. I want to see if his phone is in it. You know he leaves that shit unlocked. I want to see if he has any pics of that bitch in his phone. Hand me his coat," I said as I pointed to the coat.

"Dude, you know how he is about his coat," Adrian responded.

I reached over, grabbed the coat, and pulled Marc's phone from the inside pocket. I turned the phone on and scrolled through the images. There were only a few pics on his phone, but the most recent one was the girl he was dating, and she was naked.

"Dude, we hit the jackpot. Look at this shit," I said as I pointed the phone's screen at Adrian.

"Look at the big titties on this bitch. Damn," I said as I looked at the photo again.

"Damn, dude, she's fucking hot. Nice tits," Adrian said.

"Dude, watch and see if they're coming. Let me know if you see 'em," I said.

"Okay."

I texted all of the pics of her from Marc's phone to my phone. After I received them on my phone, I erased the text message from Marc's phone so he wouldn't know. Satisfied at our new pictures of the chic with big titties, I put the phone into the coat pocket of Marc's jacket and draped it over the back of the seat.

"Dude, that bitch has nice fucking tits. Did you see those big fuckers?" I asked Adrian.

"Yeah. Send me that shit, dude. Spank bank. Damn," Adrian smiled.

I opened my phone's images and looked at the other pics of Marc's girl. She was pretty damned cute. Looked like a Puerto Rican. She was skinny, had big tits and a pretty face. I looked at the other pics with her clothes on, and she was still hot. While I was texting the pics to Adrian, I heard Marc and Joey coming down the hallway. As soon as they walked up Adrian started acting all nervous.

"Well, you guys about ready?" Adrian said as he stood.

Everyone went back to class. I spent the rest of the day thinking about summer. Summer was so much more enjoyable than winter. In the winter there was nothing to do, really. In the summer, time flew by, and it was so much more fun. Everyone was always out doing things and having fun.

After school, I texted a few people copies of the pic of Marc's girl and her big titties. Later that night I had about five or six people ask for a copy of it, and I texted it to them. During the next few days, people blew up my phone asking for it. After about a week, it finally stopped. People probably started getting a copy of it from other people instead of getting it from me.

Maybe a month or so later, Marc called me. He asked me to meet him and said he wanted to talk about a summer surprise party for Joey. Joey's birthday was in the summer, so it was no big deal, and we decided to meet at 8:00 p.m. When I pulled into the parking lot, I noticed Marc was sitting in his car. I pulled up beside his car and got out. As Marc got out of his car, he pulled off his jacket and tossed it into the seat. He ran his hands through his hair, and slowly walked toward me.

It looked like he was going to give me a bro hug. And then, all of a sudden, he started screaming.

"You stole pictures off my phone of my girlfriend and sent them to everyone in school. You're a piece of fucking shit, Marcus," Marc screamed.

He was shaking. I could tell he was ready to fight. I knew I needed to settle him down before he did something stupid.

"Dude, I just. Well, I just. One day, you and Joey went to the bathroom, and Adrian and I…"

"I already talked to Adrian, *I know what happened*," he interrupted.

As he talked, he circled around me nervously.

"Dude, she's just a bitch, bros before hoes. C'mon dude, we're bro's," I shrugged.

I didn't see him swing, but I sure felt his fist hit my mouth. I saw a flash of light, and everything went black for a second. He kept hitting my face, over and over as he screamed about respect. When he finally got off of me, I had teeth in my mouth. My face was throbbing and I could feel blood all over my arms and face.

"She's not a bitch, she's a woman. And you need to learn about being respectful. And, the fact that people are human fucking beings. You don't have to respect *her*, you don't know her, but you should *treat* her with respect. And if you were truly my friend, out of respect for *me*, you would not have done what you did. You know, shit like this from people like you can ruin someone's life for fucking ever, you dumb fuck."

Curled up on the ground by his feet, I looked up wiped blood from my face.

"Don't ever talk to me again, Marcus. *Ever.* I said the same thing to Adrian. And you are personally going to go to everyone in school and ask them if they have a copy of that photo of her. If they do, you're going to see that it's deleted. You're going to watch them do it. *Everyone*. And a month from now I am going to ask around. If anyone still has a copy of it, I am going to find you. And we will do this again, *understand*?" Marc growled.

I stood up slowly.

My head was spinning and throbbing. I nodded my head and spit my teeth into my hand. As he stood and stared, I dropped the teeth into my pocket. I wiped my face with my hand and looked down.

Blood.

My lips felt like grilled hot dogs. Over grilled hot dogs.

"Do you understand? I asked you a fucking question, and I want an answer," Marc snapped.

"Yeth!" I responded.

"And. Don't ever speak to me for any reason. *Ever.* As long as you live. If I have a reason to talk to you, it is going to be to beat your ass again, Marcus. That's the only reason I will ever talk to you again. Get those photos found, and get them gone. And when you talk about this, if you do, don't say *Marc's an asshole*. Say to yourself or others, *I was wrong*. Because you were."

With those last words he got into his car and drove off.

And he was right.

I was wrong.

16

WHO DID THIS?

MICHELLE

"Look at her, lady. I know she has a mask on her face, but go back there and look at her and then come back here and look at me. Try and tell me we aren't related. I'm her cousin. I'm going back there," I cried as I shook my phone toward the nurse's face.

The lady at the desk in the emergency room wouldn't let me into the area where Britney was. They had pulled the ambulance up to an entrance and immediately took Britney into the trauma section. There was a special desk in this particular section of the hospital, and the woman was obviously in charge of acting like a buffer between the people waiting and the patients. She had advised me repeatedly I must wait in the waiting room. According to her, only family was allowed to go into the unit; and sometimes no one was permitted. I was attempting, unsuccessfully, to convince her I was family.

"Ma'am, I am going to walk back there. I am sorry. If you want to stop me, I suppose you can *try.* I have had a fucking awful day," I said as I wiped tears from my face.

"I found her in her garage hanging from a fucking bed sheet. I climbed a rickety ladder and carried her to the top," I paused and began to cry uncontrollably.

"I…" she began to speak.

I held my hand up to stop her. I felt compelled to finish. Still crying uncontrollably, I tried to speak.

"I held her in my arms. I held her in my arms," I blubbered.

"And I untied the rope and tried to carry her to the bottom," I wiped the tears from my face with my arm.

Sobbing, I continued, "And I got her to the ground, and I tried as hard as I could to save her. If she doesn't live, it's going to kill me," I sobbed.

Filled with emotion, shaking, and with my voice cracking, I turned and tried to walk. I stumbled at the first step. I felt weak and dizzy. She turned from the counter, walked around her work station, walked over to me and touched my arm. When I started to pull away, she spoke softly and lightly gripped my forearm.

"Hide your phone in your back pocket, honey. Let me help you get back there. Hold onto me. I will show you where she is. We will tell them you're her sister, okay?" she smiled.

I nodded. Still sobbing uncontrollably, I wiped my face with my arm and pushed my phone into my back pocket. When we got to where Britney was, there were two staff members working with her. She was lying on her back, completely still. I touched her hand, and she felt cold.

As I began to sob, the doctor turned toward us, and looked directly at me.

"Sister," the receptionist whispered to the doctor.

She put her arm around my shoulder and pulled me toward her as she gave me a hug. I began to cry again. With my head on her shoulder, I sobbed. She held me for some time as I cried, thinking of Britney hanging in the garage. Silently, I wondered if I performed the CPR correctly. I questioned if I possibly hurt her when we fell, and if maybe hitting her head on the garage floor caused the injuries. Soon, I realized I tried as hard as I could to do everything possible.

I began to pray, and as I did, I stopped crying. I pulled away from the receptionist and wiped my tears. Silently, she tapped my shoulder with her hand and turned to walk away.

"Thank you," I whispered.

"Debbie," she smiled over her shoulder as she walked through the partition.

I stood by Britney's feet and rubbed them as doctors checked her statistics. The weight of responsibility was heavy, and I began to feel guilty for Britney being in the condition she was in. As I stood at the foot of the bed, number two from my list came to mind.

God will give you more than you can handle, so you can learn to lean on Him in times of need. He won't tempt you more than you can handle, though. So don't lose hope. Hope anchors the soul.

As I continued to rub her feet, I prayed. I closed my eyes and got lost in prayer. All of the sounds, the annoying beeping, distant moans, the screaming; all went away as I prayed. I could hear nothing but the sounds of my thoughts. I felt at peace and even felt lighter on my feet. Britney's feet felt cold and smooth in my hands. I continued to pray, rubbing her feet as I did. I desperately wanted to make them feel warm. After a few minutes I opened my eyes, feeling as if I could accept whatever God's will happened to be.

"You're her sister?" the doctor turned and asked.

"Yes, sir," I responded as I nodded my head.

"She is in a coma. We will need to run some additional tests. There may be swelling of the brain – potentially from the asphyxiation, depending on the amount of time that she," he paused.

"Well, we need to run some tests. It may be something she comes out of soon, it's hard to tell at this point. We will know more after the tests," he nodded.

He turned and began to speak to the other staff members.

I can find no serenity until I accept that person, place, thing or situation as being exactly the way it is supposed to be at this moment. Nothing, absolutely nothing happens in God's world by mistake.

Kid repeated that phrase to me a thousand times. I closed my eyes and began to repeat it in my mind over and over as I rubbed Britney's feet.

When things happened in my life, I always tried to look at what transpired, big or small, and learn from it. Once, while texting and driving, I almost had a collision. I stopped texting and driving. I had seen boys pass around pictures of girls in school and quickly realized how disrespectful and shallow people can be. I would no sooner send someone a naked photo of me than I would rob a bank. I always tried to consider the possibility and probability of something happening. If I had control, ultimately I could rely on myself. If it was out of my control, I must rely on others. In my opinion, other people cannot be relied upon. When I was forced to rely on others, I eventually become disappointed. I suppose different people can be relied upon for different things.

I believe people could learn a lot from the way I perceive things.

When I chose to do something, regardless of the magnitude of the decision I made, I always tried to think how it may affect others and the impact it could potentially have if things didn't go the way I planned. If all things pointed in a direction which was good, I would do what I had been contemplating. So far, my life had turned out well. As with all kids, I made some decisions I would say weren't necessarily great, but I did not regret them. I don't' regret anything in my life and I doubted I ever would. My life's experiences had made me who I was. If I excluded any one of my experiences, I would be someone different. I was comfortable being who I had become. As the doctors began to move Britney, I opened my eyes. As they pushed her to the elevator, I followed.

When we got upstairs, the doctors pushed Britney down the hallway. As they took her away for further testing, they demanded I remain in the waiting room. They assured me they would let me know as soon as she was done with the tests were performing. Tired, scared, and full of emotion, I waited. I hadn't been there long and I heard screaming from down the hallway. The voice was familiar, and was demanding answers.

I stood up, walked out of the waiting room, and immediately made eye contact with Britney's father.

Hurriedly, he walked to meet me in the corridor.

"What happened, Michelle? Who did this?" he asked frantically.

Crying, I stood and stared. Incapable of speaking, I continued to sob. As he embraced me in an effort to provide comfort, the response came to me, but I stood silently.

"Who did this?" he whispered again.

I clenched my jaw.

You did.

17

POMEGRANATE SKATEBOARD

FAT KID

I spread the letters across the desk and sorted them by date. As I separated them, I made stacks based on month and year. Slowly, the reality of sitting in prison came back to me. My father and I had exchanged letters the entire time I was in prison and the pile of old mail before me stood as proof. I kept all of the letters we exchanged and cherished them and the memories associated with them.

When I was a child, my father and I were never really what I would describe as *close.* He was always my father and I was always his son; but I continually felt as if something was missing. As I grew older, I dismissed it as guilt combined with my own feelings of worthlessness. I never felt I made my father as proud of me as I wanted to. Regardless of what I may have accomplished, I never believed it was ever good enough in my father's eyes. Looking back at all of those years and accomplishments now, under a retrospective microscope, I wondered how much of my feelings of inadequacy were simply me wanting or needing praise I never received.

The human mind is a difficult thing to understand. It's an extremely complex piece of equipment, without a doubt. Everything which had been developed since the beginning of time was created by the human mind. In realizing technological advancements made in the last two hundred years alone, it becomes quite staggering. A person cannot look around them without seeing cars capable of traveling at speeds up to two hundred miles an hour at a rate of 25 miles per gallon. Cars were once nothing more than wooden wagons. How could one not be impressed with the capacity of the human mind?

A make-shift log cabin constructed out of tree limbs, mud and leaves two hundred years ago had developed into structures hundreds of stories tall which are capable of withstanding high winds and adverse weather. Additionally, everything within the car or building was or had been developed and manufactured by the human mind. Every computer, phone, capacitor, brake caliper, wrist watch, microwave, door knob, air conditioner compressor, carpet fiber, diode, stereo speaker, can opener and light bulb was a result of the human mind having made advancements. Every year, every decade, every new generation, every century, we continued to make measurable growth.

Having an understanding of the mind's ability to develop such feats makes it more difficult to consider the fact we can't identify and make minor adjustments in our perception of childhood memories. If we were able, we might make major adjustments to our character defects as adults. It stands to reason it would be simple. In theory it is. It takes honesty, open-mindedness, and the capability to actuate one's thoughts or beliefs.

When I was a child, my life was so simple. All I had to do was stumble through a day, not kill myself, and go to bed. Another day started when I woke up, and with it began a reiteration of the same thing, only on a different day. The weather was great in San Diego and we had no real seasons to speak of. In my opinion, my life was quite simple. Almost perfect.

Get up, get dressed, and get started. Simple for even a dip-shit like me.

"What do you want for your birthday, son?" My father asked.

"A skateboard," I responded.

"What? A skateboard? Why? Are you a hippie? A skater?" he asked as he stared down at me in disgust.

Looking up at him in admiration, I wondered if I had made a bad decision. I wanted a skateboard, and all of the kids in the neighborhood had one. I had ridden my friend's skateboards and had become quite good at doing so. The thought of having my own thrilled me to no end. I was quite certain I could get through the remainder of my life with nothing else if I had a skateboard of my own.

"Well, we'll have to see. Anything else?" he asked as he lit another Salem cigarette.

Feeling somewhat uncomfortable of what I may receive instead, I provided a little reassurance of a skateboard being my only desire in life.

"No, sir. Just a skateboard," I said sheepishly as I twisted the toe of my sneaker in a circle on the floor.

"Well, it's coming up here before long, in a few weeks I think," he said as he exhaled a cloud of smoke.

Wondering if he remembered the date of my birthday for sure, I felt compelled to remind him.

"The thirteenth, Pop. It's on the thirteenth."

"Thirteenth, huh? Yeah, sounds about right. Well, go play. We'll see. Your mother will have dinner ready soon. Go out and play in the street," he said as he turned and walked into the kitchen.

Go out and play in the street.

He used to say that to me all the time. He would jokingly say maybe a car would hit me. As a child, I remember wondering if he really wanted a car to hit me. And if he did, why? What could I have possibly done to make him feel that life, for him, would be better if I were run over by a car? I lived my life wondering whether or not my father loved me the way my mother did. But, no matter what, I always respected my father. I always admired him. And I always looked up to him. I am sure I embarrassed him on many occasions, but he never embarrassed me. In my mind, my father was like a king. Everyone went to him for answers, me included.

"Let's go to the pomegranate tree," my eight year old sister said.

She pointed across the field, toward the tree which sat behind our home. My brother stood by my side with a stupid look on his face. As a child, he always had a stupid look on his face. Our house was in the middle of the block. We had a huge field between our home and the school which stood behind our home. In the field at the end of the block was a series of trees and several of them were pomegranate trees. The fruit was free for the taking, and they were bitter and sweet. The issue with the pomegranates was the juice. It was worse than grape juice for making stains on clothing. Being seven years old and eating a pomegranate without getting covered in juice was difficult, if not impossible. My siblings and I had ventured to the trees many times, and had been in trouble for smearing our good school clothes with pomegranate juice, effectively ruining them.

We raced to the pomegranate tree. Getting there, my sister and I plucked the pomegranates from the tree and sat eating them until we were full. My brother, three years old at the time, required our assistance with about everything he did. To satisfy this requirement, we took turns shoving the pomegranate seeds into his mouth. Eventually, we ended up in a pomegranate fight, and were smearing the fruit all over each other, laughing the entire time.

I took some and painted stripes on my brother's face. My sister painted stripes on my face. I, in turn, rubbed a few in her hair and on her shirt. My shirt was next, and my brother's soon followed. Around the time when we were exhausted and almost sick, most of the stains had dried. Now the stripes and stains were a permanent part of our skin, clothes and hair. Standing and staring at each other, we admired our work. I think we all realized at the same time we were going to be in some deep form of trouble as soon as we got home.

My mother was as understanding of a human as could ever exist. If she were home alone, her response to seeing the mess would have been, *Well, let's get some soap. And take those dirty clothes off before your dad gets home and sees them.* The problem, with this particular day, was the fact that my father *was* home. We wasted as much time as we could, but eventually we had to walk home. We did so, laughing and poking each other along the way. My father was bent over landscaping in the front yard when we got home. We noticed him as we came around the corner of the house and into the front yard. Immediately, we froze. Like little concrete statues, we stood motionless. As fathers always do, he knew we had done *something*. He looked up from his landscaping and saw the three of us standing there, purple from head to toe, and he screamed.

"What in the fuck have you three little idiots done? You've been down at that fucking pomegranate tree again, haven't you? What in the absolute fuck did I tell you about going to that God damned tree?" he screamed as he stood up.

He was across the front yard from us, about fifty feet away. Standing there petrified, I tried to remember just what it was he said about the pomegranate tree. I remembered nothing at all. As I often did, I was drawing a mental blank. I suspected as always, he would remind us.

He didn't disappoint me.

"I told you if you went there again, and spread that juice all over your stupid selves, I was going to beat your little asses. And believe me, that's what I am going to do. Do not ever, *ever,* go to that fucking tree again. Not for any God forsaken reason. It's off fucking limits. Do you understand me?" he screamed as he began to walk toward us.

And it all came back to me. We weren't supposed to go to the tree for any reason. He had told us many times, but the last time he told us he made it very clear. Obviously, however, not quite clear enough.

"Yes."

"Yes."

My younger brother nodded his head. In retrospect, I don't think he spoke until he was five or six. He didn't need to, my sister and I spoke for him.

"Do you understand me?" he yelled again, now about ten feet from us.

"Yes, Sir!" the three of us responded at once.

I knew we forgot something. *Sir.* We were raised learning to respect our elders. I addressed anyone that was or even appeared to be an adult *Sir or Ma'am.*

My father was a former Marine; six foot tall, muscular, and about 180 pounds. As we grew up, he taught us respect. We were instructed to act as if we had discipline, always. He wasn't abusive or mean, and never was violent toward us. But he demanded we be respectful, and we were disciplined if we were not. As a child, I could not imagine treating an adult in any manner which could be perceived as being disrespectful.

Our heads hanging, we walked up the porch and into the house. My mother, hearing the commotion, had come to the front door and stood waiting for us. We walked up the steps, past her, and into the house. My father stayed in the yard. Our mother got us changed into clean clothes, threw our stained clothes in the washer, and attempted to clean us up the best she could. I don't recall much else about that night, but I clearly remembered our discussions at the dinner table.

Sitting at the table, as my father looked at our purple faces in disgust, I wondered. I wondered about the punishment we were going to receive, about my birthday, and ultimately how many more years I would have to wait for that skateboard.

"I'm sorry father, for the pomegranates. And for Matt's face," I said as I looked at my purple-faced brother.

My father looked up from his meal and responded as he shook his fork at me, "That's alright son. *Don't let it happen again.*"

And, I didn't.

Growing up, regardless of what happened in our home, and I do mean *regardless*, we always knew we could speak to our parents about it. As an adult, I look at that one item as being the most important thing about growing up that kept me from eventually coming unraveled. No matter how difficult of a situation I put myself in, and regardless of my age, I always knew I could talk to my parents about it. And they always listened. They made it a point to calmly discuss the ins and outs of what it was I had done - pertaining to the situation being discussed. At times, they explained their opinion of I should have done, considered, or thought. But, growing up, I never wanted to keep anything from them. This freedom and open line of communication, this *one thing* made a difference in the way I grew up.

I never had a desire to run away from home. I never had an urge to commit suicide. I never lied to my parents or tried to cover something up. Communication, I still say today, is the key.

As I spread the letters out, I tried to decide what it was that I was actually trying to do. What I hoped to accomplish. I spread them over my desk and looked at the pile. He had sent a letter every few days, without fail, for almost three years. He wrote me regularly, no exceptions. No lapses. I couldn't count on much as I sat in prison. I lost friends, I lost touch with my family, I lost my job, I lost pride, and I lost my freedom. I gained a relationship with my father I never had growing up. A relationship where he told me he was proud of me. I sat in prison, of all places, and my father said he was proud of me, and he meant it. His letters continued to come, with regularity, and I looked forward to reading them. I looked forward to his letters more than I looked forward to anything else I received. I would forfeit food, water, exercise, and phone calls before I would have forfeited his letters. During this time, he recalled things I had done as a kid I grew up certain he didn't even notice. Things I didn't know he knew. Things I was positive he couldn't or didn't remember. But he did. And he made sure in the letters that he wrote I knew he remembered.

My father was proud of me.

I wondered when the last time Britney's father said he was proud of her, or the last occasion he took time to give her a hug. I wondered when he last made reference to something she had done and said, *your accomplishments made me proud.*

214

Maybe the prison Britney was in now would make the difference.

The first time I rode the skateboard, I did so with a smile on my face. A purple smile, as I was still stained by the pomegranate juice.

18

GUILTY MINDS

MICHELLE

What happened to Britney changed me - the understatement of a lifetime. I could see changes in how I looked at things, my reactions, and how I perceived day-to-day events or happenings. In making comparisons to before I found Britney, these changes were drastic. Some things which seemed important before no longer mattered. Yet other things which were not important all of a sudden became so. I felt as if I had either done something wrong or simply didn't do what I should have. Britney had been in the hospital for a few days and was still in a coma. Although the doctors attempted to assure me I had saved her life, it was difficult for me to see it that way. She was not alive. She lay in a bed, surrounded by people crying, and she couldn't acknowledge anything. She was fully comatose.

Minor swelling of her brain, they explained. And there was no real way of telling the extent of the damage as a result of oxygen being cut off to her brain. Time, according to the doctors, would tell.

I challenged the decisions I had made. *What if I would have gone to the garage first*? She probably wouldn't have even had time to hang herself. What if I had sent Kid the pictures when he first asked? My

217

procrastination could have cost Britney's life. These thoughts consumed me, and became part of my daily thinking. I had not gone back to school, and felt as if I was incapable of doing so. In two days, everything seemed to change. My parents had expressed a greater concern for what my brother and I did, and appeared to be a little more relaxed in their expectations of us. Because it had only been two days it was difficult to tell if they were really concerned for our safety, or if this was a knee jerk reaction any parent would have following a suicide of a close friend of the family.

It also troubled me how Kid appeared to change as well. He had shared with me the story of his loss of a girlfriend to suicide. We talked at length about his feelings associated with the loss. I harbored the same feelings. Contrary to our earlier discussions about *broken people attracting broken people,* he had been more distant for the last few days. I suspect he now felt as if he had lost two people to suicide. In addition to feeling as if I let myself and Britney down, I knew I let Kid down, and that didn't sit very well with me. Letting down other people hurt me far more than letting myself down - it disappointed me greatly to disappoint others.

On the evening of the suicide Kid and I talked at length of his similar feelings after his loss of his girlfriend. He indicated he had spent his entire adult life attempting to make up for not identifying and preventing her suicide. After the suicide, he made every effort to *save people,* feeling if he did so it would make the pain go away. Ultimately, he uses his internet blog solely to assist people, in hopes the feelings associated with the loss of his dead girlfriend, *and the incident,* would fade away. According to him they never had.

I could become comfortable with the thought of living my entire life feeling the way I do now. Having a better understanding of how Kid had lived his life, and the feelings he possessed caused me to feel sorry not only for him, but for every survivor of suicide. Other people who have been forced to live with the loss from a suicide certainly feel the same way. The victims of suicide are clearly the survivors.

And the pain is crippling.

Although I had not seen it, my parents indicated a suicide letter was found. They said Britney's father intended on allowing them to see it.

I had no idea what to expect or if the suicide letter could actually provide me comfort. To be quite honest, I expected nothing. I felt knowing Britney's thoughts prior to the suicide would do me no good now. I was filled with guilt in so many ways. I was willing to bet I was already more knowledgeable about whatever her letter contained than anyone would be even after reading it. I was aware of the problems she was having long before the day came. For years she had been fighting feelings of worthlessness and bulimia As a result, she had little, if any self-esteem. The lack of self-esteem in my opinion may not be totally attributed to the manner in which her parents treated her, but without a doubt was partly a result of them never providing her with any form of assurance they were even aware of her existence.

As teens, it seemed we all had issues with our parents, but Britney's parents provided her with material things, and not the care and affection a child expects and deserves from a parent. In my opinion, no amount of money could buy the comfort felt from a hug, or the reassuring words *I am so proud of you.* It was and will always remain disturbing to me to think that a once a month hug accompanied with such a statement could save a life or lives. What a small price to pay. I did wonder if parents knew in advance where the minds of their children would eventually lie, what they would be willing to do to prevent the suicide of their child.

To think a little praise expressed to a fractionally overweight daughter might prevent her from suffering from bulimia or anorexia was sickening at best. Most teens grew out of eating disorders by the time they were in their early twenties. The codependency and seeking praise from a sexual counterpart, from what Kid explained, lasted a lifetime. Some of his stories of where codependent girls wound up – physically, mentally and psychologically – made me feel sick. It saddened me to think a different manner of raising a child could make such a difference.

Children don't come with handbooks. Generations grow up, and raise generations who eventually grow up, and the new generation grows up to raise yet another. To look at the changes from 1913 to 2013, we have made technological advancements that couldn't even be imagined. As a whole, the mental stability of a high school student, however, has plummeted. Drug addiction, low self-esteem, alcoholism, prostitution, pornography, bulimia, teen pregnancy, pre-marital sex, deceit, theft, lying, manipulation, anorexia, depression, codependency and the list goes on and on. At seventeen, I was familiar with a great percentage of the problems teens suffered from. I felt most could have been stopped by a parent who may have chosen to spend a few more minutes a month simply caring. Thinking about what may have prevented Britney's suicide caused me to lie in bed and cry endlessly. In considering the amount of people on earth who were or would eventually feel the way I felt over the loss of a loved one due to suicide caused me to hurt.

And it hurt deeply.

In a sense, I believed it got down to trusting. As infants, we're reliant on others. We learned early on to trust our parents. We were even told *not* to trust others. *Never trust a stranger*. As toddlers, we continue to develop this trust. We eventually became children, and we trusted our parents, wholly. We developed faith they would *always* be there for us, to assist us, make decisions for us, and provide us with guidance. As teens, because we trusted they had done all they had the power to do, when things fell apart, we naturally wondered.

If our parents were the people we trusted the most - and they didn't have the answers - who might? We had placed our parents on a pedestal, and there they remained. When they failed, we failed.

Lying on my bed, I logged into Tumblr and wrote a passage.

Parent,
As I am growing up...
Provide me with love, and tell me you love me.
Provide me with guidance, and show me the way.
Provide me with affection, and tell me you care.
Provide me with reassurance, and tell me you are proud of me.
And as I grow older, give me some freedom.
With the freedom, trust in me the way I have trusted in you, and I will make decisions to make you proud.
Your child.

19

THE INCIDENT

FAT KID

We'll clear the main room. If they're not in there, there's one bedroom on the right. The laundry's on the left, that's it. Both rooms face front door. Bedroom is about a ten by ten, and it isn't even supposed to have furniture.

There's one exit visible in the front room, on the right side.

They have weapons?

No, no weapons.

So, we're in, secure the room, get them zip-tied, and it's over. In and out, five minutes.

You good?

Yep. I'm good.

The door swung to the left. The first shot was fired as soon as the door opened. Fire was returned in self-defense. Weapons fire continued from both directions. When the firing ceased, there were two dead bodies in the main room of the house.

It sounded simple.

It was anything but.

The incident kept me from being remotely close to normal for my entire life. I dreamt that dream in detail, over and over. It happened repeatedly, nightly, until my mind shut down and stopped allowing me to recall it. The end result was I stopped dreaming entirely. Not one. Not even a simple pink elephant on a picnic table, or a walk in the park. *Nothing.* Ever. My psychiatrist explained my mind still processed dreams every night, but same mind which processed them would not allow me to recall a single one, regardless.

It's some form of defense mechanism, she explained.

Either way, I was pleased when they finally stopped. Relieved was more like it. Things didn't change as a result of the dreams stopping as I had hoped. When they ceased, I anticipated measurable recovery. It never came. I continued to live with guilt, tremendous guilt. An unbearable guilt which words have no ability to accurately explain. To attempt to describe it would be impossible.

Although the dreaming stopped, the day-to-day thoughts never ended. The dwelling, constant second-guessing myself, replaying the event over and over in my mind and trying to piece together what could have been done differently never ended.

I lived every day with a weird inner belief if I did something extraordinary, if I performed some form of absolute magic on a helpless person, the slate would be wiped clean and the guilt would be gone. I believed God, in appreciation for the grandest of good deeds, would take away my pain and suffering. Remove the guilt. Eliminate the daily reminder I had lived and others had not.

Survivor's guilt.

If I had to do it over again, would I?

I used to ask myself daily - actually a few times daily. In the early years, my response used to be *no, it was self-defense.* Anyone with any form of training or understanding would have done the same thing.

Today, and in recent years, I'd certainly respond differently. I would have held my hands in the air, taken a round to the chest, and died right there in the front room. The guilt was overwhelming. Guilt turns to pain for those of us who may have a reasonable amount of common sense. I like to think I possess a tremendous amount of common sense.

Therefore I live with a tremendous amount of pain.

There was always suicide. It was an option to end my pain. I felt it wouldn't be fair for those who lost their lives for me to bow out of this world by my own hand. I believed I owed it to those whose lives were lost to continue enduring the pain. It was the least I could do.

Or.

I could make right with God.

I believed God had another plan for me - because try as I might, the guilt continued.

When the dreams finally stopped I was relieved. I felt if the constant reminder was eliminated, I would recover over time. Although it had been a decade of no dreams, the guilt remained – as strong as ever. Over the years I continued to be grateful for my mind choosing to cast the dreams aside.

Not one dream in over a decade.

Until now.

I woke up and sat up in the bed. Initially, I was a little uncertain of what had happened. When I cleared my thoughts, I walked into the kitchen and took a pen out of the drawer. I had no idea why I had walked to the kitchen for a pen, but I sure ended up standing there. So, with the pen in hand I walked to my desk, got out a post-it note, and wrote down my summary of the dream.

On a fucking post-it note.

It was 3:20 a.m. The time of day I was certain of. I always looked at my watch whenever I woke up. It was some odd habit. As soon as I awaken, I had to know what time it was. So, at 3:20 a.m. I had a dream, wrote down the high light, and took the pen to bed with me.

As I attempted to become comfortable in bed, I stared at the ceiling for what seemed to be an eternity; realistically it was maybe fifteen minutes. I reached toward the nightstand in the dark, and fumbled for my phone. After finding it I sent Michelle a text message.

Michelle. Good news. I will tell you later. Maybe in a week or two. I will swallow this and see what it tastes like. Talk tomorrow or the next. Kid.

I continued to lie in bed until I fell asleep, which I suspect took thirty minutes. When I woke up the next morning, I felt rather odd. I wasn't sure as I was waking up if what I had thought happened actually happened. I was pretty sure I had a dream. Uncertain if I either had a dream that I dreamt and wrote it down on a post-it note in the dream itself, or I had dreamt, and later, in real life, wrote it down on a post-it note - I walked to my desk and looked down at the piles of paper.

Sure enough, on the desk lay a post-it note with my handwriting on it.

Fuck.

It had actually happened.

I sat at the desk for a considerable amount of time and tried to decide if I wanted to continue to dream. I did miss dreaming, but I didn't miss all of the things associated with it. I had the recurring nightmares associated with *the incident*, which I wasn't interested in reliving. Also, as a child and as an early adult; from time to time I had dreams which would end up being reality. They were a forecast of sorts.

Some form of view into the future. I really didn't like thinking about the *looking-into-the-future* dreams. Truth be known, they kind of freaked me out. The *future* dreams, as fate would have it, were as different when compared to a normal dream as night would compare to day. There was no misunderstanding when I had one of them. Any time I had one, I knew exactly what it was. In most, I could sense what the characters in the dream were thinking and feeling. Easily, I would immediately identify it as *one of those dreams*.

I stood up from the desk, convinced I had no interest in ever having a dream again

I wandered into the bath room and got on the scale. A perfect 319. Not bad for morning weight. I was pleased. Smiling, I got off the scale and brushed my teeth. I hopped in the shower and got dressed to start my day. I imagined a cup of coffee was in order, a few emails, and a short talk with Michelle to see how she and Britney were doing.

After Britney's suicide attempt I had called the hospital and left word for someone to call me if there was a significant change, but my experience told me I couldn't always rely on the staff at a hospital. I hated hospitals. I hated the staff. Pretty much everything which had to do with going into a hospital freaked me out. Generally speaking, I could last all of about ten minutes in one. I was worried about Michelle. She was merely 17 years old and had been through a tremendous amount in the previous three or so days, and it worried me. She was a strong girl, and I wanted her to be able to live the rest of her life without the daily guilt I had spent a lifetime harboring.

Still somewhat confused from the events of the previous night, I stumbled from my house to the elevator, and went downstairs to the parking garage. As I approached my parking stall, I stood and stared. I had forgotten the incident with the smashed passenger side window and the fact my car was at the dealership being repaired. As I looked down at the unfamiliar keys in my hand, I remembered the BMW dealership had graciously provided me with a new M5 to drive while they fixed my M3. I unlocked the loaner car, tossed my bag in the back seat, and fired up the engine.

The 600 horsepower engine roared as I pulled out of the garage.

Attempting to maintain any reasonable speed in the loaner car was nothing short of impossible. It had a six speed transmission and six hundred horsepower. I wondered who in their right mind could drive a car like this without being arrested. Within a few minutes I was headed up the entrance ramp to the freeway. I stomped the accelerator pedal and smiled as I merged with traffic at 110mph. A few short minutes later, and I was exiting the freeway just a few blocks from the coffee shop.

Parking the car in the lot felt surreal. I had not been there since the day Britney hung herself. For the last three days I had literally sat at home and wallowed in the guilt associated with the suicide of my former girlfriend, and of Britney. I had not shared my increased degree of guilt with Michelle, nor did I feel that there was any value in doing so. I grabbed my bag, got out of the car, and headed for the coffee shop to start my day. As I approached the front door, I turned and looked at the vehicle admiringly as I considered the possibility of a new car and the false sense of pleasure associated with it. One hundred and twenty thousand dollars would be a small price to pay for a little potential peace of mind, especially if it traveled at 200 miles an hour.

I admired the car for a few more moments as I contemplated thoughts of ownership, and then reluctantly walked inside.

I stepped in line and pulled my phone from my pocket. Checking it, I found no missed calls or text messages. I expected Michelle was sleeping late and was probably still deeply depressed. As I stood in line, I heard a familiar voice call out my name.

"Kid, the usual?" Liz asked.

"Yes please, Liz. Thank you," I responded with a smile.

Liz was about five foot six. She varied, depending on her mood and the time of year, from 105 to 115 pounds. She had auburn hair which when I met her was to the middle of her back. She had cut it a few years prior and it remained the shorter length, which to her shoulders. Her skin, regardless of the season, remained smooth and pale. I looked into her eyes on the first day she worked at the coffee shop and quickly identified her as a person who could use a friend. Over the years we developed an odd friendship, but a friendship none-the-less. No one really understood Liz, but she wasn't a person to understand. She was a person to experience and absorb, and I had spent the last four years enjoying doing so. As I studied her I reached into my pocket and fumbled for my money clip.

"I've got this one, Kid. Glad you're back," she smiled.

I thanked her and walked to the station to receive my drink. As I waited, the barista nodded and smiled. Soon, he handed me my drink and wished me a nice day as he welcomed me back. I walked to my normal seat, sat down, and got out my laptop. After powering it up and logging onto the Internet, I logged into my email account.

No new emails?

Feeling empty, I sat and looked around the coffee shop.

I contemplated what I was feeling and attempted to decide what it was exactly. I had a feeling of serenity and accomplishment. Try as I might to be perceived as a repulsive complete asshole, people seemed to like me. Maybe for *who* I was, not *what* I was. A person would be hard pressed to find anyone who had the capacity to be more appalling than me. Yet. People who were exposed to me, or had an opportunity to experience and absorb me, liked me. I now sat as proof my weight didn't matter. Being obese, having a foul mouth, appearing arrogant, short-tempered, anti-social and having an ego the size of the Madison Square Garden obviously wasn't enough.

The few people who actually knew me liked me. I looked around the coffee shop and grinned.

This being fat business isn't doing the trick.

I sat in the chair, weighing 320 pounds and but one chocolate bar away from a heart attack. My natural weight would be 185 if I didn't try to be obese. For me, it was hard work being as big as I was. It took tremendous planning, eating, and lack of exercise to be the Fat Kid. I was certain my problem the day of Britney's suicide was a heart attack. I didn't like thinking about it now that it was over. As I sat and surveyed the coffee shop, my views on life began to change.

The heart attack from a few days prior was making me feel strange to be alive, and be appreciated. Maybe it was Britney's suicide? I considered the possibilities of the dream making me more an emotional wreck than normal. I couldn't decide. As I thought about the dream I decided I was overdue for a long drive.

A 200 mph drive.

Grinning, I logged off my laptop, powered it down, and placed it in the bag.

On my way out the door I noticed the new trash can beside the entrance. I stepped a few feet away and tossed my empty cup at the opening. *A complete miss.* I steadied my bag over my shoulder, shook my head, and walked to the car. I backed out of the stall and shifted into first gear. As I released the clutch and began to roll forward, it was obvious to me just how comfortable this car really was.

Within minutes I was back at my condo.

Standing in the elevator, I looked down at my shoes. The soles were worn through. The toes were ripped off and flapped when I walked. Whenever it rained, the water soaked through the bottom of them into my socks. I could not bring myself to spend the money on a new pair. I had this particular pair forever, and I was attached to them. I lifted my foot, and looked at the side. I could see my sock through the opening that was worn through the inside of the shoe. I lowered my foot to the floor just as the elevator opened on my floor.

I walked into my bedroom and packed a quick bag for the road. Khakis, white tee shirts, socks and toiletries. Road trips often relaxed me in a way nothing else really could. I felt I was able to think better on the highway. And the faster I drove - the better. After zipping the bag closed, I lifted my head and looked around the condo. I inhaled slowly through my nose. Nothing at all looked familiar. It was as if I were standing in someone else's home. I exhaled as I continued to look around, trying to remember just how long I had been living in this particular space.

My laptop on one shoulder, and my overnight bag on the other, I walked into my office and grabbed the post-it note. I carefully folded it and placed it in my pocket. As I headed toward the door, I gazed around my condo. Feeling as if I had forgotten something, I stood and blankly stared. One more pass through the house revealed no necessities. Passing the kitchen counter on the way out, I stopped.

I stood beside the kitchen looking down at my raggedy shoes. After another deep breath, I exhaled and turned toward the door. I reached into my left pocket and gripped my chocolate supply, more out of habit than necessity. As I pulled the door handle to exit, I paused. As if rehearsed, I dipped my right shoulder and dropped my laptop on the floor of the entrance. I stood for a long moment staring down at the computer bag. Slowly, I pulled the chocolate bars from my pocket and dropped them beside it the bag. Feeling oddly satisfied, I looked up, locked the door, and left.

20

TRUST ME

MICHELLE

Finding Britney hanging in the garage had become part of who I was. Feelings of finding her haunted my every thought. The recurring thought *what if I would have…*

The *what if* thoughts didn't necessarily start in the garage. What if I would have sent the pictures to Kid earlier? What if I would have identified some of her issues or taken her seriously earlier in life? The guilt and the wonder consumed me.

While it was becoming increasingly difficult to do so, I continued to go to see Britney at the hospital. I felt I had to go there. It wasn't a feeling of respect which made me go; it was more out of necessity - and probably a little guilt. Sitting there, I would rub her feet - filled with hope she would wake up - changing every one of my thoughts to some form of an odd dream. Each time, I left filled with disappointment and even more guilt. I continued riding the emotional roller coaster, wondering how long it, or I, could continue to last.

My talks with Kid had been far less frequent and I could not decide if it was him or me who made our communication seem awkward. He had initially tried to determine how he became involved. He wondered and second guessed how Britney could have lived in East Brunswick as a dear friend of mine and realistically found him by mere happenstance.

I had become far more understanding of others after Britney's suicide attempt. I began to listen to my brothers, and actually consider what they said. Consideration of my friends' wants, needs and general comments regarding life had become second nature. In the past, I was always quick to judge and somewhat slow to comment. Everyone was entitled to their opinion. Now, I found myself more apt to actually listen, and have no feelings of condemnation regarding a thought, feeling, or opinion that I may not immediately agree with. Britney's incident made me a more diverse and understanding person.

I had developed a better understanding of what Kid had been feeling his entire life. It was easy for me in the past to try to explain to him how I understood his feelings. I know now I did not truly understand them before. Not really at all. It was impossible. Experiencing the loss first hand had caused me to feel the same types of feelings others experiencing this level of loss would feel. Britney may not have been dead, but she wasn't alive either. As I stood and rubbed her feet, I was constantly reminded of what I had lost.

I had lost her.

Although I could not be certain, I expected her parents felt the same way. I would imagine the guilt associated with being a parent and having the same level of loss would be tremendous. For a parent, the feeling of responsibility following the loss of a child to suicide would last a lifetime.

If Britney would have been killed in a car wreck or by some other natural means, I was quite certain I would have been over it. Not to sound morbid or lack a degree of compassion, but it was true. Following her death I would grieve, later accept the death, and eventually recover. If she did not wake up, or if she passed away, I felt I would never actually recover.

Suicide, as Kid suggested in the past, cuts to the bone.

In a matter of months I would be in college, and the process of becoming a responsible adult would begin. At some point in time I would become married. God willing, I would have children. I suppose all parents believed they were doing what was necessary to provide everything their child needed or expected throughout the active raising of their children. I prayed my exposure and understanding to what life offered me would allow me to make decisions which would prevent my children from feeling as if suicide was some form of means to end a pain they were incapable of resolving.

The feeling of pain never leaves. With every beat of my heart, I was reminded it remained. It festered within me like an infection. Life's antibiotic for pain associated with how we *feel* is communication - communication with people who possessed or had endured the same feelings or exposures in life. I needed exposure to people who had felt the depth and degree of loss I felt.

Suicide survivors.

Broken people helping broken people.

21

SEMPER FI

DAVID

The time following Britney's suicide was extremely difficult. As a whole, the community began to change. Parents were more attentive of their children. It was an odd mixture of being more guarded yet providing more freedom. Parents, teachers, bosses - almost everyone - seemed a bit more careful of what was said, done, requested or recommended. It was difficult to believe a suicide could bring a community closer, but it sure seemed it was happening.

I had met with Dr. Baritz once since the suicide and twice after Michelle and I talked about my heterosexuality. Initially, when I told her I was heterosexual, she didn't accept it as fact. The more she listened, the more receptive she became. I told her about Michelle's friend Fat Kid, and she had reservation about his clairvoyance, but agreed with his diagnosis regarding fear of failure. She seemed somewhat disappointed she hadn't caught it earlier, but we had some very meaningful discussions regarding my fear of failure, and we were working on making measurable progress.

She said knowing was half the battle to conquering the problem.

In the last six weeks I had given considerable thought to what I wanted to do with my adult life. I felt as if I was a new person, and I witnessed changes in myself daily. I was less stressed about day-to-day living, and had been exhibiting far less OCD tendencies. I still tugged on my pants, but wondered if it had actually become habit or if it was a subconscious issue. The fact I was conscious of it now was a step in the right direction. Michelle was instrumental in my realization of some of the things about myself I never would have realized on my own.

Good friends, friends who really care, are a once in a lifetime thing. The thought of this school year ending and our friends going in different directions was a difficult thing for me to come to terms with. We carry our memories with us for as long as we choose to, and I intended to carry the memory of my friends with me for a lifetime. The realization of becoming an adult and needing to make changes in my life to do so was now a reality.

Progression.

As a child I learned to walk, talk, and read. Eventually, I began school. As school progressed, at the end of the school year - every year - I feared the upcoming year. Inevitably, I was going to learn something new, and the not knowing what was next scared me. I would be required to do something more; become more intelligent, to be more adult like. Every year, I would ask someone - an upperclassmen for instance - a question like *How difficult is fifth grade? I heard it was really tough.* I would wonder as the new school year approached if I would even make it through it. Every year I felt the same way; and every year I made it on to the next. Before long, I needed to learn to drive. I was certain I would be the one kid who never learned. My first time behind the wheel of a car was a scary experience for all of those involved. Again, I was certain I would not be able to master driving. In time I did become a better driver, and now I drove as well as any other senior in high school.

We reach points in time in our lives which require us to make progress toward being responsible; a responsible teen, responsible high school student, responsible adult, responsible college student, responsible employee, and a responsible parent. I now felt the change from high school to becoming an adult would be the first actual step I would take as an *individual*. I fully understood I had made progress my entire life, but this step would be the first I would take *alone*. Doing something alone scared me, and I doubted I was alone in this feeling. I would guess now, knowing what I know, we all have a little fear of failure. Some simply have it more than others.

I was ready to make decisions which would allow me to make progress in life. I wanted these decisions to be the basis for my evolution into what would be the best possible person I could become. I wanted to feel as if I had done *something*, and stand proud of myself regardless of whether or not anyone else was proud of me. The more I considered my future, the more I began believing I had the ability to accomplish anything, within reason, I decided to achieve.

I had three scholarship offers from colleges, and my parents were beginning to question my intent for the future. It was about time for me to make a decision and begin plans to relocate to my college of choice. I was not necessarily scared, and although I did not fear the changes, I feared making the changes *alone*. No differently than the changes I feared as a child going from first to second grade, I now feared advancing from high school to college and doing so alone. At least as a child, we had summer to prepare for the change. As an adult, there were no summer vacations. As Britney's friend Marc says, *time passes, and things change.*

After Britney's suicide, my parents became very supportive of me. To my initial surprise, they indicated regardless of the decision I made regarding my future, they would support me. It was comforting to know wherever I decided to go, or whatever I decided to do, they would back me. Based on my belief of their support, I decided I wanted to do what was truly best for me, and not what they may expect of me. My new realization of who I was needed to be considered in my decision making, and I struggled with this to some degree. To be quite honest, the decision came at a difficult time in my life, because in many respects I felt like an infant. More accurately, I felt as if I were in the infancy stages of understanding the abilities of a new me.

I felt as if my parent's decisions in raising me weren't necessarily great ones. Compared to other parents, they had little or no experience when they raised me, as I was an only child at the time. They made decisions with no way of knowing the effect. A trial and error, I suppose. I harbored a small degree of fear I would do the same thing. I had no desire to raise children in the exact same manner my parents raised me. The bad memories of my growing up would not be repeated in raising my children. I would like to think we are not a product of our childhood or of our parents, but a product of the environment that we are exposed to - and our ability to discern right from wrong.

I asked God for the ability to make decisions regarding his will, and his understanding of what was best for me. I fell asleep after a few hours of reclining, praying, and thinking. Normally, I would fall asleep in five minutes. This particular night was different. When I woke up, however, I was ready for a new beginning. A step into what would be a new world, a world which would welcome me, and give me the capacity to succeed and measure my successes.

I got up, showered, and got dressed. Afterwards I walked downstairs to talk to my parents.

As I walked into the kitchen, I smelled my mother's cooking. Although I didn't normally eat what she cooked for my father, I decided on this morning I would. We could eat together as a family.

"Mom, I will take some of whatever you're cooking, it smells good," I said as I leaned over and kissed her cheek.

"Oh, good morning, David, how did you sleep?" she asked.

"Great, thank you mother," I responded as I walked toward the table and sat down.

"Your father will be in soon. He went to shower. He just got home from his morning run. I will add some eggs for you," she said as she cracked the eggs into the bowl.

I sat quietly as my mother continued to cook. As my father came into the kitchen, I was finishing reading the paper. He sat down about the time my mother carried the plates to the table. As she placed the plates on the table, my father spoke for the first time of the morning.

"Scrambled eggs, bacon and wheat toast. Now that's a man's meal, son," he said.

Mentally, I shook my head, knowing now that my father had serious shortcomings. "Yes sir, it sure is," I responded.

Quietly, we sat and ate. As we did, I began to talk of my future and of the decision I had made the night before.

I alternated glances between my mother and father as I spoke, "Mom. Dad. I have been thinking about my future, about my offers from colleges, and about what it is I am going to do. Can we talk?"

With his mouth half full of eggs, my father looked up from his plate and responded, "Let's hear it son. Just spit it out. Isn't that right Mary?"

"Yes, Joseph," my mother said without looking up from her plate.

"Well, I have considered what I think all of my options are, and what each one offers, and I have made a decision," I looked at both my mother and my father independently, shifting my gaze back and forth as I spoke.

"There's no disrespect intended in my decision, but I have been reminded since my eighteenth birthday that I am now an adult, and I am expected to act as an adult. My decision, I am afraid, has been made."

"Well, Christ. Let's hear it son. Jesus. Enough with the fucking production. Where are you headed?" my father said as he picked his teeth with his fork.

I pressed both palms firmly into the edge of the table, "I'm going to the recruiter's office after we're done eating. I am going to be a Marine."

My mother let out a barely inaudible, "Oh my."

"Son, becoming a Marine isn't something you do for anyone other than yourself. Don't do this for me. Do you understand me?" my father asked as he pushed his chair away from the table.

I stood from my chair. As I did, my father began to stand.

"Sir, this is a decision I made for me. I am doing this for me, it has nothing to do with you. I'm doing it all alone, with no help from anyone else. It's what I want, and I feel it's where I belong. My decision is final. I am not willing to discuss this."

My father opened his arms and hugged me. And for the first time in my life, he told me something I had waited a lifetime to hear.

"David. Son, I am proud of you. I'm proud to be your father."

And as I hugged him, for the first time in my life, I was proud to be his son.

22

THE RIDE

FAT KID

I had lived the majority of my adult life not necessarily respecting figures of authority, especially police. Generally, I tried to treat people in a position of authority with respect, and it wasn't always because they deserved it or had earned it. As a young adult I respected authority, but later in life things changed. I was taught as a child to treat people with respect, and *most* police officers were people; but it took a really down to earth cop for me to truly treat him with respect. I had no earthly idea what a cop would have to do to actually *earn* my respect.

"Did you realize that you were swerving from lane to lane?" the officer asked as soon as I rolled down the window.

I stared at my reflection in the officer's mirrored sunglasses.

"I did not, no," I responded as I attempted to plug my telephone into the phone charger.

"Well, I suspect you did not realize it because you weren't watching the road," he responded as he pulled his glasses down his nose a little bit.

Attempting to plug the cord in and get my phone charging, I didn't respond immediately, nor did I feel the need to do so. I never quite understood the feeling of necessity to kiss a police officer's ass. It seemed everyone did so for fear of some form of repercussion if they did not. I was not one of those people who felt it was even close to necessary. I was never intentionally rude unless they were complete assholes, but I wasn't unnecessarily nice either.

"Sir," he paused and lowered his sunglasses even more.

Now, glaring down at me over the top of his glasses, he continued, "You were weaving in and out of your lane, speeding, and you did not immediately pull over when I activated my lights and sirens. Additionally, it appears you were attempting to elude me. I will need to see your driver's license, proof of insurance, and registration."

I thought for a moment before I responded. I hated cops, and he was no exception. They certainly all weren't idiots, but they all *acted* like idiots. I was driving a car with a dealer's license plate on the back. Obviously, it was either a demo, rental, or a loaner car. The window sticker was still in the rear window. And seriously, trying to elude him? The car could easily go 200 miles per hour. I hadn't tried. Had I, I would have succeeded. I contemplated pressing the gas pedal to the floor and leaving him and his ridiculous glasses standing there. By the time he realized what had happened, I would be four miles away.

Instead, I responded.

"*This* car is a loaner car. *My* car is in the shop. I do not have a registration, as it is not my car. Also, I do not have an insurance card, *because it is not my car*. Lastly, I wasn't attempting to elude you. I didn't see you," I responded as I placed the cell phone, charger inserted, on the passenger seat.

"Well, maybe if you weren't fucking with your phone you would have seen me, and I would not have pulled you over. I'll need to see your driver's license please," he said in a monotone voice.

From time-to-time, something happens which causes us to realize we need to become humble. Humility can be a good thing, in moderation. Acting humble or swallowing a little pride can be tough, depending on the circumstances. I was feeling as if I was being fed my pride with a stick as I tried to muster an answer for this guy.

You're going to love this.

"Sir, I have a driver's license, I just don't have it with me. It is inside the glove box of my other car, the one in the shop," I responded apologetically.

He removed his glasses, folded them, and placed them in his shirt pocket. After studying me for a long moment, he responded.

"You are required to carry your license with you at all times. Are you aware of that?"

"Yes, sir, I am," I responded as politely as I could force myself to.

He placed his hands on his hips and tilted his head to the side slightly, "Well, why are you in *this* car while your license is in the glove box, of all places, in the *other* car?"

His right hand rested a touch lower, close to his service weapon.

"Sir, it's a really long story. I apologize, but it is where it is."

"I want to hear it. In fact, I am going to *require* that you tell me," he said as he raised one eyebrow.

Although it probably didn't, it seemed as if his hand crept closer to his pistol.

I blinked my eyes and stared.

So be it.

"Well okay, you asked," I breathed.

"I run an Internet blog where I help people get through problems in life they may not be able to get through alone; alcoholism, drug addiction, teen pregnancy, suicide, bulimia, anorexia, obesity, bullying, and parental issues. And, here's the story. A few days ago, I was certain I was going to die from a heart attack. Sitting in the parking lot of my favorite coffee shop, my heart began acting funny and I started to sweat. I've considered death a lot, and have always wanted to die in a manner that left a mark – a big mark. Say, something which would cause people to stop and pay attention or at least make them gasp in disbelief. So, I was sure I was going to die on this particular morning, and when I did I wanted to create a huge fuss at the coffee shop I was going into. I wanted the paramedics to have a hard time identifying me when they arrived, so I left my ID in the car. When I stumbled into the coffee shop, I tossed my car keys in the trash on the way into the coffee shop, making it more difficult for them to find the ID," I paused for effect.

He stood, attentive and silent, and stared at me. He apparently wanted more, so I gave it to him.

"Later, while in the coffee shop and after reading an email, I realized a girl who I had been communicating with was in the process of committing suicide. I desperately needed to contact a certain someone immediately, but to do so, I needed my cell phone. As luck would have it, it was also locked in my car. Frantic after receiving the email and realizing her fate rested in my very incapable hands, I ran outside to the trash can. After dumping the contents, I couldn't find the keys in the trash, so I picked up the can and threw it through my passenger side car window. After the window shattered, I retrieved my cell phone," I hesitated, and he continued to stare in apparent disbelief.

"I then called someone to attempt to save her. She was found hanging in her garage, and is now in the hospital. My car went to the shop to have the window repaired. And along with the car, the driver's license, which was still in the glove box. The repair shop loaned me *this* car, and I drove off from the dealership, never realizing my ID was in the car which was being repaired," I paused and inhaled a deep breath.

"I bet you're glad you asked, huh?" I focused on the top button of his shirt and waited for a response.

He pulled his glasses from his shirt pocket and grinned, "You couldn't have made that story up."

Placing the glasses back onto his face, he continued, "Have a nice evening, and stop fucking around with your cell phone when you're driving."

I watched in the side view mirror as he walked to his car and got inside. I sat and waited for what was next, certain the event was far from over. It couldn't be over, he had not written me a ticket yet. As his car pulled away, he turned to me and nodded as he passed by. Speeding away from my stationary position, his car got smaller and smaller until it eventually disappeared. As I started the engine, I wondered why all police officers weren't a little more understanding, compassionate, and human. As much as I hated to admit it, this had been a pretty reasonable lesson supporting unnecessary stereotypes. All people should not be placed in a mold or category. Everyone is an individual. Still stunned, I reached into my left pocket and confirmed the existence of my post-it note.

As I did, I realized he was actually a cop *and* a human being.

Pulling away, I sped up to 80 miles per hour and set the cruise control. Thinking of the police officer actually being human was both comforting and disturbing. The thought of liking a cop was unsettling to me. I hated cops. But this officer was different. I guessed the time had come for me to practice what I preached, so to speak. We can all be a little prejudiced, but realizing just how much was rather enlightening. As I made a mental note to not categorize people or have preconceived notions about them, my phone rang. Looking at the screen, I realized it was my brother.

I let it ring ten times before I answered.

"Hello," I said, acting as if I did not know who was on the other end.

"Hey brother, we're getting together this weekend. I'm going to barbeque and everyone is going to be here. We were hoping you would make it this time," he said in his typical cheery tone.

"Yeah, I will be there," I said flatly.

"Dude, you didn't even ask when it was going to be. Are you coming or are you going to say you're coming again and not make it?" he whined.

Little brothers, regardless of age, are always little brothers. They look up to their older siblings. As children, my brother and I grew up as friends. As we got older, we became best friends. For several years as young adults, we were inseparable. As we got older we had grown apart. Truth be known, I had grown apart from my entire family, and from people in general. My brother never quite understood what happened to me, or what changed. No one really did. I just separated myself from my friends, family and loved ones. Over time, it happened after I got out of prison. As much advice as I could give others, I could not force myself to fully understand or correct the thoughts or feelings I harbored.

"When is it?" I sighed.

"It's Saturday at noon, the day after tomorrow. Are you going to make it?" he asked in a wishful tone.

"Yes, I'll be there. Listen, I have to get. I am right in the middle of something important," I said sternly.

"Alright brother. See you Saturday," he said gleefully.

The entire time I was in prison, I couldn't wait to get out and see my family and friends. I counted the days until I could see everyone, and dreamt of the things we would do together. After I was released, it quickly became apparent my mind wouldn't allow me to get close to the people I once loved. I believed I had subconsciously developed a deep fear of separation. The fear was so deep seated and so profound, I would not allow myself to be attached to or care for anyone. This fear also prevented me from allowing anyone to become attached to me. Since prison, I had not been in a meaningful relationship. I had tried several times, but as soon as I felt truly attached to someone, I ended the relationship. I also became so distant from my family I really preferred to never see any of them again. I literally had to force myself to visit.

When I did finally see members of my family, I always enjoyed it. This enjoyment would turn into a craving for more, or a desire to return back to normal. This would soon resort back to the self-imposed separation, which eliminated the potential for future pain. Becoming fat and repulsive soon followed my recognition of these problems. Exiting the freeway, I began thinking of my brother and I as children. Slowly, I began to smile.

As I parked the car in the parking garage, I began to feel sick. The visit certainly wasn't going to be easy, but I felt it was necessary. I reached into the console of the car and retrieved a piece of gum. After I chewed on it for a moment, I got out of the car, closed the door, and looked at my reflection in the window glass.

Change isn't always easy, I told myself as I walked away.

Walking to the elevator, I looked down at my shoes. The soles, barely attached, flopped when I walked. I lifted my right foot, and looked at the underside of the sole. It was worn through. I continued walking, wondering about the probability of me actually buying a new pair of shoes. When I got to the elevator, the door began to close. Just before completely closing, a hand grabbed the door and stopped it. It then reversed and opened, revealing an almost empty elevator.

I got in and began to push button for the third floor. As I reached for it, I noticed it was already illuminated. The gentleman in the elevator was about six foot two, two hundred pounds, and balding. Holding a bouquet of flowers, he looked at me through small rimless glasses, and did not speak. I stepped to the corner of the elevator and smiled. During the short two story ride, he looked up and down my frame as if he were sizing me up. He focused on my shoes for a moment, and mumbled something. I considered giving him a piece of my mind, and later chose not to. The elevator reached the third floor and the door opened. As it did, he motioned for me to get out first.

As I walked down the hallway, I could hear his footsteps behind me. I didn't give him the satisfaction of seeing me turn around. If I heard his footsteps get much closer, I would turn around and let him know about encroaching into the space of my bubble. I continued to walk toward 316, looking at the numbers beside the doors, but not fully turning around. When I got to 316, the door was closed and I could hear people speaking inside. Laughing, talking, and having what appeared to be a good time. I stepped beyond the door to 317, and took a deep breath.

As I stood in front of 317, the man with the flowers stopped as well. As I motioned for him to pass by, he looked at me and smiled as he stepped into the door marked 316.

I reached into my pocket and checked for the post-it note. After confirming its existence, I took a deep breath, and stepped inside.

Change isn't always easy.

23

I CAN FLY

BRITNEY

I felt myself rise above the body that lay beneath me on the floor. I watched as Michelle stood and ran outside the garage. As she returned to the garage, frantic, she talked on the phone. She began to perform CPR on my lifeless body as she screamed my name. Although I watched the entire time, I felt nothing but calm. I tried several unsuccessful times to reach out to Michelle to touch her, call her name, and tell her I was alright.

I watched as Michelle cried and got into the ambulance behind my body. Oddly, I could feel what Michelle was feeling. Although Michelle and I had never been extremely close friends, we had been good friends. She was not only concerned with my welfare and my well-being, but she truly felt responsible for what had happened to me. I could feel Michelle's pain as the ambulance pulled away. I tried to wake myself up, to make myself breathe, sit up, or speak, but I had no control over my body at all.

As we entered the hospital, I became strangely comfortable with what I had become, yet I wanted to return to my former life. I tried to float to where I could touch Michelle as she cried and pleaded to be allowed to accompany me in the emergency room. When she claimed to be my sister to gain access to where my body was, I began to cry.

The fascination of being alive in a spiritual sense soon evaporated when my father arrived. As my body lay in the bed and the heart monitor beeped, my father sat and cried. He didn't speak, but I could hear what he was thinking. I could feel what he was feeling, his pain, his regret, his wonder, and his shame. As he sat in the chair and wept, waiting for my mother to arrive, he offered to God to trade his life for mine.

I desperately tried to cause my spiritual self to become one with my physical self. As my father wept, I wept with him, regretting the feelings I had. I regretted the hatred and the selfishness I had felt. Feeling my father's love for me was the greatest gift I could ever have received. His love for me filled my heart.

My mother arrived and wept uncontrollably. My father comforted her, and although she did not speak the words, she blamed my father over and over for what had happened. She began to believe she knew all along I was unhappy. She felt as if she knew this was going to happen, and she blamed my father. I wanted to comfort her and tell her it was not his fault.

Later that night as they sat and wept over my body, the guilt they began to feel was tremendous. They took full responsibility for what happened. The guilt began tearing them apart. Their love for one another was beginning to dissolve as they stood over me. Each time a doctor came into the room my father began to hope deeply for my recovery. Each time after speaking to the doctor, the hope soon faded and the guilt returned. I desperately wanted to reverse what I had done, but my spirit and my body remained separate; incapable of making a connection. I felt if I could just touch my body and fill my body with my spirit, I could be alive again.

As the days passed, when there was no one in the room with my body, my spirit would wander to my childhood memories - memories of my mother brushing my hair and my father holding me in his arms. Their fascination with me as a child was incredible, and those feelings of love and pride filled me and gave me warmth.

After five days, Marc came into the room alone. He laid his leather coat beside my body and wept. As he cried, I felt his love for me. Not a love which was expressed through thoughts or words, but a love that exuded from his every pore. Like my father, he offered his life to God in exchange for my recovery. He asked God to take his life if I could not recover. Regardless of where my body lay, Marc wished to be with me in spirit. As he stood and wept, I cried uncontrollably.

Michelle arrived while Marc stood over me. She introduced herself. The gratitude Marc felt toward Michelle was uplifting. He thanked her verbally, but the appreciation he felt inside could not be expressed. His heart swelled when she spoke, when she wept, and when she told the story. Michelle humbly stood as Marc mentally placed her on a pedestal. As Marc left, Michelle picked up his coat, and offered it to him. Marc explained he no longer needed it, and asked that she leave it in the room beside me.

The next day, Marc, Michelle, and my mother were in the room talking. The guilt felt by each person was unbearable. They each felt as if there was something they could have done to prevent my suicide. In spirit, I felt guilty. Guilty for being selfish, for not understanding, for not realizing as Marc always said, *time passes and things change*. Pleased to see Marc in the presence of my mother, I yearned to live, to be alive, and to physically be able to proceed in life.

If I were able to live life again, I would do so with appreciation and vigor.

My father entered the room holding a bouquet of flowers. As he did, he turned and hugged Marc. As they touched, my father felt affection for Marc. He felt love. Feelings of what could be between Marc and I began to fill my spirit.

I wept as they hugged.

As my spirit floated above my body, I filled with regret.

For the first time, I felt as if I could touch my body.

In spirit, I closed my eyes and prayed.

And an odd warmth began to fill me.

24

TALL PEOPLE

FAT KID

In my mind, almost everyone on this earth was the same height. As a mass of people, they exist, shoulder to shoulder. What they know is what they see. And they all see the same thing; only what's directly in front of them - because they are all at the same height and the same eye level. Living each day and seeing what's directly in front of them, and the exact same as the person beside them, they stumble through each day blind to the rest of what exists. From time to time, a tall person is born. The taller people grow up, and have a different perspective, a different field of vision, and they see all there is to see. With their heads held above the crowd of the masses, they are aware of all there is to know. All seeing and all knowing, they watch the ignorant and happy people below them blindly exist. The knowing, the truth and the seeing scares them. It hurts them and binds them. The tall people live, bound each day to decide whether or not to expose the masses to what they are incapable of seeing. Above the crowd, their eyes see everything which emerges beyond the heads of the shorter masses. Inevitably, in their life's travels, another tall person becomes visible in the distance.

And.

They both blink and stare in disbelief.

I opened the door to the room and walked in.

"Oh my GOD!" Michelle screamed as she raised her hands to her face.

Assuming now the man carrying the flowers earlier was Britney's father, I extended my hand toward him and offered a handshake.

"I'm Kid, I spoke to your daughter through an Internet blog. I stopped in to see her," I said as he extended his hand to meet mine.

"The pleasure is all mine," the man said as he shook my hand.

"Michelle has told us a lot about you and what you have done for our daughter. We appreciate you calling Michelle. The phone call saved my daughter's life," the man said as he gestured toward Britney.

As his wife approached, I extended both of my hands toward her, lightly cupping her hand between mine. She smiled and nodded as our hands touched. I nodded in return.

"You must be Marc," I said as I turned to the younger man in the room.

As he cleared his hair from his eyes he offered his hand.

"Thank you for everything you've done, sir," he said as he shook my hand firmly.

I smiled and released my grip. I turned to face Michelle. She looked embarrassed, mad, and angry all at the same time. I had sent her a text message earlier and explained I had a surprise for her.

Earlier in the week we had spoken, and I expressed the same thing to her. When we spoke she had also indicated she had a surprise for me. I had not, however, told her what the surprise was. I was certain she imagined our first actual meeting would be a little different, and not so much of a shock.

258

"We need to talk out in the hallway, Kid," she said in a very matter of fact tone.

In her combat boots, jeans and a light colorful top, she turned and went through the door. She stood on the hallway side, holding the door as he tapped her foot on the floor. In person, her eyes and her attitude were much larger than I ever imagined.

"You fucking asshole, you just show up. Simply stroll in here unannounced?" she half screamed.

"Listen Michelle. As you can probably imagine, I have been driving for a few days. I was coming here all along. And no, I did not tell you. It was to be a surprise. Not *the* surprise, but one of them," I said quietly.

"Well, I don't like it. And, as you say, you can *write that down*," she said as she pointed at my face with her index finger.

Wow, this girl had guts; and an attitude as big as mine.

"I apologize, Michelle. If I have offended, embarrassed, or placed you in an awkward situation. It wasn't my intent," I whispered as I opened my arms, offering to hug her.

As if we had been old friends reunited after a decade, she hugged me. As she did, she cried for a brief few seconds and stopped. Breaking our hug, she turned and wiped her eyes.

"Let's walk and talk," I said as I began to walk down the corridor.

"Do you know where the cafeteria is?" I asked.

"Duh, I've only been in there a hundred times. Follow me," she said as she quickly stepped half a stride ahead of me.

"So, what's the surprise, asshole?" she asked as she walked briskly, her head turned slightly my direction.

"Well, I have several," I said as we got on the elevator.

"Let's discuss them in the cafeteria. Nice boots, by the way," I smiled.

"Fuck you Kid," she said as she pushed the button to the first floor.

"Seriously, I like them. They remind me of some I had back in the day," I said as I stared at the boots admiringly.

We stepped off the elevator and walked down the hallway together like old friends. I had no awkward feeling being with her. We walked side by side as if we had known each other for years. Michelle was wise beyond even her own comprehension and certainly wise beyond her 18 years on earth. We had been friends for almost a year at this point, and even though we had spoken on the phone for countless hours, and shared photos of ourselves, I still expected this to be awkward.

It wasn't even close.

We entered the cafeteria and each got a cup of coffee. Although it wasn't remotely close to the Americano at my coffee shop, it was sufficient for the occasion. We walked to a vacant table and sat down across from each other. We studied each other for a moment and Michelle broke the silence.

"So, how was your drive and what is the surprise? You go first, and then I will let you know mine," she said.

"Well, I kind of have two, so let's go back and forth. How's that? Me, you, then me again," I laughed.

"Fine," she said sharply.

"Well, I guess I will just get to it then," I sighed.

"As I told you on the phone, I had one of my dreams. After years and years of nothing, I had one. It revealed several things. Most importantly, Britney is going to wake up, Michelle. She is going to wake up and I think she will be fine."

"Are you fucking kidding me? You came here to say that? I don't know whether to tell you to fuck off or say thank you. Jeez, Kid. I can't tell her parents that. Do you really expect me to believe that? I mean, I know you have certain gifts, but fuck. Seriously, Kid? You had a dream. And you really think it's going to come true? Really? I don't know what I think about this," she said as she shook her head.

"Listen Michelle, I have never had a dream like this and *not* had it end up being true. Or real. Or whatever you want to call it. And I don't want you to tell her parents anything. If everything goes as I think it will, she will wake up while I'm here today. I want to leave as soon as she does. I do not want to be here after she wakes up. There will be too much embarrassment and lack of trust on her part," I said as I extended my arms across the table to hold her hands.

She was beginning to shake. As she reached out and held my hands, she began to speak.

"That makes sense. I never really thought about it that way. Kind of admitting to her parents that she talked to *you* about suicide and didn't talk to *them*, right?" she said as she squeezed my hands.

"Exactly. Oh, and the drive was great. Most of it was between 120 and 160 miles per hour. Well, except for when I got pulled over in West Virginia. Potentially, I could have received ten tickets, but the cop let me go," I grinned.

"I hate cops," she said as she rolled her eyes.

Yet another thing we have in common.

"This one was nice. He made me look at things differently. I will have to tell you the story later. So what's your surprise?" I asked.

She let go of my hands and sat back in her chair. A smile began to appear on her face, and she looked intently into my eyes. With her eyes, she smiled almost a prideful smile. Slowly, she stood from her chair, turned to the side, and began to speak as she started to lift her shirt from her waist.

"After all of this happened, my parents and, well…" she paused as she continued to lift her shirt.

"All of the parents started to pay more attention to their kids. To listen and ask questions, probably in fear of their kids having suicidal thoughts. My parents apologized for the tattoo comments and said if I wanted to get one, I could. So, I did. I couldn't wait to tell you, and to show you," she said as she lifted her shirt and revealed her new tattoo.

As I looked at it, I tried to act as if I had no idea what it was going to be. It had been done in a fancy script, but it was clear what it said. Still swollen and apparently new, the tattoo was gorgeous. Michelle was a piece of work. Her first tattoo wasn't going to be a butterfly or some flower. As she held her shirt up proudly, I read the words out loud.

"Stay Human. That is absolutely gorgeous Michelle. And I must add, quite appropriate. Where did you get the idea?" I asked.

"Well, I had a dream one night. It was the night my parents made me so mad. There was this guy. He was in prison and he was mad at the authorities. It was a really weird dream. Different than any other I have ever had. It was like I could actually sense what the man was thinking and feel his pain. The dream was extremely clear and vivid. Not like any other. Anyway, he got out of prison and there were all of these rules. One rule said he couldn't get a tattoo. Oh no, not this guy, he said fuck it and went and got one anyway. And when he did, this is what it said," she said as she pointed to the tattoo.

"It just fits, don't you think?" she grinned.

"It certainly does. More than you know. Kind of puts everything in place," I said as I stood up.

262

"Well, what's your other surprise?" she asked as she lowered her shirt, still glowing with pride.

I reached into my left pocket and retrieved the folded post-it note and handed it to her. She reached toward the note, and took it in her hand as she rolled her eyes. As she looked down at it I noticed it was covered in pocket lint and dirt. It had been in my pocket for several days, and it showed. She began to unfold it, and turned it over to read the two words I had written on it.

"Are you fucking kidding me? But. How did you…"she paused and stared at the note.

"Kid, what the fuck? What's going on? This is crazy. It's freaking me out," she said as she looked up from the note.

"I had a dream. In it, Britney woke up, and I saw *that*. Clear as day. I wrote it down to prove it to myself, and to you," I said in a somewhat apologetic tone.

"Kid, you are truly an amazing person. You just are. You're different. And this is crazy. Oh my God, she *is* going to wake up, isn't she? When?" she asked as she stood from the table.

"Probably now, or as soon as we get back. If my dream was accurate, and it appears it will be, I'd say right about now," I said as I stood.

"We need to make sure we're done talking, because when she wakes up, I have to go," I sighed.

"Kid, this just blows me away. The *reading people* as you say, the dreams, your ability to understand, to offer advice. You're just so, well, I don't even know how to say it," her voice trailed off as she started thinking.

"Michelle, damned near everyone on this earth is the same height. They all see everything the same. From their vantage point, they all see each other. A literal mass of people seeing only what is in front of them. They live unaware of anything they can't see. And they can't see beyond the person in front of them. Every now and again, a tall person is born. They, from their vantage point, are *all seeing*. They're all aware, and they see all there is to see. I am tall. I always have been. You are as well. You're tall, Michelle," I said.

I stood and waited for her to respond. After a short pause, she did.

"Kid, I am not tall. Not like you. You have those dreams, you have a gift. I may be smart, or intellectual, or intelligent, but I'm a kid, and I know *nothing* compared to you. You have dreams that come true. You see what others don't, you are taller than anyone. If I had those dreams, man..." she hesitated and shook her head.

"I'm telling you. If I had them, then we could talk about being tall," she nodded her head and smiled as she rolled her eyes again.

"Stop rolling your eyes, you're going to make yourself sick. Remember our *broken people* conversation?" I asked.

"Yes. Why?" Michelle responded.

"Well, I am by most standards, broken. You say gifted, I say broken. I stand above others. I see as far as there is to see. And I could see you standing above the crowd from San Diego. You're tall. You'll realize it one day, you certainly will. And when you do, it will flow through you like an infection. You will feel compelled to help others, open their eyes to what you know, and what they are incapable of seeing without your assistance. But Michelle, I am broken. And broken people attract broken people, remember? That's what has drawn me to you," I said as she listened intently.

"Well, I don't know Kid. Those dreams. You're way beyond what I can imagine," she said as she straightened her shirt into place.

264

"Well, shall we?" I asked as I pointed toward the hallway.

We both began walking toward the hallway. I turned and looked at the table where the post-it note lay. The side I had scribbled on faced upward. The two words I had written were clearly visible.

Stay Human.

As we walked by the cafeteria exit, I threw my coffee into the trash can and chuckled lightly to myself, thinking of the steel dildo I had thrown through my car window. We continued to walk down the hall without speaking. I was certain as we walked Michelle was digesting my tall people speech. She was thinking. Probably realizing, if I was correct, Britney was going to wake up. As we got off of the elevator and began walking down the corridor, our walk slowed slightly. Subconsciously, we were probably both a little reluctant to actually arrive at the room. An anxious fear, I assumed. As we rounded the last corner, we saw several staff rushing down the corridor. At the same time, we turned and looked at one another. Turning back to the corridor, we watched as they rushed into Britney's room.

I opened the door, and the room was hysteric. Laughing, crying and praying. I stood in the doorway, knowing it was time for me to go. Britney, half sitting up, spoke two words as we stood in the doorway.

"I'm hungry," she said.

I don't know what she may have said before or after those words, and it didn't matter. I released the door, stepped into the hallway, turned toward Michelle, and shrugged.

"I guess I'm done here, Michelle," I said as I opened my arms for one last hug.

"Oh my God this is so exciting, but the room is insane. There are people everywhere. Why so many doctors, I wonder?" Michelle asked.

"Who knows," I said as I stood waiting for my hug.

"Well, I suppose I could walk you to your car," Michelle offered.

"That would be nice," I responded as I hugged her.

We held the embrace for a moment, in a form of celebration.

"So, what are you going to do now, Kid?" she asked.

"I guess I am going to go to my brother's house for a party," I smiled.

"You're actually going to visit your family?" she asked as her eyes widened.

"I guess so," I responded.

"How long did it take you to get here," she asked as we began to walk down the hallway.

"How long to get *here?*" I asked.

I thought for a brief moment and finished responding,

"A lifetime, Michelle. *It took me a lifetime.*"

25

DAMN, THAT'S ONE TALL BITCH

MICHELLE

Tall people.

What I wouldn't give to be tall.

To have those dreams and to be tall. To be tall and a doctor. I felt it would put me in place to make a huge difference in this world; to truly make my mark. To do what so many others would not be capable of doing. As we walked to the car, my mind was racing the entire way. I was overwhelmed with all of what had happened. Finally meeting Kid. Our talks, long-winded discussions, his advice and meeting him in general was a pleasant surprise. I thought of Britney's attempted suicide, and how everything eventually came into place for all of us.

Kid's dream.

My tattoo.

His knowing of my tattoo before I got it and his knowing of Britney waking up.

I thought about what Kid said when we were walking away from the room. He said it took *a lifetime* when I asked him how long it took him to get here. I think he meant a lifetime of guilt from his girlfriend who committed suicide was all released when Britney woke up. Maybe additionally he was making progress in life through all of this. As we walked side by side, I realized the entire time he had not eaten any chocolate.

I looked at his khaki pants, and focused on the left pocket. I saw there was no rectangular bulge, and I wondered.

A lifetime.

Entering the parking garage, Kid pushed the button on his key and unlocked the car he was driving. He opened his arms and we embraced for a minute. As I stood outside the car, he opened the door and got inside.

Quickly he started the car, and rolled down the window.

"I better go if I am going to get to this party on time," he grinned.

"I guess it'll be goodbye for now Michelle," he said.

Standing outside the car, I leaned down and looked in the window.

"Bye, Kid. Before you go, will you at least tell me your name? I know I've asked a million times. And a million times you've said no. But, will you *now?*" I shrugged.

He smiled and shook his head.

"Well, I'll tell you what. You can call me the same thing everyone else who actually knows me calls me. It's not my given name, but it's all my close friends or family ever call me. Hell, my own father hasn't called me by anything else since I was about twelve years old, how's that?" he asked as he looked at me through the open car window.

"Fine, Kid. That'll be fine," I said angrily.

Actually, I appreciated the fact he would tell me anything personal about himself.

As I stood outside the car, he revved the engine and backed up alongside where I stood. As I heard him shift the car into gear, he rolled forward slightly and stopped.

"I got to get Michelle, or I'm going to be late. The next time we talk, just call me by my name. It's Hoot."

As he waved and pulled away, I thought…

Hoot?

I know that name from somewhere…

ACKNOWLEDGEMENTS

The contents and events depicted in this book are fictitious. The characters are fictitious as are the events. There are, however, some portions in this book which are a reproduction of items my friend Michelle Basilious provided (or stated) to me in conversations we had regarding life, living it, and what our respective thoughts were on any given day as they pertained to a circumstance or sequences of events.

Michelle proved to be wise beyond her years, and as I attempted to assist people in their need to have someone to lean on, Michelle often provided an opinion from that of a female perspective. Frequently she would take some time to consider her responses, often taking a few days before she gave an opinion.

Other times, she would immediately provide a response.

Her opinion was always considered, but not always implemented.

One weekend, I had a girl get in touch with me I had never met. She received my telephone number from a friend of a friend. Frantic, she attempted to speak to me initially, but each time she tried, she was overcome with emotion.

This emotion filled silence continued for over an hour, and we then actually began to communicate, albeit slowly and one-sided. I learned through the course of the conversation (which lasted almost eight hours) that she was bound by her husband and gang raped by his friends. This happened over the course of a few days. Against, if I even need to state this, her will. She was in and out of consciousness for two days.

Eventually she was released. In shock and extremely poor health, she contacted me from a remote hotel room.

I struggled with this event entirely, and how I should handle it. I fought with this more than I have with almost anything in my life.

Vengeance.

At what point does one administer his own form of justice to someone the court will undoubtedly not punish properly? The punishment for this particular crime, regardless of what was imposed by the court, would not be sufficient for the crime committed.

Although I could not speak to Michelle about the particular person, the events, or the intimacies of this conversation, we spoke for some time in general about God, law and the difference between what is right and what is wrong. I shared with her my thoughts of feeling a need to resolve the issue with the caller's husband on my own. When the smoke cleared, I sat in a coffee shop and thought.

And I made a decision on my own.

"Put up again thy sword into his place; for all they that take the sword shall perish with the sword."

I decided, for once in my life, it was not my responsibility to resolve this issue. I contacted the authorities, called in a few favors from some friends in law enforcement, and the issue was dealt with in a manner which was in accordance with law.

Michelle, as always, proved extremely useful in her ability to convey her understanding of the message of God in a manner I could listen to and accept. I have always struggled with attempting to do what is right (in my mind), and always hoped it was what was right in God's eyes.

I did not know these things could be in line with one another.

Until now.

Michelle's independence, stubborn nature, and lack of willingness to give up proved useful throughout the above described event, and many others just like it. I have spent my entire adult life running. Running from whatever it was that made me feel uncomfortable. Often, if something made me feel too comfortable, I ran as well. Michelle and Michelle's way of communicating caused me to listen. Finally, I stopped running.

I stopped right after I ran to the tattoo parlor and got another tattoo. An Arabic number three on my left wrist. To me - a sign of completion - the trinity. The Father, the Son, and the Holy Spirit.

I have heard many times, and I do agree, *God works in mysterious ways*. His speaking to me through an eighteen year old female for six months caused me to listen, consider, and ultimately apply his wisdom (and what I believe his intent was) to the above described event, and many others that followed it.

Some of what was shared between the 'real' Michelle and I was used, with her permission, in the writing of this book. As I stated above, the events in this book, entirely, are fiction, every bit of it. Nothing depicted in this book happened in part or as a whole. Described below is my best recollection of what my reproductions are of Michelle's ramblings to me.

Depending on which version of the book that you are reading, and what manner you are viewing it may not necessarily correspond accordingly, but in the chapter entitled "Fuck Oatmeal," the *Stay Human* tattoo was a tattoo idea Michelle had. Although this phrase or tattoo idea isn't copyrighted by her or anyone else for that matter, the idea of her getting the tattoo originated from her thoughts. I applied it to this chapter as a sort of dedication to her. In the same chapter, the sign on the door was of her mind and her making.

In the chapter entitled, "Cups", the discussion regarding the KKK, medicine, and prejudices between Michelle and David, for all practical purposes, actually happened between Michelle and I.

It was reproduced in the book in the best manner that my mind could recall. This was used, once again, as a dedication to Michelle and my agreeing with her very human understanding of these things that so many other people are incapable of grasping.

In the chapter entitled, "Broken People", the email between Michelle and Kid which goes into a discussion regarding broken people is an exact reproduction of an email between Michelle and me, short of a name change.

In the chapter entitled, "Dude, you're creeping me out", the list of "Things I've Learned in My 18 Years of Life" is an exact reproduction of a list of things Michelle developed. This list was not created for this book, but developed throughout Michelle Basilious' life; over many years, many tears, and much thought. This was a list she held and still holds dear to her heart, and for good reason. From what she told me, she spent many hours in her bed at night crying as she added items to the list and made the necessary adjustments.

As I stated in the opening of the acknowledgements, the events, the conversations, and the opinions in this book are fictitious, and are an element of the imagination of the author. The sentences, emails, and list the author describes above are the extent of the items which were used from the author's life, and applied to this novel. Remaining conversations in the book regarding these items, or reiterations of these events or items, are all fiction.

Michelle Basilious, however, is very real. For what it is worth, contrary to how she is depicted in the book, she loves oatmeal.

Maybe, if you hold your hands to the sky, and plead with God for the answer to a question you have never been able to resolve, she will appear.

When she does, you better be ready.

The author

ABOUT THE AUTHOR

Scott Hildreth resides in Wichita, Kansas. He is broken. Although this book and the characters depicted within it are fictional, the contents of this book are based on his experiences in life and his exposure to the human race. He continues to expose himself to broken people daily as he frequents his favorite coffee shops. His advice is typically based on statistics, and will always remain free.